Fisher's Hornpipe

Fisher's Hornpipe

TODD McEWEN

HARPER & ROW, PUBLISHERS, New York
Cambridge, Philadelphia, San Francisco, London
Mexico City, São Paulo, Sydney

A portion of this book appeared in *Esquire*.

None of the characters depicted in this novel represents
any specific person, and all the incidents are imaginary.

FISHER'S HORNPIPE. Copyright © 1983 by Todd McEwen. All rights reserved.
Printed in the United States of America. No part of this book may be used or
reproduced in any manner whatsoever without written permission except in
the case of brief quotations embodied in critical articles and reviews. For information address Harper & Row, Publishers, Inc., 10 East 53rd Street, New York,
N.Y. 10022. Published simultaneously in Canada by Fitzhenry & Whiteside
Limited, Toronto.

FIRST EDITION

Designer: Sidney Feinberg

Library of Congress Cataloging in Publication Data

McEwen, Todd.
   Fisher's hornpipe.

   I. Title.
PS3563.C362F5   1983   813'.54   82-48684
ISBN 0-06-015164-1

83 84 85 86 87 10 9 8 7 6 5 4 3 2 1

To I. Schenkler

To describe the bottom of all the universe
is no enterprise to undertake in sport.

—Dante

I had three pieces of limestone on my desk, but I was terrified to find that they required to be dusted daily, when the furniture of my mind was all undusted still, and I threw them out the window in disgust.

THOREAU, *Walden*

Fisher's Hornpipe

I WALDEN;
Or, An Accident in the Woods

But when you raise your head, when you see the trees standing there as they always have, when you see a goose up in the sky and you feel the freezing air hardening the deep insides of your nostrils, you realize the goose, seemingly hanging in front of a cloud, is flying, actually straining to fly at the moment. If in a rush of cold air and dizzy fear you were suddenly taken right up next to the goose, if all of a sudden the goose's PRIMITIVE EYE nearly FILLED YOUR FIELD OF VISION and you felt the cold air rushing around you and the goose, and below you were the fields, white and tiny and terrifying, you would hear the goose grunting and heaving, a sound that does not reach you on the pond. It is very hard work to fly, the goose is using all her energy to fly, you're right up next to her, she's frightened but flying, sighing softly with each downstroke of her great wings.

We stood in the middle of the ice on the most depressingly frozen winter's day. It was sunny but it was sunlight for the dead Earth we're supposed to inherit in a million years. You prayed for wind, for rain, for any molecular motion that might dissipate this raw sunlight which impossibly outlined everything and terribly etched the overwhelming cold right through your eyes into you. The thick clear ice on the pond boomed and whined, settling and resettling on the life under it. Fish, little, swimming, cold, under the ice, were perhaps deceived by the sunlight in which we stood and wished they could warm themselves in it. Skaters had made scratches and piles of powdered ice on the clear surface. We walked across a corner of the pond, the ice screeching but never buckling. It can't buckle said Donald. Harvard man. I stood and shivered and abstracted as usual my mind wheeled from my cloud journey at the side of the goose to vague stupid historically inaccurate thoughts about Concord and Lexington and Thoreau. I'll bet he's still here I thought characteristically unwilling to avail myself of the lessons of history or even those of mortuary science.

I then heard a quick tapping from beneath the ice. It was Thoreau. His beard was filled with dead fish. His skin was grey, the great mournful eyes red and worried. He was reaching up to the undersurface of the ice with a stick, banging, looking at me. I signaled to him, nodding, Yes I see you! He beckoned to me and I walked a few yards so that I stood just over him. He had no clothes on. I don't know how he was able to breathe. Thoreau reached into a hollow log there under the water and pulled out a waterlogged placard which read GO GET MR EMERSON! in big red letters. He pointed animatedly in the direction of Concord and bubbles came out of his mouth. I nodded and smiled and held up my hand in assurance I understood. I didn't think it was extraordinary. He needed help. I began to walk away backwards smiling Yes help is on the way Yah uh huh. The big eyes narrowed suspiciously. He didn't believe I would really go get help. I was just like all the others who nodded and smiled and went back to their cars and drove back to Boston, stopping for a steak somewhere, forgetting the waterlogged Genius of America back there in the pond. But no, I'll help. I will. I'm stepping backwards smiling waving don't worry gesturing Don't you see? But suddenly my foot hooks a block of ice left by a fisherman and I slip! I see my feet, comic, high in the air in front of me! I flail my arms! My head hits the ice very hard, my eyes close after a second, I am unconscious.

Apparently I pray when injured. I opened my eyes experiencing a small involuntary orison as I saw Donald bending over me. Two fishermen were also leaning Yankee faces into view. I looked at Donald and wanted to say something to him in the split second before he asked me a question but couldn't. Can you hear me? he asked. Yes. I felt watery. As though I was made of broth, my features and perceptions floating like vegetables on top of me. Can you get up? I moved my legs. One of them was under the other. I slowly pushed my shoulders up with my arms. I felt blood running down the back of my neck. Donald and the fishermen helped me stand. Donald poking at the top of my head. You're cut he said Can you make it to the car?

They helped me along the trail. How different things look after an accident that doesn't affect them. I was afraid. How long have I been out? Perhaps I've really lost my legs. It's all anesthetic. I could have asked these questions, speech felt possible. But things looked so odd. It's probably all an hallucination. Soon a doctor wearing a speculum and a white coat will start poking me and calling me by some unfamiliar name. Now then Mr MacGillivray. No it's Fisher. White gowned figures in the background whisper He thinks his name's Fisher! Donald holding his head in his hands in the waiting room. A

Hitchcock nightmare from which I will not escape until I get involved with a blonde and climb around on some famous monument. These thoughts became repulsively tangled in the strands of my hair caught in the big bleeding gash in my scalp. How horrible I thought, pressing a rag to my head in the car. I hated the idea of my HEAD being OPEN.

But I was all right. I could walk into the emergency room and tell them what happened. Although I omitted mentioning Thoreau for the moment. They put me on a cart and wheeled me into a draped alcove. Then the stitching. The needle going in and out of my scalp for God's sake. Nearing and leaving the confused ideas about what had happened. My desperate prayers for no true brain damage but for a new way of being! To get up off the gurney and see my way clear. To become skilled in the use of high quality hand tools, something to do with the fine arts. To become pure, fascinating, Great. But my luck is not that kind of luck.

Whaddya wanna do? said Donald Should I take ya home? Well said Fisher. The two stood in the hospital parking lot, Donald with his hands in his pockets, Fisher's head wrapped in yards of gauze. As it was Sunday, Fisher was unshaven. He looked handsome unshaven which was just as well as he nearly always was unshaven. His beard was demoniacal. As soon as he shaved it, it grew back. Had he ever been able to shave his face smooth, no one would have recognized him. Are ya hungry? said Donald. Yes I could eat said Fisher. To the Bonanza! said Donald. The Bonanza! said Fisher. They started toward Donald's car but jumped back in fright as a huge battered car swept past them with a HONK! It's nice to think you can survive serious head injury said Fisher Only to be run down in the hospital parking lot. He had read once of a man who survived a three hundred foot fall into a quarry only to die watching television twenty years later when a truck went out of control and crashed through his house.

Fisher and Donald drove through Boston. Out Route 93. To a big highway steak restaurant Fisher had always feared. Steak! thought Fisher Steak and fries and a milkshake and a salad and a beer. No. Possibly. Fisher, William Fisher. Boston. To my left, Donald my friend. My extremities move and feel at my command. Aw bump on the head, big deal. Are ya feeling OK really? said Donald. I feel thought Fisher Like an audience. But that doesn't make sense. To put it that way will only alarm him. I don't know said Fisher.

A fat man in a maroon suit with an armload of plastic menus. Big menus. He looked at Fisher's head and then at Donald. Two? he said. Yes said Donald. The fat man led them through the clamorous Bonanza to an orange upholstered booth decorated for Christmas. He gave them their menus with great pride. He looked at Fisher's head again and then went away. I could brain you thought Fisher With this heavy glass ashtray and then you would have to wear a bandage too.

What do you want? said Donald. Steak! shouted Fisher. Several customers turned to look. Be quiet said Donald They'll think you're a nut. Steaaak whispered Fisher hiding coyly behind his menu. Great selection here he said examining the colored photographs of dishes—for those who preferred to order by grunting and pointing. Fisher punched Donald's arm and pointed at a picture of steak. Nguuh! said Fisher. Yeah yeah OK said Donald. Fisher jumped as a rusting battleship of a woman docked at their table. Yeah? she said. Burger special please said Donald. She made marks on her pad. What's he want? she asked Donald after looking at Fisher's bandage. This is an outrage! said Fisher I can order for myself. OK honey said the waitress. Why not be courteous thought Fisher Instead of hiding in the kitchen eating French vanilla ice cream by the gallon and snubbing people in a rage over your dirigible-like body? William what do you want? asked Donald poking Fisher. Grilled T bone medium rare and a side salad with blue cheese. And a beer! said Fisher. She looked at his bandage again and scrawled and then went away. What's the matter? said Donald You look funny. Oh said Fisher They all think I'm mad or sick or something just because I shouted Steak. I know said Donald. But I always shout said Fisher. I know said Donald. Think of all the people who are sick and don't wear bandages said Fisher his voice rising. I know said Donald Be quiet! Relax! Sorry said Fisher. I felt all right when we left the hospital he thought But now I'm creating unrest. It's them. They're scared of my bandage.

The big waitress brought food to Fisher and Donald. Fisher began to munch loudly. His salad was made up of the hardest of tiny lettuce hearts and dried up old stems. He took a large gulp of beer. Watch it said Donald. You watch it! said Fisher. Yeah well I'm a doctor said Donald. It's just as well because you make me sick said Fisher. They ate in silence. Vaudeville was dead.

What a perfect meal for the hungry and injured thought Fisher Even though tomorrow I will have forgotten its texture. It's a standardized texture, steak of this nature. The same texture as its glaring color photograph on the menu. Oh Mr Steak! You look just like your pictures! And the golden fries, I can't eat this slop. This is what everyone's eating here. God I wish I were at home with my violin. Eating cold cereal peck upon bushel—pining for the hot meal I am ever too lazy to make. I'm so behind in my practicing. It's terrible. I shouldn't try to play the violin thought Fisher I should just be shot and stamped on and buried in an unmarked grave. He stopped chewing and stared into space. At this moment he realized he had no clear memory of the proper position of his fingers on the violin. Oh God thought Fisher It's happening. The terrible effects of the accident. He took the last bite of his steak and felt hot pink worry rise up his neck and bloom in his ears. He took his last swallow of beer. Not bad said Fisher.

Nope not at all said Donald Wanna go? Yes said Fisher Let's go. Donald waved at the waitress who was eating a giant piece of fluffy cake behind a partition. She put it down and steamed toward them. Could we have our check please? said Donald. She added up the figures, her tongue appearing briefly at the corner of her mouth. Trying to escape its saccharine prison thought Fisher Poor devil. She put the bill on the table. Thanks she said thickly. Then she was off, a tired luxury liner moving down the ways. Bon voyage said Fisher.

Fisher and Donald approached the cashier. The fat man was all smiles. Thank you sir he said taking the oily check from Donald. Six eighty five sir thank you he sang to the merrily jingling bell of his voracious machine. Donald handed the man three dollars. That's my share said Donald. Thanks very much sir Merry Christmas sir said that fat man. Fisher was feeling in his back pocket. Oh no he thought It's shrunk. No, it's not even there! He felt in his other back pocket. But after you check your back pockets you know it's not there. His hands flashed through all nine of his pockets in a balletic flutter. The fat man was looking at Fisher's bandage and his fumbling, the yellow restaurateur's smile gradually fading. Fisher turned to Donald. I don't have my wallet he said. I'm calm, so calm he thought. I lost my wallet Donald I must have lost it at the hospital said Fisher not looking at the fat man. Oh *no!* said Donald. Don't overdo it said Fisher. That three was all I had said Donald starting to laugh. What! You got no money? the fat man said. Donald seeing the man's meaty fists stopped laughing and put his hands in his pockets. Red, he looked at Fisher. Are you sure that's all you've got William? said Donald paternally. Yes sorry I'm sure said Fisher. The fat man was turning dark as his maroon suit. What are you guys a couple a bums? he said mirthlessly. Ya God damn kids ya come in here with no money ya bums! That's what ya are ya crazy bum you! he spit up at Fisher. Fisher turned to study himself in a gold flecked smoked mirror. Perhaps you're right he thought. His bandage showed traces of blood from the stitched wound. He had not noticed it before but his clothes had been dirtied and his jacket torn in the accident. A twig protruded from a small hole in his shirt. He hadn't shaved that morning and his skin was dirty and clogged. What's to distinguish me thought Fisher From those tall guys who hang around Harvard Square at night in Air Force overcoats, matted hair, a week of stubble and acid shocked eyes reddened by booze which they disdained so heartily when they were in community college? You're right you miserable fat slob thought Fisher I am a bum. But no said Fisher turning back to the boiling face I am not a bum. My name is William Fisher and I am an administrator at the Institute of Science and I play the violin. The fat man's eyes popped and he seethed. And this continued Fisher Is my

friend, who will soon be a fully qualified physician. So I am
not a bum. Ya bum! the man yelled You ever come in here
again I'll show ya somethin! Fisher turned to see Donald
backing toward the door. The fat man took a moment to
ease himself painstakingly down from his high stool and
advance on Donald. What's the matter with you? said
Donald laughing again I paid! The bill is six eighty five
shouted the fat man An you gave me three bucks! Your
friend the bum with the bandage he's got no money! I
should call the police! Look he's just had an accident said
Donald. Fisher came up behind the fat man and ran
neatly around him, pushing the door open for Donald.
The fat man charged at them, elephantine, in the vestibule. God damn it! he trumpeted. No no not yet Sahib
said Fisher to Donald Wait until he is most excellently in
your sights Sahib, this is what the Rajah does. What! said
Donald. Fisher pushed open the door to the parking lot
and he and Donald ran toward Donald's car. The fat man
stumbled out of the door to the curb. Ya basteds! he called.
Donald got in the car and unlocked the passenger door.
Come on he hissed. That fat waitress is eating you out of
business! Fisher yelled at the billowing host Get back inside! Quick! Fisher jumped into the car. Jesus said Donald
turning on the motor. Huh! That's my wife! the fat man
yelled You fuckin bums don't talk to me about my wife!
That does it! He lurched toward the car. Donald backed
out of the parking space just as the fat man reached it. As
Donald slowly maneuvered his big car toward the highway the fat man beat his fists on the trunk. Get outta that
fuckin car! he shouted You don talk to me that way! Come
back here! It looked as though it would be difficult to
appease him.

Fisher stared back at the man who was becoming a

small jumping up and down speck as they drove back down Route 93. Where's your God damn money? snarled Donald. I don't know, the hospital or the pond said Fisher. Cripe if you've lost your wallet said Donald. Fisher stopped smiling and tried to feel concern. My *wallet* he thought. There wasn't any money in it anyway. Just my bank card but they have wisely taken anyway any credit I ever had so a fat lot of good that's going to do anyone. And what does Henry David Thoreau know about using a credit card anyway? He probably doesn't even believe in them. The old crank. Don't worry I'll take care of it said Fisher.

They crossed the Charles and Fisher felt flat and low as they cruised the crowded Christmas encrusted streets of Back Bay toward his house. Fisher lived on Newbury between Exeter and Gloucester. The interests of innocent parties forbid giving the exact address. If you don't know Boston God bless you. Newbury was filled with shoppers dead with fatigue from goggling at boutiques. Donald stopped the car. Fisher got out. Donald looked at him carefully. Are you OK William? Fisher looked at Donald. Wild of eye. Yes I am Donald. Thanks for taking me to the hospital. Sorry about the incident said Fisher. That's OK said Donald But you'd better call the police about your wallet. Police! thought Fisher. But then Donald was nervous. A nervous Harvard man! OK said Fisher. He slammed the car door and waved. He started across Newbury only to throw himself back against the car as a giant coupe swerved down the street narrowly missing him. Fisher shook his fist at it. See ya! he called to Donald starting across the street again. As Donald pulled out into the traffic he worried about Fisher. He was able to do this and drive at the same time because he went to Harvard.

Again I reach this side of the street alive thought Fisher
Although what really is the point? Fisher lived on his side
of Newbury Street only by the merest chance. One side
was the same as the other. The same shops, the same
pedestrians, the same confusion abounded. In fact Fisher
knew there was a man who looked very like him living in
what would have been Fisher's apartment in the building
across the street. Many times Fisher had considered talking to him but in the end decided it would only do to
knock him down and run off. As Fisher now climbed the
steps of his apartment building a window on the third
floor slid open and the creaking old voice of his landlady
dripped down on him like death. Hey what happened to
ya head? called the landlady. It's war! shouted Fisher
quickly ducking into the vestibule and fumbling for his
keys. What! came the muffled query. Fisher opened the
inner door and ran inside slamming it hurrying toward his
apartment. As he groped for that key he heard the landlady open her door on the third floor landing. Don't slam
the door I keep tellin ya! she screamed. Fie! yelled Fisher
slamming his own door and inside leaning against it panting. Safe! He stumbled toward his bed and fell across it.
  Fisher kicked his shoes off and got under the covers
with his clothes on, a feeling he found both exciting and
discouraging. He wearily laid his head down on the pillow
but rose up with a yell as he had lain squarely down on his
fresh wound which prickled. He muttered and rolled
about in the bedding. The bed was turmoil, Fisher could
not make a bed. Except during adolescence when he suf-
fered from a peculiar form of sleepwalking in which he
often awoke to find himself sitting on his bed which he
had made perfectly in deep sleep. Better than beds are

made in the best of motels. But I shouldn't lie down now thought Fisher I should make a pot of tea so strong it makes you bark and I should get out my violin and practice. It was two o'clock in the afternoon and Fisher feared that when he woke up he would feel sick as a dog. Naps did that to him. Outside the brick sidewalks and townhouses of Newbury Street and indeed all the bricks of Boston were cooling in the stiff breezes blowing through town. In another hour the sun began to set as Fisher nodded on and off. The sun thought Fisher Should never bother to rise on Boston because it will never ever warm the God damn place up. The sun is 11,000°F but it can't warm up Boston from October to August. You failure! Fisher said to the sun knowing it was nowhere in the vicinity.

Fisher woke some hours later in the cold Boston night and began to anger as the events of the day crowded in on him before he was ready. Particularly the memory of his accident. But of course this has happened to me said Fisher aloud Today is Sunday and Sunday is horribly inescapably bad wherever you are. SUNDAY is always the same but every week YOU are less and less. Sunday is a gigantic Clock of Doom which bloodily measures the slow deaths of great and small in town and rural principality alike. Pinning us all to the sweaty mat of life under its incalculable weight Sunday grinds your guts away with mechanical glee and the imperceptible movement of its pitiless minute hand. Sunday is the fat bully of the school, MacGillivray, sitting on your chest and moronically laughing with repellent idiot breath in your face ultimately breaking your arm and your sternum thought Fisher. I hate Sunday. In tossing about his bed which was now a hopeless mess his eyes lit on a box of matches. And this was an excellent example this box of matches of the Rules of Sunday. You can't enjoy yourself, you can't use your interesting new wooden matches on Sunday unless you have used up all of the old ones, the package of which bores you to tears. On Sunday you are due not an iota of pleasure. My nice new intriguing obscure brand of wooden matches! Fisher called out in the dimness. Were I to use them before the old matches are done it would be a heinous violation of the Rules of Sunday and result in a blizzard or nothing but Baroque music on the radio or even a phone call from my uncle! Fisher shuddered and writhed in his sheets which were beginning to mummify him. But part of the Rules of Sunday are the things you must do, the tormented individual actions. You must go to the toilet and discover you are out of tissue. You must attempt to make an omelet and watch it burn to death in the pan. You must go out on the porch freezing in casual wear and look for the *New York Times* only to find it chewed and defecated upon by the neighborhood pedigree. But the kitchen. The altar of Sunday. You must go to the kitchen and insult yourself with its indignities. You fling yourself on its damp rinds and grounds. There is something erotic and weird about Sunday. You crawl with driven inevitability toward the kitchen just as the first half fish half mammal dragged herself up onto the beach at Atlantic City or wherever it happened.

Hell! shouted Fisher stubbing his toe on a kitchen chair, falling against the dirty old porcelain sink and banging his ribs. There was frost in the kitchen. The apartment was slowly freezing. He forced himself to reconnoiter in the cupboards which were dankly dustily empty and in a rage he stormed back to his bed where he again lay and shivered. Fisher was determined to sleep Sunday away, thinking that once it was Monday the awful events of the day might reverse themselves. At the witching hour his head might miraculously heal. But even if it didn't it would at least be Monday and he could go to his warm office and show off his bandage. After struggling with his head and clothes and the counterpane in a series of small convulsive fits he again fell asleep. But he tossed and turned in his bed and woke grumbling from time to time. When he did so he was dismayed for his eyes seemed always to open on some object in the room which he disliked. God damn it said Fisher throwing himself disgustedly into his pillow.

In fact Fisher disliked all physical objects. He had been trying over the past months to rid himself of as many as he could. This had led however only to a plethora of neurotic systems which hounded him every waking and sleeping minute. On this night Fisher's bedroom contained his bed, a chair, a cheap radio, a desk made from two oxidizing file cabinets and a door stolen from the basement, a music stand, and in the corner his violin, Mr Squeaky. Musically Fisher was worse than untalented. But he hated his job and a deep seated hatred usually gives rise to wild imaginings. Fisher really thought he was a capable amateur violinist. But he was lamentable. A horrible *scraping* fiddler capable of playing off key only a handful of simpleminded traditional tunes. By ear, with a group of grumpy organic food enthusiasts. This was Fisher's chamber group, the adroitness of which he extolled to anyone who questioned him when he was carrying Mr Squeaky.

Awake again! said Fisher Even though I have eliminated every object possible from this apartment the ones that remain have taken on qualities of their departed brothers and they are keeping me awake. I could live without that desk said Fisher suddenly sitting up and peering about the room. Then he wondered if he would be able to sleep without a bed. Then he said It would be just me and my violin and my music stand and my notation paper and the Three Essential Pens and my music books. Now that would be the way to live! he shouted. He briefly considered sleeping every night in nine or ten fresh paper towels. Who am I kidding! howled Fisher I've got ten blankets on my bed and I'm freezing! He sank back onto his bandage. Yaaah! he yelled. He came to rest on his elbows. It is a sadistic love I have for you he said to his possessions All I want in life is my violin. And the Three Essential Pens. I want you naked! he shouted at his apartment. The new creed. Living Minimalism. Of course I like things, we are born to love and to cherish things. But I like them best to burn and chop up. Look at that horrible chair. I don't need you! he shouted. If I got rid of you tomorrow I could really get something done. I could learn so many études. So many difficult passages if I threw out the chair and perhaps the desk. Now there's an idea, there's bravery talking! Fisher again threw himself into the unquiet sea of bedding, pummeling the mattress in frustration. I'm kept awake by *things* he moaned. But suddenly chastened he thought Who am I to complain?

Fisher had known a man who was completely dependent for sleep on a physical object. A Sleep Machine which when electrified produced a Whir-r-r! and a seductive pink light. This Sleep Machine was made in Liechtenstein or Monaco or some difficult place and when one night it ceased to function and had to be deported to its country of origin the man began to crack. Every day he appeared at work looking more haggard than the day before. He took to drinking six or seven double rob roys for lunch, shaking constantly and snapping horribly at his colleagues. Apparently the *Schlafensmechanik* got lost in the *Luftpost* for it never returned. But long before it might have the man was led away screaming after trying to kill a sleep researcher. This unfortunate had told the poor man there was *no physical need for sleep* and showed him scientific proof: some baboons had been kept awake playing basketball for 900 hours and had then gone on to procreate normally.

Fisher always heaved with laughter at this story and as he heaved he rolled over on his bandage and Yiiih! rose up with creeping flesh. He glared around the room. Finally as unknown to him Sunday became Monday he fell back and drifted into a restless suspicious sleep.

II Thoughts of the Protagonist

Fortunately Bill Fisher's accident out at Walden hasn't
kept him away from work, and besides it's easier to spot
him in the hall now with that big bandage on his head!
Speedy recovery, Bill!
from the Institute newsletter

Yes fortunately *smashing my head open on the ice* hasn't
kept me from my job thought Fisher My *job* here in this
big *building.* Heaven forfend. Who says it was an accident anyway? Fisher brooded, drooping at his desk like a
crippled zeppelin. Alone here in the think tank, Fisher
had nothing to think about. Although to make up for it all
around him were thinking furiously. He was surrounded
on his floor by men with intermediate degrees, atop another floor of men with lesser degrees, and above were
two layers of men with advanced degrees pipes tweed
jackets and individual sinks in their offices for their coffee
things. They were all dreaming. At least they were all
sitting with their heads in their hands, just like Fisher. But
they were thinking about something other than sitting
there with their heads in their hands. Or at least they
were supposed to be. Fisher thought of the Institute as a
big yeasty Pie of Science. A baklava of ideas. His office was

small and grey and he did not even have it all to himself. For behind a crude partition of the 1950s sat a man with a middling degree who shouted at Fisher periodically. Fisher and the man (a Professor Smith) pretended they had separate offices but it was a mockery. If Fisher wanted to smoke he was obliged to go to the "smoking room" which had been set up by the chairman of the Institute *anti*smoking group. A bench, a pail. Pictures of lungs. It was ludicrous. I'm hungry, I'm thirsty thought Fisher. I wonder if the phone is going to ring.

Certainly it will ring he thought If I take my violin and sneak downstairs to the vending machines. The vending machines! That's where life is lived. Downstairs in the great Basement of the Institute. Below the warm flaky layers of dreaming professors. The steaming dough of pining wistful men who are no doubt at this very moment dreaming up rude genetic engineering surprises for all of us. Or, most of us. Not them. But beneath lay the real world of the Institute, the rough and tumble world of the Basement.

The Basement is very hot in winter. When you enter the Basement you keel over with the powerful ammoniac smell of the great printing presses of the Institute. Wide avenues accommodate forklifts and even small electric trucks carrying shipments of cold drinks to the inhabitants of the bowels. You hear the rumble of Motors! And if you stand in the middle of one of the grand boulevards of the Basement you can watch the trucks trail off into the distance. Sometimes the Basement is like a mine. Blank haggard men drive trams, cart their fellows off to the bowels where numerous he-man services are performed for the fluffy dreamers in the warm layers above. Men are

grimy here. Fisher wondered if they had ever been upstairs, the grimy men who stood around the vending machines pouring their pittances into them. Sometimes he
entertained them with his violin (or so he thought!) the
men in coveralls dancing tarantellas and the odd schot-
tische in the infrequent pools of light in the dark Basement tunnels. I must remember to practice thought
Fisher. Sometimes you hear the dirge of a Basement fu-
neral. You're not supposed to see them but there is
hushed talk of seeing them. Pallbearers in black coveralls
tow the deceased off to the bowels on one of the electric
carts. They sing a dirge to the beat of an empty industrial
drum. When Fisher thought the phone was not going to
ring and the dreamers around him seemed so stupefied by
their own yeasty warmth that they would require no ac-
tivity on his part he always headed for the Basement. For
a rip roaring look at burly men grappling with real problems. Not the weird enigmas hourly conceived and immediately patented in the dough above.

But Fisher's responses and indeed his determination
had been dulled by his accident and he had not the initia-
tive to go to the Basement. He sat staring fuzzily at his
calendar. He usually did entirely too much. Normally he
quivered in anticipation of his next duty. He was known
for lightning responses: I'LL GET RIGHT ON IT! NO PROB-
LEM! LEAVE IT TO ME! But now the complainers see a new
me thought Fisher As they file in their druidic stream past
my desk. He met their eyes with a blank stare born not
of defiance but of numbness. Dulled, I am hopelessly
dulled and simplified forever by hitting my head! he
thought. *Where's your report? You usually write a twenty
page report!* He couldn't remember how to respond to the

complaints or ? if there had been complaints. My only clear thoughts Fisher told himself Are of my violin. But this wasn't true either. The plain little tunes he had learned before Saturday were jarred apart by the accident Sunday. Sunday! wailed Fisher When will my responses return to normal? Be quiet! Smith snapped from behind the partition.

I wish I were home thought Fisher I love it at home. It was there Fisher imagined he played so sweetly on Mr Squeaky. I can do anything I like at home not just play with emotional abandon but also write incisive social commentary and understand Locke and Pollock he thought. When Fisher was at work he just wished he were home. But when he *got* home he began immediately to agitate about work. About the budget and the uranium report. On a typical evening he sat down, stood up, sat down, stood up, danced about, sat down, stared disconsolately at his violin, stood up, made tea, sat down, tried to draw, crumpled up the drawing, stood up, banged on the radiator for heat, sat down, wrote *idea about a guy who hates his job* on a pad, liked it, hated it, crumpled it up shrieking I own too much blank paper!, stood up, searched the apartment for things to throw away, sat down, glowered at his furniture. Two black men who had had themselves surgically turned into women and who were prostitutes and who loved each other lived above Fisher and they often raged at each other through the night. And above them lived Fisher's hammerhead shark of a landlady. I hate it at home thought Fisher. At least everything at work belongs to someone else and I have to live with it all, no question of Living Minimalism here! Although Fisher had quietly flung two old chairs out a stairwell window one quiet spring morning and nobody said anything. Save the police and the widow of the fellow they hit. And it's warm here said Fisher. At home he shuddered unendingly in the infinite cold. The only exercise he got was walking to bars and beating a weak tattoo on the radiator. He would get out his violin and play a few notes in the frigid air and then shaking give up for the night and lunge for the kitchen where he cowered and snacked in fear. Fisher dreaded the nightly giving up, the dragging of the television set from its closet hiding place, the animal feeding on cookies and beer. Whimpering softly. But it's not so bad, my home thought Fisher. Soon I will have got rid of everything I don't need. I will have nothing but my violin, the Three Essential Pens, music books and notation paper. And my music stand. Fisher bought pens and new types of paper every week. I'm sick he thought I'd like a new pen right now, my accident hasn't helped that I see. Fetishes will limit and destroy you. Although you've got to dog your manias within reason. But why said Fisher isn't it obvious to them I'm a violinist? That I don't belong here? Why isn't it plain as day? Why am I not *transformed?* Perhaps it would be plainer if I could shake off this post injury lethargy and when they came in with their damn budget I grabbed it and jumped up on the desk and swung from the light fixture oo oo oooga like an ape! And ripped it up and started to eat it! Hunched up on my desk with the bright eating eyes of monkeys in zoos. Fisher slumped forward at his desk. Footsteps in the corridor. This is not helping he moaned. The budget. Now, *now* there is work to be done and I haven't had any candy. And I haven't run off to the Basement to be by myself for just a few stinking minutes. The telephone rang. Fisher swayed, hands on ears, Laughton in his tower. Ohhh the bells!

Fisher reached for the telephone and pricked his hand on the point of a pencil extending from a tea box which sat on his desk. Ow! said Fisher into the receiver. William? said a woman's voice. Fisher thrilled until he realized it was the voice of his paramour, Jillian Hardy. His relationship with Jillian was fraught. Fraught with cultural baggage, bagged with clinical frottage. You'll see. He didn't like it and neither did she. Jillian? said Fisher. Yes said Jillian How are you? Not too well actually said Fisher I hit my head. Huh? said Jillian On what? Walden Pond said Fisher. Eh? said Jillian. I went out there yesterday with Donald and I slipped on the ice and hit my head said Fisher I needed ten stitches. Stitches! said Jillian My God William my *exams* are coming up. What's that got to do with it? said Fisher knowing full well. Well why do you do these things to me? said Jillian. I didn't do it to you, I did it to me said Fisher annoyed. If I'd done it to you you'd never let me forget it he thought Besides I didn't do it, it happened. Honestly William said Jillian Now I suppose I have to take care of you. Don't bother! said Fisher. Listen said Jillian I don't like this tone you take with me all the time now. As he listened with resentment to Jillian a gaseous cloud began to build up in Fisher's entrails. I have to change my chair! he wanted to shout. I don't know what tone you're talking about he said in a low squeal. Yes you do said Jillian. I have to—yiii! said Fisher beginning to sweat with it all. William? said Jillian Are you . . . in pain? Ooog said Fisher I'll talk later. Well! said Jillian I was only trying to be sympathetic! I'll talk to you tonight growled Fisher. Don't count on it! shouted Jillian. They hung up on each other. Fisher ran for the door and hurried down the corridor. He lost his balance a moment—Gawwd!—as he slipped on a soapy puddle that was being lazily slopped at by a janitor. He righted himself and gained the men's, audibly relieving himself in the cool cavern once inside. Fisher was nothing if not discreet. Christ! came a plaint from a closed stall.

AN ORRERY OF BOSTON

The Boston which features in this narrative sits at the bottom of a great bowl. Perhaps a natural bowl of geology such as the great crater Los Angeles sits in? You can think that if you want! But Boston rests at the bottom of a huge toilet gentle reader. An actual Bog.

From August to July year in year out this thunderbox is sate on by a Being so grand, so huge no one has ever seen him or really named him. It couldn't be God as God is merciful. But from this seat the Being can survey the eastern seaboard, Appalachia, the way west, Ohio, maybe Pikes Peak on a clear day. You work it out. (If say the toilet were 20 miles high and the Being of human proportion, his eyes would be nearly 100 miles in the air and he might be able to see Hawaii. Of course the eyes being so huge would gather more light . . . it could see deep under the ocean for one thing.) Enough! The point is that all that is known meteorologically astronomically and metaphysically in Boston is the walls of this monstrous latrine (on the east of which is the fresco of the Berkshires) and The Ass (they've named that!) of the Being. The Bostonian's sky is dark, his horizon porcelain, his environment water ice and effluvia from August to July. All they see hear feel and smell is The Ass. The Ass! Squatting resolutely above. Producing a continuous unholy cacation which the hapless populace term rain and snow. But how can that be rain which smells of dogs and how can that be snow as black as pitch? The names are merely out of consideration for strangers. After so many years of this the Bostonians haven't any real decorum left. Only a lot of tiny pleasures in the face of this onslaught. They're not kidding anybody. Knowledge of their awful lot is etched on their faces along with the doubt.

The Institute of Science sits dead in the middle of this Boston, itself looking like it might have been extruded from The Ass more or less a century before. Spreading gray across several acres near Boston Common, at the edge of Back Bay but too indifferent to ooze in.

Fisher felt he could not return to the heartbreaking smallness of his office. He decided to go on an errand assigned him by Smith. It was quite a distance to the library. Fisher did not know how to hold his hands while walking there. If he put them in the front pockets of his trousers he looked too nervous. If he put them in his jacket pockets he looked as if he were trying to impersonate junior faculty. If he put them in his back trouser pockets he looked like a juvenile delinquent. From time to time during this journey Fisher distracted himself from the hands problem by looking out a window at Boston, the low grey buildings of the Institute rising like plantar warts. Fisher wondered why on such mornings the city didn't freeze solid. But perhaps then he thought The warts would fall off. It's all carefully constructed. Some morning I won't show up and they'll go to my apartment with a crowbar and find me frozen to my bed. Fisher began to mumble imprecations against his landlady but found he had reached the library. He went into it. Behind the desk was a librarian typing. *Miss Mapes* read the sign. Fisher stood and gaped at her.

From the top of her delightful windswept ponytailed auburn hair to her athletic legs and feet encased in pennyloafers and green knee socks, Fisher found her beautiful. She typed efficiently too. Next to her was some kind of amorphous Christmas decoration she had brought in. Fisher drew a slip of paper out of his pocket and looked at it, then back at her. I love you thought Fisher clearing his throat. Do you have *Mitochondria for Moderns?* he asked meeting her eyes as she turned at the croaking. The eyes were pale blue and riveting. I'll see she said turning to her desk. I want you thought Fisher I want a preppie. I want to be taken boating on Daddy's sailboat and drink gin and tonic and have weekends to ourselves in the big house in Connecticut. Aisle 40 said Miss Mapes after consulting the library catalogue. Thank you very much said Fisher who turning abruptly walked right into an Oriental student. He pardoned himself and walked toward the stacks *followed* he thought *by slanted eyes of hate.*

Aisle 40 was an attractive aisle and Fisher enjoyed walking down it. He found himself surrounded by books about life in its simplest most pitiful forms. Passionate plankton, the drama of the diatoms. He stopped at the appropriate shelf and searched for the book for which Smith lusted. Fisher was coordinating Smith's latest book for the press. This meant typing and retyping hundreds of pages of tiny equations. Fisher found *Mitochondria for Moderns* and took it off the shelf. It was a foxed old book filled to bursting with formulae. Fisher's blood cooled remarkably. I'm going to have to type this he thought All of this. He looked up and down the aisle and seeing no one he put the book on the floor, resting it on its edges like a pup tent. He took a box of matches from his pocket and quickly set the book afire. He bent over and blew on it to encourage the flames which quickly took to the dry old pages. Fisher stood back and admired the bonfire. He kicked at it slightly to keep it away from the books on the bottom shelf. As he stood contemplating the crackling book an alarm bell sounded. He jammed the box of matches into his pocket and turned to leave. Only to see Miss Mapes running toward him up the length of Aisle 40.

What's happening? she panted reaching him. That book's on fire! said Fisher pointing at it and adopting a worried look. What! she said. Panic stricken. It was the strangest thing said Fisher turning to follow her as she began a rapid trot back to her desk. He watched her bottom jerk in her khaki skirt. It was warm said Fisher Almost hot when I picked it up off the shelf. As Miss Mapes ran she turned around and gave Fisher a queer look. But a believing look thought Fisher. And then it just burst into flame he said.

Miss Mapes reached the counter and unclasped a small fire extinguisher from under it. I've got to save the library! she shouted Fire! Students from other lands looked up at their desks not understanding. ¿Inferno? Que . . . ? Miss Mapes ran back to Aisle 40 followed by Fisher who from the rear again admired her horsy build through the classic lines of her conservative dress. He watched her bend over and flushed with excitement squirt white foam on the smoldering book which really had already burnt up. The bell was still ringing. Miss Mapes emptied the entire extinguisher on the little black pile, then daintily stepped over the tower of suds she had created. She came back toward Fisher and looked at the steaming mess. You say it was hot? she asked him wrinkling her fine eyebrows. Her eyes sparkled like the Delaware in spate along waving fields of grain the tips of which were her freckles (just a few). Yes said Fisher Hot to the touch and then it ignited. They walked back toward the desk. Lucky thing I happened to pick it up said Fisher Or the whole place might have gone. I'll have to call the head librarian said Miss Mapes. Fisher watched her brown hand athletically dial the telephone. She spoke briefly and in another minute a man who smelt of ambergris was standing in a tie next to Fisher. What is it Alison? he asked Miss Mapes. *Alison* thought Fisher. A book has burned up Mr Ropp she said. What! said the man who had been eyeing Fisher. It was spontaneous combustion said Fisher unasked. Mr Ropp's eyes narrowed alarmingly. Books don't do that sir he said keenly And who may I ask are you? Ah Fisher William Fisher said Fisher I'm an administrator in Engineering. Ropp looked Fisher up and down in a dismissive way. Was it an old book? he asked. Yes said Alison It was an old biochemical text. It was almost alchemical joked Fisher again unasked It was so old. Very funny said Ropp Spontaneous combustion in my library. Yes said Fisher Everything's going to Hell these days. Mr Ropp looked penetratingly at Fisher and then turned to Alison. Turn off the alarm! he said Sakes alive! Then he walked away. As he went into his office he called to Alison Make out a report! His eyes disappeared attempting to plumb Fisher's soul.

Alison turned a wonderful smile toward Fisher. The alarm was still ringing. I'll need your telephone number she said. 2197 said Fisher. And then she said What's your home number? 490 2770 said Fisher astonished. She looked up and smiled at him warmly, magnificently. I'll call you about it she said smiling. Her meaning was unmistakable or so Fisher believed. He blushed and smiled and stumbled backwards. Yes OK fine he said. He turned and headed for the door. I don't believe it he thought Alison

Mapes may dial my personal number. But as he opened the door he was thrown to the floor by a powerful stream of water, he was knocked and buffeted back into the library by a torrent of water! which roared into the room. As Fisher battled the raging cataract and with spare brain sections tried to deduce its meaning he heard voices yelling and Alison screaming Stop! Stop! A moment later it stopped and as Fisher got uncertainly to his feet with stinging skin and ringing ears he saw the gaggle of Latins which comprised the Institute fire brigade. They all wore yellow slickers and sou'wester hats and they were as wet as Fisher. The four of them stood holding a huge dripping hose and looking at Fisher with reticence. Alison ran up. What's the idea? she said looking for some reason at Fisher. Don't ask me he said in exasperation Ask *them!* Alison looked at the fire brigade. De larm one of them said We had de larm. Fisher looked down at his clothes which had the dull rich colors of clothes that are fully saturated. His shoes were bathyscaphes. I don't believe this said Fisher. Sorry man said another member of the brigade. Fisher looked at Alison and was dismayed to see she might laugh. Scarlet, he immediately walked past them all and out into the hallway. His bulging shoes squelching on the stone floor. He rounded a corner, then stopped and looked out a window at the frozen town. I am wet he thought. He didn't know what to do. He couldn't go home, it was 20° outside. He began to walk back to his office.

He got strange stares in the halls. Man is not in his element thought Fisher In the forests the mountains or on the seas. Or deserts the Arctic or the Antarctic. Man's element is the office. All our striving. The office. It's infernal. But who says you're supposed to like your element?

Who's asked brittle stars if they enjoy inching along the dark sandy bottom? Who knows if the iguana is pleased with a bed of sun baked guano? It's dangerous, questioning people's element. They get nervous as Hell. Dullards! Fisher fumed Haven't you ever seen someone soaked to the skin before? On to the office. A sallow woman put her head out of her office and with a toothy smile said Oh is it raining? Fisher considered hitting her with one of his shoes which easily weighed two hundred pounds but how to lift it? It was all he could do to walk in the heavy wet clothes. He slogged up to the door of his office and went in. Immediately a voice from behind the partition.

Fisher! Where's that book? They didn't have it! yelled Fisher It's gone! He sat down at his desk and reached for the lamp. As his hand touched the switch he received an electric shock. Yaaah! he yelled. Be quiet! came a shout We're working! As he sat and sagged Fisher's clothing began to rain down over the chair and onto the floor. Over the steady drizzle he considered various ways of drying his clothing. I could go to the Basement and straddle a steam pipe he thought. I could go stand by the photocopy room exhaust. He looked about the room and noticed the radiator. He decided it would be easiest, all things considered, to take his clothes off and hang them on the radiator which raged dull red in heat all winter long. Are you liable to be working for some time? Fisher called over the partition. Shut up, can't you? came the reply. Right thought Fisher. He made a sign for the door which said I'M NAKED INSIDE, tore it up, wrote another which said OUT TO LUNCH and hung it on the door, locking it then from the inside and turning off the overhead light. He took off his shoes and socks, trousers shorts jacket shirt and undershirt and hung them all on the long radiator. They began to hiss and to fill the room with vapor. Fisher sat down at his desk and tried to come to grips with the feeling of being naked at it. If the phone rings I'll be talking to them naked he thought. If I agree to certain budget items while naked I could perhaps use that as an excuse to change our policies in midterm. A way of getting out of the inevitable April jams. A board of government auditors. But you said equipment for this project would cost only $10,000. *Yes but I was naked when I agreed to that.* What! But what about this completion date? *Sorry but I had no clothes on when I promised you that date.* I was naked, naked in my office!

Fisher! a voice called. Fisher jumped and banged his bare knee against the desk. What! he cried. Don't get testy with me the voice said What's the matter with you? I'm naked Fisher thought I'm busy he said. What time is it? the voice said. It's one said Fisher. Order us lunch in the dining room for two said the voice. Right said Fisher. So I am going to talk nude on the phone he thought. He dialed the Institute dining room. Hello? said a tiny voice as if from the bottom of a tureen. Is that the dining room? said Fisher I want to make a reservation for two. Do you know what I'm wearing? he thought. What name? said the tiny voice, upset, drowning in the soup. Smith of Engineering said Fisher. The voice hung up suddenly. Fisher hung up and looked at the pool of water around his chair. It's all set he called. For God's sake be quiet! said the voice.

Fisher reached up and very carefully this time turned on the desk lamp. He was distressed to discover he had need of the men's. The clothes were still sizzling on the radiator and he heard people passing in the hall and saw their shadows on the frosted glass of the door. Even if I made a dash for it after waiting until the hall was quiet he thought With my luck I would collide with Brenda Moran just coming out of her office for a late lunch. Fisher pictured slipping on that morning's soapy spot and shooting naked past the men's through the stairwell and out the plate-glass window onto Arlington Street. I will have to wait thought Fisher. Little soldier. His clothes were somewhere inside the thick cloud which filled the room. Fisher decided they were not dry. Then to his horror he became aware of noises made at the ends of meetings coming from behind the partition. Fisher realized the inner office door was about to open and in panic his mind supplied wild pictures of fantastic routes of nude escape but the door opened and out came professors Brown Jones and Smith.

The three men stopped and looked at the naked Fisher. Say! said Brown. Wow said Jones. What the Hell? said Smith. Wait! said Fisher jumping up I was just about to go to the bathroom. Not in here you won't God damn it! shouted Smith. Fisher! said Jones What's the matter son? What's all this steam in here? said Brown. My clothes are all wet said Fisher I got soaked in the library and I had to take them off and put them on the radiator. How in Hell could you get soaked in the library? said Smith. It's those Latins said Fisher. What *Latins?* said Smith. Suddenly Fisher could not find words. The three men looked in unison from Fisher's head bandage to the radiator and back to Fisher in his nakedness. Let's get out of here said Jones. OK said Brown. Put your clothes on for Christ's sake said Smith. They made for the door and flung it open alarmingly wide. Fisher saw Brenda Moran in her office across the hall although she did not look up. Smith was the last one out. I'll talk to you later he said to Fisher angrily. I'm telling the truth! said Fisher as the door slammed.

Now chilled he sat down in his chair.

Naked thought Fisher I have been discovered naked in my office but even so I feel dulled and alienated. Fisher reached out to the radiator and touched his coat which looked as though it might be dry. It was soaking wet. Fisher got up and struggled to wring out the heavy clothes, unleashing a freshet onto the floor and out under the door. He put the crumpled clothes back on the radiator and sat down. The telephone rang. What? he said lifelessly. Mr Fisher? said a voice straining to speak beyond its intrinsic importance. Yes? said Fisher. This is Security. You call this security? Fisher thought. What do you want? he said. Well uh Professor Smith tole us you might not be feelin too good Mr Fisher an uh he wants us to come an see you an take you home maybe. Good Christ said Fisher There's nothing wrong with me, I've just taken my clothes off that's all. Silence. After I got drenched by those damn Latins! What Latins sir? said the voice. Ah now you're interested! said Fisher The fire brigade! Why doesn't somebody call the fire brigade? he shouted. He's hysterical all right said the voice to someone else I never handled nothin like this, what do ya do? Calm um down said another voice. I'm calm I'm calm said Fisher I'm trying to tell you the God damn fire brigade hosed me down in the library and I came up here to dry my clothes. Doncha have any spare? said the voice. A spare set of clothes? howled Fisher I work in an office! The air and light are filtered and processed, there is no weather here. If you worked up here would you keep a spare set of clothes sergeant? Uhh . . . no sir said the voice. And to the other voice: I dunno, maybe he's OK. Fisher fumed as he looked down at his naked legs and the pool of water. Well fine said Fisher If you call the library they

will tell you I was drenched with water there earlier
today. He wanted to add Unless they are part of this too!
but remembering Alison he didn't. But sir said the voice
What about this uh bleedin bandage on ya head? Professor Smith said that uh . . . My bandage has nothing to do
with my behavior! shouted Fisher slamming the phone
down. He decided he should put his clothes on, wet or no.
He got up from his desk and went over to the bubbling
radiator and reached for his socks. A knock at the door.
Who iiis it? said Fisher musically. It's Alison Mapes. From
the library said a voice. And so saying the voice produced
a hand which opened the door!

No! shouted Fisher as Alison put her head into the
room and looked at him with an open mouth. Fisher
whipped a sock modestly in front of himself. What do you
want? he whimpered seeing Brenda Moran about to get
up from her desk across the hall. I . . . I . . . said Alison.
Close the door! said Fisher. She moved into the room and
shut the door. Your clothes are off said Alison looking
Fisher up and down with demure enthusiasm. Get out of
here said Fisher. His fantasies about Alison stampeded to
a far country. But all of a sudden she was beside him. Ooh
you're nice she said rubbing his chest. Fisher recoiled
from her icy hand. What are you doing! he said stumbling
back against his chair Seduction isn't possible under these
conditions. She laughed. Horsily, clubbily, oh so prettily.
I was just trying to dry my clothes off said Fisher They got
wet, perhaps you remember. Don't you have any spare?
said Alison wrinkling her nose and advancing again. Certainly not said Fisher You're the second person who's
asked me that. Why would someone who works in an
office have spare . . . But she was at him again, rubbing his
chest. Fisher was now in the corner. Proverbial and con-

crete. I have a dryer at home said Alison. No said Fisher I'm going home . . . to my home . . . uhh . . . she was still rubbing. . . . What time is it anyway? I've noticed you said Alison I think you're really neat. Ah well be that as it may said Fisher I have a confession to make. That fire today, I . . .

Another knock at the door. Louder. Fisher froze in terror and looked at Alison who was beginning to laugh again. The rich babbling of young maidens at a yacht club luncheon. Fisher? said a deep voice Fisher! What? said Fisher. Open up said the voice. Who's that? hissed Fisher to Alison who was withdrawing into a different corner with her fist in her mouth. Choking with hilarity. Fisher looked at her in fear and realizing the voice outside thought the door was locked, grabbed his wet trousers from the radiator and jammed them on, stumbling toward the door.

Fisher opened the door a crack and looked out to see Smith standing there with Victor Jowls, the Vice President of the Institute, who surveyed Fisher's naked chest with interest. Yes? husked Fisher. Are you all right Fisher? said Smith who it seemed had hoped Fisher would answer the door clothed. Yes I'm all right said Fisher keeping the door drawn against him. He looked at Jowls whose hairline was being pursued by his eyebrows. What I've been trying to say said Fisher Is that I got wet and took off my clothes because it was lunchtime. Jowls's eyes narrowed. You know said Fisher Because there was no one around. Jowls looked at Fisher's head and a light came into his eyes. I had to dry them off! said Fisher Look there's nothing wrong with me, stop staring at my head! I'm shouting at the Vice President of the Institute he thought And I have only pants on. Jowls and Smith looked at each other and then back at Fisher. What's in there? said Jowls quietly. Nobody! said Fisher Nothing! Now you listen to me said Jowls frowning As Vice President it is my responsibility to determine whether or not you are capable of carrying out your uh Institutely duties. My what? said Fisher. That is your employific . . . your *Institutional* duties said Jowls. Your job said Smith. Right! said Jowls. Fisher you know you're in a sensitive position as regards use of radioactive materials said Smith nervously. I'm well aware said Fisher Of the radioactive materials you keep in your desk *Smith* he thought. Smith could never be bothered locking things up. People like you have got to be normal said Jowls. Fisher seized the opportunity to appear sane. Don't we just! he huffed. He pointed his head upward in what he hoped struck Jowls and Smith as an attitude of trustworthy indignation. Gentlemen said Fisher I'm normal as the day is long. As he said this he suddenly realized it was the shortest day of the year. But! he continued quickly I have a budget and a monthly report to write so if you will excuse me I think this enough of banter. Much as I enjoy it. Fisher shut the door firmly in the faces of the two men. He switched on the overhead light and turned on his typewriter. He began to pound repeatedly on the *x* key, and to harrumph. He saw the silhouettes of Smith and Jowls against the door. After Fisher had typed two or three bogus lines they went off. Arguing. He stopped hammering on the machine and put it off, turning to Alison in the corner. You're really interesting she said. That was the Vice President said Fisher. You handled him marvelously said Alison walking toward him. Don't touch me! said Fisher Your hands are cold. She went instead to the typewriter and typed. Then she walked to the door and to Fisher's dismay flung it wide

wide wide and with a merry laugh went quickly away down the corridor. Fisher hurried to close the door but as he did so Brenda Moran looked up from her desk across the hall. Hey where's ya shirt? she called. I don't know said Fisher slamming the door.

He went to the radiator and began to tussle with his damp clothes. Slowly he pulled them on. They were so heavy he began to stoop. He put his overcoat on and pulled the piece of paper from the typewriter. *Alison* it said. *Call me.* A number. He put it in a pocket. He groped under his desk for Mr Squeaky. Pneumonia is an agonizing death he thought. He turned off the overhead light and banged out the door down the hall and down the stairs. He dragged through the big lobby. The lively intellectual atmosphere of a columbarium he thought. He staggered out to the street. A chafing cold wind howled off the bricks of Boston and immediately started to turn Fisher's face into a sloughing white parchment.

III | The Moaning of the Bar

Fisher decided to trudge rather than walk. As he trudged he mused on the pre Christmas bustle of Boston. There is no earthly reason for people to bustle in Boston he thought. They bustle because they know Boston to be a city of 600,000 and they feel bustle is required. It seemed to Fisher that everyone in Boston always did everything the same way. He wondered that the streets and sidewalks were not striated with a thousand ruts. Drive work eat. Drive work eat. Drive work eat. Eat drive eat. Eat drive eat. Eat drive eat. Boston! On his blackest days Fisher resorted to the hypothesis that Bostonians had no free will at all. Boston a debased puppet theater on a big chain drive. People moved up and down the street by pulleys cleverly hidden under them. Looked in windows, brayed at others, all mechanical, all dummies. Funny faces jerking back and forth. To walk down the street was to live in a ratchet driven cartoon. The same shooting gallery every day. With a BONK! and then a WHIRR! and then a BONK! and then a DING! A monstrous toy. The Pilgrims crossed the glass Atlantic in their clockwork *Mayflower*. And all under the effluvient Ass! Cold nipping flatulence if such can be imagined, called a cold raw wind in Boston. Sending the residents scurrying for their imitation winter clothing.

Although I should go directly home thought Fisher as he trudged I need a Guinness. This meant he would have to walk wet as he was through Boston and over a bridge to Cambridge. Fisher did not like Cambridge. Nor did he like to take the T. He liked to walk and he liked Guinness. As he warmed to the decision for Guinness Fisher tried to trudge quickly. But this he found impossible. And he thought One is not sexually attractive when trudging. Save to a pretty depressed bunch. He then attempted to combine his scholarly world weary trudge with a bold walk brimming with virility and ended up jouncing awkwardly up the street. Fortunately he met no one he knew. Traveling this way wet Fisher with violin passed through the Public Garden up Charles Street over a bridge and up a long avenue to the door of the Evening Star. The Evening Star was a Cambridge bar with vague Irish intimations where the entertainment was not, as in many Cambridge water holes, a houseplant riot nor a turtlenecked guitarist, but the ever present possibility of personal molestation.

In Fisher's mind the country of Ireland was not so much a country with the usual accouterments (people, handbills, factories, cars, magazines, sheep, sauces) as it was a great unitary biomass, a brown and green tufted nodosity softly breathing in and out, a mole on the face of the globe, its processes of photosynthesis and excrescence culminating solely in the production of Guinness Extra Stout. He dotted its contours with loamy fields sprouting proud rows of barley and with leafy glades where hop vines clung lovingly to delicate strings twined in inventive cat's cradles by a happy peasantry. On the banks of twinkling blue rivers singing farmers sacked grain morning till night. On the brows of gentle hills in Fisher's Eire gay windmills sailed powering cogged wooden machinery within which did something or other. Steam locomotives painted turquoise pink and gold called at Victorian country platforms, loads of barley and hops flung into open cars by the adoring serfs. The trains chuffed slowly through shimmering dales to a Dublin fashioned after the Emerald City of Oz. Singing midgets unloaded the sacks with glee and trundled them into the maltings and storerooms of the great Brewery at St James's Gate. Plump pink men, each at one with the worn handles and whistling steam jets of the antique machinery he tended, worked in high rooms under arched windows of sunlight, stirring live things in mighty vats with dedication and giant wooden spoons. The slumbering brew foamed delicately in its tubs, passed in copper pipes from kyrie to sanctus to agnus dei and finally dropped sensually to the racking room where each open mouthed soldier in an army of kegs and brown bottles thirstily awaited his turn at the gushing pipe of ecstasy. And this hearty river of life which began as the pollen streaming through the Irish mornings to the hop flowers and became the barley cars flying along the little railways and the wort coursing through the arteries of St James's Gate and the bottle barges on the Liffey and the kegs in liners on the Gulf Stream found its way to the Boston docks and up Massachusetts Avenue through the tap and into the watering mouth of William Fisher. Ireland may in fact be like that although current accounts suggest it is slightly otherwise. But to Fisher the concept of Ireland was inseparable from its great stout and would ever remain so.

Fisher's Hibernicizing was interrupted by a dark hand which grasped his shoulder with determination. Yo Fisheh said a deep black voice What happen to yo haid mah man? Fisher turned to behold Fat Leroy. While hardly Irish (although in Celtic fuzziness many of the Evening Star regulars called him Fat *Leary*) and certainly not an example of negripulchritude, Fat Leroy was nevertheless a respected ringer at the Evening Star. He could wield his bulk threateningly (Mah bodah is a register weapon he boasted often) and so was one of the unofficial bouncers of the place. At times the Evening Star was filled with unofficial bouncers exclusively. I fell on the ice Leroy said Fisher drumming his fingers on the bar. Mm mm mm! said Fat Leroy Yo ah would be mo careful in future Fisheh. He always said in future. Yes thank you Leroy I will said Fisher In future. With a glare Fat Leroy moved off down the bar. Fisher's relationship with Fat Leroy was one of timid joking. Fat Leroy had stepped between Fisher and some obstreperous unofficial bouncers one night but Fisher had since come to the conclusion that it had been just a fluke. There was no telling with Fat Leroy.

Fisher stared out at the cold night and engaged himself in blanching at his workday. When all is said and done he thought I have acted quite normally and all this about my bandage is wind. If I hadn't hit my head I could have taken my clothes off in my office without it becoming an issue. It's so unfair. We're all judged by our wounds. All is vanity and vexation of spirit Fisher said to the bartender. Yuh said the man. Fisher stared at the glass of black stout and tried to establish a system for drinking it. Every time I hear someone order a whiskey I will take a gulp thought Fisher That will work out nicely. Whiskey!

said a gruff voice almost immediately and Fisher raised his glass to his lips. He drank deeply and as he replaced the glass on the bar another voice said Whiskey! As Fisher lifted his glass a third nasal chant of Whiskey! That's two gulps thought Fisher beginning to drink. Whiskey! Three thought Fisher just finishing the first. Whiskey! Whiskey! Whiskey! Whiskey! Whiskey! Fisher put his glass down in disgust. There was some kind of absurd whiskey pandemonium going on, it wasn't normal. His systems usually came to naught.

Fisher felt a pressure on his right elbow. He turned to see a tiny dirty man smiling up at him and pawing the tip of his violin case with a filthy hand. Mister my buddies and I been noticin ya said the little man. Oh? said Fisher. Yah we been seein ya in here said the man. Hm said Fisher beginning to worry. We was wonderin if ya could give us a tune on yer viol said the little man picking at Fisher's sleeve. Fisher hesitated for the little man was unknowingly asking for a great commitment. At moments like this Fisher knew he was no musician. But why *prove* it to a bunch of drunks? Yes all right said Fisher his stout warmed brain flashing a murky picture of his hand on the fingerboard which was however intended to be a warning. Fisher's relationship with his brain was poor. He grabbed his violin and the little man pulled him to the back of the Evening Star.

Four big ruddy men at a table. Hi! said Fisher. The men looked away. A tune said one of them. Well I'll give it a try chuckled Fisher Although I'm just learning. This ain't no students bar sonny said the biggest of the four. Quite coldly. So! thought Fisher It's a putsch. Play or be pummeled. As he opened the case and picked up Mr Squeaky he began to sweat recalling the numerous warnings he'd been given against straying too far to the rear of the Evening Star.

But the real trouble began when Fisher put his violin under his chin and raised his rosined bow and thought: ? Try as he might Fisher could not remember how to begin any of the artless tunes he whistled and fussed over constantly. As he shut his eyes he could not recall a one. He softly brought the bow down on the A string and not finding the opening of a tune he pretended he was warming up. Sweat poured down Fisher into his already wet clothes. For two full minutes he ran trembling hands up and down the scales of E G A and D and found not one portal to any melody. Egad. He tramped his feet under the table in vain search of rhythm. Well get on with it! said one of the ruddy men. Sweet God thought Fisher They're getting ready to kill me. I've I've I've had an accident said Fisher See? It's affected my playing. See my bandage? He moved to indicate with his bow but instead knocked over somebody's whiskey. A horrid glower from the assembly frightened Fisher into sawing lifelessly at the strings again in gibbering despair. Dissatisfaction now spread rapidly to the bar. What's that eh? said someone. Dillytant! said another. Fisher shut his eyes and commanded his hands to play something without him. No response. He was hardly that kind of fiddler being no kind really at all. A broken picture of Walden lit up his inner eye and Fisher then understood it really was the accident.

I can't play tonight gents said Fisher hurriedly reaching for his case. No sooner had he laid Mr Squeaky to rest but Fisher felt a strong grip at his neck. Why don't you just take a little walk right on home sonny? said a guttural voice. Wait! said Fisher as the grip lifted him to his feet by the neck I'll sing you a song! He was released and stood shaking looking at the red men who it seemed might be stayed by this offer. To take out a fiddle in the Evening Star and not play lilting Irish music! What an idiot! Fisher cleared his throat and shivered in his damp clothing. An Irish song I learned off a Pete Seeger record said Fisher then inhaling to begin. But a monstrous growl rumbled through the group and the grip grabbed Fisher this time by both neck and pants and sped him toward the door. Hey! shouted Fisher What's the matter? Haven't you guys ever heard of Pete Seeger? The door, looming! Leroy! howled Fisher banging his head on the door as he was catapulted into and through it. He landed in an unnatural sit on the sidewalk and as he turned to look back he was struck squarely in the forehead by Mr Squeaky, in case. The door shut with a bang. Great thought Fisher getting up more or less in a spasm. Make friends the world over with folk music.

After looking up and down the avenue Fisher began his walk back to Boston violently shivering as the winds roared at him. God the Irish thought Fisher drifting up and down the freezing boulevards. With their Guinness their Jungian music their raven haired white skinned colleens and their soft lilting voices they are put on this earth to put us to sleep and lull us toward Death! To charm us into a stupor and then hit us over the head. Filled with resentment he gripped Mr Squeaky and as he finally reached Back Bay he was snarling and glaring at passersby. An old woman took flight as Fisher came up behind her at a street corner, blue bump on forehead bloody bandage peeling off Grrr! As he neared his apartment he saw a light in it. Jillian! he thought And I smell of Guinness and am wet. Jillian! Of course I could make up a fantastic explanation. But no. I have been supernaturally victimized today and that is all. My bandage has nothing to do with my behavior.

Fisher walked up the steps of the three story house. To his dismay he saw his landlady in the vestibule. Wondering no doubt how to open my mailbox thought Fisher. He pushed the door open viciously against her. Yeow! screamed the landlady. Oh good evening said Fisher. Watch where ya goin she said. Then: Whaddya doin lookin like that? she whined Ya all wet. I got soaked at work said Fisher An accident. You smell like beer said Fisher's landlady I think you drink too much. I will lift my violin and beat her brain out thought Fisher. Involuntarily his arm lifted the case slightly. An another thing she rasped Stop playin that thing so late at night! I will dispose of the body in the furnace thought Fisher. In this way he remembered the furnace had not been working for weeks. When are we going to get some heat around here? said Fisher. Just never you mind! said the landlady shaking her penurious withered fin at Fisher You ask too many questions! And listen she said Who's this girl who keeps comin in here? She's always in here, I didn't give her no key said the landlady. She is my girlfriend said Fisher And every night two floors beneath your old Vaporub sodden bed we do it! It! Fisher stared ferociously at his landlady who stared back as he put his key in the lock. Wait a minute you don't talk to me that way come back here! I can't said Fisher I have to go get pneumonia, I'm late already. He slammed the door. Don't slam the door! And stop puttin ya dirty fingas on the glass! shouted the landlady furiously searching her rotting coat for her own key.

Fisher opened the door to his apartment and went inside slamming it even harder. Don't slam the door! came a faint cry from the vestibule.

Fisher turned and seeing Jillian standing right next to him stumbled over his violin case. What was that all about? said Jillian. That suppurating old troll said Fisher She gives me a pain. God William what happened to you? said Jillian in exasperation not sympathy. Nothing said Fisher Nothing has happened. But what's that bump on your head? said Jillian putting down a half chewed wad of feminist law briefs. I told you I had an accident said Fisher Remember? On the phone? Jillian looked from Fisher's loose bandage to his forehead. Why didn't they dress the one on your forehead? That said Fisher Is new. I just got it. He sat down. The ceiling light began to beat down on him. He hated the light in his apartment. There wasn't any during the day and at night there was only a 500 watt bulb which clubbed you unmercifully. Intense annoyance filled Fisher's forearms with dull pain. Jillian looked at him. When are you going to buy an iron William? she said You look like a real bum. Thank you sneezed Fisher. You're all wet said Jillian. Yes sneezed Fisher again It so happens I met with a second minor accident. As well as the third. Is it raining out? said Jillian. No at work said Fisher. It's raining at work? she said. She did not come over to Fisher to offer any physical consolation he reflected. She just sat and asked him questions. Truly a barrister in the making. What happened? she said. There was a fire in the library and I was squirted by the brigade said Fisher. William why are all these things happening to you? Are you sure you're all right? What kind of American are you! cried Fisher Just because I have a bandage on my head! Give a guy a break! I don't use my bandage as an excuse for anything. She got up and went over to him. You're shivering she said. Damn right said Fisher It's twenty degrees out and I'm soaked to the bone. You smell like beer said Jillian. Do you mind? said Fisher *I have a bandage on.* I was wet and I wanted a drink. So I got one. At that place? said Jillian. Yes said Fisher. Why don't you ever take me there? said Jillian. Because you wouldn't like it said Fisher You like places with plants hanging all over and matching homosexual waiters in neat little red aprons. Thanks a lot said Jillian. Fisher got up and started toward the bathroom. Where are you going? said Jillian petulantly. To the solarium said Fisher equally so.

Jillian Hardy was a tall girl with long legs dark hair and a stunning face. But her face often stunned with the greediness of the sounds it made rather than with its beauty. A disquieting face, the kind of face in which the muscles are always slightly bunched in dissatisfaction. Dissatisfaction firstly over the unattainment as yet of high personal income and secondly over historical masculine injustice. Fisher had taken Jillian away from a pudgy blond overachiever named Mohrdieck and had spent a deal of time lately wondering how Mohrdieck could be induced to take her back.

Fisher got into the bathtub and turned on the hot water tap. I have decided he called to Jillian To take my clothes off in a stream of hot water. But a rush of cold water shot out of the nozzle and drenched Fisher who began to tremble. There isn't any hot water called Jillian. Hell! said Fisher I'm going to kill that old crab I swear it. He stepped out of the tub and stood once again in drip-

ping wet clothes. He then saw he was still holding his
violin. I need dry clothes he said quietly. Why don't you
just go to bed? said Jillian. Because I'm going out said
Fisher shuffling to the bedroom I'm playing tonight.
You're kidding she said following him After I came all the
way over here from Cambridge? Who asked you to? said
Fisher beginning a titanic struggle with his wet clothes. I
was going to call you after I got home he said falling
against the wall as he attempted to take his trousers off.
Jillian stalked out of the room. Stalk away said Fisher Stalk
stalk stalk. You are driving me crazy he thought Not my
bandage. The clothes clawed at him. It's circumstance.
Awful divine retribution for God knows how many of the
sins I've committed. The water in Fisher's shoe had
created a tremendous vacuum which bonded it to his foot
as if with glue. It's retribution and Jillian Hardy. I can't
stand it! he shouted pulling at the shoe with all his might.
He fell to the floor tugging at it. In the front room Jillian
turned on the radio. Later tonight you can hear real Tas-
manian musicians discussing women's music urban planning and their upcoming concert at Symphony Hall.
Would you turn that shit off! yelled Fisher ripping his
sopping shirt off his back and throwing it to the floor with
a loud slap. The radio went off. Savage sounds of packing
up came from the other room. Going somewhere? said
Fisher. Yes home you idiot came the reply. Should I come
over later? said Fisher rooting in a bureau drawer. If you
want! Slam of door. Furious key click. Furiouser slam of
outer door, stamping down on steps. Far up in the night
an anguished cry: Don't slam the door I keep tellin ya!

Ah thought Fisher Alone with my thoughts and my
wet violin. My violin is wet! He picked up the case and ran

to the kitchen. I'll put it in the oven at a low heat, it will revive. Hills of London do the same. Hot fiddles, heat em up, one a penny two a penny. Fisher whistled. He turned the oven on but there was no sound. Now there's no gas! cried Fisher sinking to his knees in impoverished urban desperation. If I wanted to kill myself I could not! Oh I could place my head in the oven and wait to *freeze* to death, that wouldn't take long. He trudged back to the bedroom and began to hunt for dry clothing. He had put on a sweater and buckled his belt when a horn sounded outside. He put on a rarely used jacket picked up Mr Squeaky and turning off the vicious light he went out. Go to Hell he thought remembering the landlady's injunctions to lock the street door. Getting roughed up by a formless intruder would do you good cackled Fisher. He started across the street toward Donald's car and in doing so braved Death. The big banging cars throbbed with blood lust that night.

Donald sat motionless staring ahead smoking his pipe. Contemplating the Folds of Rindfleisch. Fisher tried the passenger door which was locked. God damn it he said violently banging on the door with Mr Squeaky. Donald jumped and hurriedly unlocked the door. Thanks said Fisher getting in and slamming it loudly. Donald immediately began to examine Fisher's bandage. Don't look at my bandage said Fisher holding Mr Squeaky as if he were a sick baby. How ya doin? said Donald starting the engine and pulling out into the traffic. Great said Fisher looking gloomily out at the store windows. Christmas. Did you go to work? said Donald. Yes I had a wonderful day at work said Fisher A girl gave me her telephone number although I will omit the secondary details. She give you that contusion too? said Donald. No I managed that all by myself said Fisher. Sounds interesting said Donald.

They drove over the Harvard Bridge into Cambridge. I hate Cambridge said Fisher It's so tidy. But ugliness rages within each brick's heart. Speaking of Cambridge how's Jillian? said Donald Do you want me to drop you off there on the way back? She stalks said Fisher. I see said Donald. Way back from where? said Fisher. Concord said Donald I thought you knew. Oh great said Fisher I didn't. Sawdust and soy pies. You could have told me, I might have escaped. Come on said Donald. Driving me there in the car, he says come on thought Fisher.

The usual Belmont fun night was under way. Along the streets teenagers hunched shoulders against the cold and put hands in plastic coat pockets. Some smoked while others gawked in pizzeria windows. Suddenly a roaring souped up kar flashed out from a side street. Jeez look at that guy said Donald. Yeah said Fisher. The bright lime kar swerved from side to side, then hit the rear of a car stopped at a red light. Jeez! said Donald. Yeah! said Fisher. The rogue kar went into wild reverse and escaped down another street. The motorist hit was now climbing out of her car and shaking her fist in the vandal's direction.

Vroom! said Fisher Vroom! Vroom! Huh? said Donald driving around the poor woman with the crumpled trunk. Batteries not included said Fisher You can drive speed demons anywhere. What! said Donald. Well how do you expect people to act when they're raised in the belief that automobiles and the human body are indestructible and of no consequence? said Fisher And the sponsors think the same of the human spirit? This is not a flying toy. What sponsors? said Donald. Tube doom said Fisher. Fated to grow up on TV in Belmont. To become a crude 17 year old. To ram an Italian woman, possibly a mother. To squeal off into the night. You mean you're *judging* that guy just because you think he's from Belmont? said Donald. Certainly said Fisher And I urge you to do the same. I don't know what you're talking about said Donald. Don't you! said Fisher. *I'M TALKING ABOUT CREEPING MIASMA.* They drove on toward Concord.

When do the stitches come out? said Donald. I hate that expression said Fisher. Any moment now. ABC CBS NBC growled Fisher And that God awful PBS. Donald there's television to eat drink wear read and think. And pot is just television. Dope! You have sustained head trauma said Donald. You son of a bitch said Fisher I'm talking sense. Calm down said Donald. Everyone thinks I'm not calm! shouted Fisher I'm just telling you what I think! Come on there's lots of good things on television said Donald. Fisher reflected. Yes he said Engineer Bill. Who? said Donald. My childhood said Fisher Don't you care? He dressed in blue and white overalls, he was a brave engineer. And he played this milk drinking game with you called red light green light. He said Green light! and you started to drink your milk and then he maliciously shouted Red light! when you were about halfway and you choked and retched your milk up onto the screen. Sounds great said Donald. You're crazy said Fisher TV is irretrievably narcotizing moron-making and bad. You're going to wet the seat said Donald. I'm so calm said Fisher. They drove.

You know Rachel does video stuff said Donald. What? said Fisher Who? Rachel said Donald Sandra's roommate. Oh Rachel said Fisher. She does video said Donald. Hm!

said Fisher annoyed at the usage "does x." And she talks about you said Donald. She talks about me? said Fisher. I mean to say she likes you said Donald. Stop the car said Fisher I'm going to be sick. Very funny said Donald. God thought Fisher Don't tell me that. Rachel!

IV Fruitlands

It was silly to call it that for there was no utopian thinking around the house save a muddled idea that cleanliness and pantomime self sufficiency might someday produce Utopia of their own accord. Cities blacks and American cars didn't fit into the argument however which was one reason why it was ignored. But Fisher and Donald called it the Fruitlands. Slapping each other in hilarity.

In the kitchen of the white clapboard house a young woman sat writing a note. To My Housemates it said. Congratulations on a very clean week. You have all done very well. The only *shirking* was on the part of Rodney who forgot to clean the insides of the holes on the tooth-brush rack again. Rodney this isn't fair to the rest of us. Please pitch in. The young woman paused to sip from a pottery mug, then continued. In the refrigerator she wrote Are 4 helpings of soy goulash (coded green), 3 help-ings of green noodles and turmeric sauce (coded yellow) and 5 helpings of the fish and root casserole which sadly was partly burned but nonetheless is edible (coded red for immediate consumption!!). She put down the blue pen she was using and picked up one with red ink. IT IS NOT FAIR

TO OTHERS she wrote TO EAT GREEN OR YELLOW CODED FOOD BEFORE ALL RED CODED FOOD IS FINISHED. She put down the red and continued in blue. There has also been a sponge problem this week. On Tuesday I found someone (who shall be nameless!!) using the light green sponge on the stove top. Again the red pen. THE LIGHT GREEN SPONGE IS FOR THE SINK ONLY AND ANYONE WHO HAS FORGOTTEN THE SPONGE CODES SHOULD LOOK AT CHART NO 12 ON THE BASEMENT DOOR. Have a nice day she wrote in blue. Rachel. She sat down at the table after posting this edict on the refrigerator. Taking a bowl of peas and a special knife from Maine she began to shell them.

How warped said Fisher who stood looking in the window. Huh? said Donald coming up from locking the car. Concord is filled with thieves. She has no interest in *peas* for God's sake said Fisher She's just doing that *to be sitting in a ladderback chair in a kitchen with a woodstove shelling peas.* Monday eh? said Donald tapping the part of his head which had it been Fisher's would have been stitched. Hilarious said Fisher. Why don't you relax? said Donald I think it's great out here. They got candles fireplaces woodstoves. Yes said Fisher It's a wonder there's any oxygen left. Perhaps that's the problem.

The residents of the Fruitlands were

1 Rachel, whose sole livelihood was the following about of mentally defective wards of the State with video equipment;

2 Sandra, livelihood unknown, distinguished by macrobiotically induced exophthalmia;

3 Rodney, assistant assistant assistant designer of com-
   puting software for a large firm with sinister under-
   ground headquarters.

Their interrelationships were confused but essentially
dull.

Fisher and Donald walked into the hallway. The door
was ever unlocked for vague political reasons on behalf of
two of the three residents and sheer density on the part
of the third (not necessarily No 3 above). Donald went
into the kitchen to greet Rachel and Fisher walked over
to a door on which hung a sheaf of bright colored charts.
He leafed through them and became appalled. While the
Fruitlands was a place of music and camaraderie Fisher
had always suspected its cheery exterior of being a front
for some sort of moral collapse. Now looking through Rachel's charts he discovered it was a tightly run totalitarian
enclave based on slavish devotion to order and cleanliness. Proof! The charts allowed time for nothing else in
the world but tidying up and the reorganization of cleaning supplies. And, once a fortnight, music. Stuffed into a
little box. Fisher found he was part of an idolatrous system. Filled with indignation he turned abruptly to storm
into the kitchen but slipped on a small hooked rug and
sailed into the stairs, banging his head on the banister
before being obliged to grab same to remain upright.

Hey William! came a voice. Still hugging the rail
Fisher slowly rotated his head to see Rodney gawking.
Nrg said Fisher. Hey I heard about your accident said
Rodney. Which one? said Fisher. He drew himself up and
stepped off the little rug. Yeh heh heh said Rodney Rachel's been making these rugs. You shouldn't have one
there said Fisher. Yeah maybe not said Rodney putting it

back in the same spot. So how ya doin? he said swinging to pound at Fisher's back which was quickly moved aside. Ya bump yer forehead at the pond too? said Rodney. No I've been trying to go one better said Fisher You know me, never satisfied. Oh said Rodney.

Hi William! said Rachel coming into the hall followed by Donald. *Hi,* what an awful word thought Fisher I can't bear it. Hi he said. I heard about your accident said Rachel Are you all right? Her dark eyes danced as she said this and Fisher thought perhaps something was in the offing and that to quell it he should slog across to her as a paralytic might and vigorously juicily buss her. But he didn't. I am whole he said. Silence. They didn't cotton to remarks like that at the Fruitlands. Mostly because they didn't get them. They disturbed them. At this point Sandra came staring into the room. Hi William she said. Fisher could not bring himself to say Hi again so he bowed low. His wound prickled and he straightened up abruptly. Agh! he said. No one understood it. That's some bump you've got said Sandra in what passed at the Fruitlands for real jocularity. Silence. The group shifted from foot to foot and each in his turn glanced sidelong at Fisher's head. Hey said Rodney Let's go play some tunes.

In the heat of a blazing birch log fire all had at once to shed their coats. Rodney ostentatiously peeled off his lumberjack's jacket. Where had his lumberjack got to? You! thought Fisher I saw you at Quincy Market in a three piece suit last week. He was about to excoriate Rodney but realized it would be an admission that he had been at Quincy Market himself and so said nothing. Donald and Rodney began to tune their guitars. The usual argument over which of them had a true A ensued. Donald being a Harvard man was able to shout Rodney down. Fisher sank into a chair in sudden fatigue. This furniture he thought Is no better than my own but the issue has been clouded by covering it all with printed muslin. He looked around him. The room was not filled with normal objects, it was filled with crafts. That is to say objects purposely made stubby humpy and crude. And warty. Unbeknownst to the inhabitants of the Fruitlands some of the objects were machine made. The walls were decorated with tangles of decomposing rope, the traditional craft of a smaller African people recently bombed off the map. The floor was strewn with more little death rugs such as Fisher had encountered in the hall. If William Morris were alive today said Fisher He'd slit his throat and not bother hunting up a beautiful knife for it either. He'd use a Christmas Greetings from Vermont letter opener if he had to. Rodney and Donald were looking at Fisher. Heh heh! said Fisher but his heart wasn't in it.

Rachel bustled in with mugs giving off brown vapor. She bustles thought Fisher What a day. Bustle. Water. Attack. The idea of beer appeared at the doorway of Fisher's cluttered conscious and began to gesticulate. With an immense smile Rachel offered Fisher a mug and he took it. What *is* this? he said. Grain coffee said Rachel flashing her teeth at him. She files them he thought. He sipped. Christ even astronauts get real coffee he said gloomily. The tuning stopped again and Rodney and Donald looked at Fisher. Hey man said Rodney We run an organic house here man. What does that mean? snapped Fisher You mean you're all carbon based life forms? Gee whizz me too! Rodney turned to Donald who motioned for a general ignoring of Fisher. Rachel's face had glaciated and she gave a mug to Sandra who as she drank became more bugeyed than before. Come on William said

Donald Let's play. Slightly embarrassed Fisher opened his
violin case. A stream of dirty water ran out onto the floor.
Jesus! said Rodney How'd your fiddle get so wet, that
can't be good for it. No said Fisher looking at the sodden
Mr Squeaky and the puddle beneath. Fisher was getting
tired of looking at himself in puddles. I'll get a cloth said
Sandra getting up. No no no the *orange sponge* said
Rachel running after her. How did that happen? said
Donald. I took a shower with it said Fisher still staring
morosely at the floor. What! said Donald. Hey I've heard
of togetherness said Rodney. Fruitlands humor. Rachel
came in and knelt by Fisher. She soaked up the brown
puddle with the bright orange sponge, smiling up at him.
Fisher looked quickly from her eyes to Mr Squeaky whom
he began to shake violently. Get out! he raged at the water
that flew from the little fellow. Hey don't shake that thing
in here said Sandra annoyed. Sorry said Fisher. He dabbed
at Mr Squeaky with the sponge. Come on come on said
Donald See if it's wrecked.

Fisher tightened his bow and poised it over the strings
and ? tried to remember again. Turkey in the Straw?
Soldier's Joy? Dvořák, Violin Concerto in A minor? Again
the searching up and down the by now atonal scales. Then
deep, rich fatigue. Once or twice Fisher felt something
coming on but the notes he produced were so singular he
sagged in melancholy. Life is unbelievable Fisher an-
nounced. It sometimes seems as though there are car-
toons on every channel. Everyone looked at him uncom-
fortably. What I want to do he said suddenly Is put my
violin in the oven! Is that a good idea? said Rodney. Hills
of London said Fisher. Huh? said Rodney. Donald studied
Fisher. I'll help you! said Rachel in anticipation of God
knows what happening in the kitchen thought Fisher.

Donald and Rodney started to argue about blues.

There's no gas in my apartment said Fisher to Rachel by way of conversation. He shut Mr Squeaky in the oven and turned the all important knob. Oh you mean you're electric? she said. No I mean there's *no gas* said Fisher sitting down. She looked at him. You have shining dark eyes thought Fisher But you put up notices and your bathroom is inexcusably clean. What a house. Nobody my age thought Fisher Should be able to keep a house this clean. They must have slaves in the basement. Fed on organic gruel.

Have you gone back to work? said Rachel. They always want to know you're working. Yes said Fisher But today I had a bad day. It was a series of accidents designed by a higher intelligence to enrage me. You have a strange view of life said Rachel. Yes said Fisher But at least it has nothing to do with my accident, I had it before that. My bandage has nothing to do with my behavior. You work at the Institute right? said Rachel. Institute *of Science* said Fisher. What do you do there? she said. I type said Fisher I phone. I write budgets and yell and sometimes I would like nothing better than to take a big bite out of my desk, chew it until my teeth fell in bloodied shards to the floor and then spit it out the window at gale force seven. But I have no window. Well said Rachel ignoring him I video-tape autistic children. You do? said Fisher I may throw up at any time baby he thought. What for? he asked. Only polite. It's part of a statewide program to use video said Rachel To integrate it into the clinical program. But what for? said Fisher rising in choler Who watches it? She looked at him uncomprehendingly. I don't know she said It's just video. What's the point of that? snarled Fisher dribbling grain coffee on himself. Calm down said Rachel

alarmed. I'm calm! shouted Fisher How come everybody
thinks I'm not calm? After a moment he met her eyes.
Her face although pinched at the corners smiled at Fisher
with the warmth of an expensive woodstove.

Listen do you have any dare I say it beer here? said
Fisher in despair. Oh man no said Rachel Do you drink?
Er well sometimes said Fisher blushing Go to Hell he
thought. Rodney came into the kitchen. Private session?
he said winking at Fisher. You too said Fisher. William
wants to *drink* said Rachel uneasily to Rodney. Ah said
Rodney. He opened a cupboard and after rummaging in
it drew out a half gallon of vodka. What's that doing in
there! cried Rachel I didn't know you had that. Heh heh
said Rodney. He poured a shot for Fisher who consumed
it animally. Rachel tried staring a hole in Rodney but he
would not have it. Intriguing thought Fisher She discov-
ers Rodney has been out of his mind on rotgut while he
tends the *organic garden* out back. The least you could do
is keep it in the correct cupboard she was saying. Rodney
lifted the big bottle to his lips and glugged. Then he put
it away. See ya he said and went back to the living room.
Having fortified himself thought Fisher For arguing with
Donald. That is amazing said Rachel He doesn't even care
what cupboard he puts it in. Reprehensible said Fisher.
I'm the only tidy person here said Rachel. And you have
beautiful lustrous black hair thought Fisher But you have
devised a system for using sponges which ranks with the
most gruesome inventions of man. I don't even own a
sponge he thought And if I did I would probably wind up
eating it on a Sunday. If I lived here I would arise daily
in my sunny bedroom and while walking downstairs to
my smoldering health breakfast I would be obliged to take
a huge dose of heroin.

Rachel was brooding over Rodney and the vodka. Fisher took the opportunity to shut his eyes. Ah but life in the rural districts he thought. The autumnal odor of burning wood. It comforts for the moment but what of the day when the forests of America are gone? Uprooted and violated not by big companies but by lumberjack jacketed Fruitlands folks laying waste the countryside to fuel their Hellish stoves. Fisher breathed heavily. The smell in the kitchen was that of the one bonfire of his childhood. The pile of wet orange leaves. The strong white smoke. The fireman who drove up, doused the fire, and slapped Fisher's father. He must have been French. Perhaps one could set aside a sum against infirmity by shipping bonfire leaves from New England to California Fisher mused. He always became commercially minded when silly with heat. He drowsed in the woody smoky smell which became heavier more evocative heavier heavier odor of burning wood and suddenly Fisher jumped up yelling My violin! My violin! Black smoke poured from the oven.

As Fisher yanked the oven open Rodney lurched in a vodka cloud into the room. Throwing Fisher aside he reached into the oven and brought out the burning fiddle. Fire! said Rodney. He dropped Mr Squeaky on the floor and jumped on him. Fire! said Rodney. It was over. Thank you so much said Fisher I could have saved him. Him? said Rachel. The violin was now a mere rise of soot at their feet, the bow a black stick. Fire! said Rodney stupidly.

Fisher began to snuffle and cry. Donald! he said. Donald came in from the doorway. Today Donald wept Fisher I have been antagonized, wrongly accused, I have had to violate my principles and tell a lie, I have been sprayed with water, embarrassed, propositioned, I had to take my clothes off at work, I have spoken with at least two women who hate me and my violin has been cremated. And you drag me out here! Here! Where all they do is drink wheat and shell peas you stinking phonies! Fisher yelled at Rodney and Rachel. Oh come on William said Donald It's nobody's fault. Fault Hell said Fisher I'm being crushed by some big thumb. And I can't play he sobbed. The only tunes I knew are scattered all over Walden Pond in little flecks of brain and skin and blood. Boo hoo hoo! Ooh how gross said Rachel leaving the room. Donald and Rodney exchanged looks intended to be knowing. I think he's been arguing with Jillian said Donald. That bitch! said Fisher sitting down. Is he drunk? said Rodney. I am not drunk said Fisher More's the pity. Come on said Donald wearily Let's go. Fisher stood up. In the hallway he angrily jumped up and down on the little hooked rug. However the next step he took, off the rug, was the first of a small number of steps (as steps in life go) which would lead him in a fairly small circle (as circles in life go) back to the Fruitlands.

V Frank of Oregon

In the car. You're too sensitive said Donald. Go to Hell said Fisher. You have to learn to relax and enjoy things said Donald. Yeah? said Fisher How can I relax in the middle of all those crafts? If you sat still long enough in that house they'd weave an ethnic garment around you. Stop said Donald. How to relax said Fisher With bowls of barley thrust at me by rutting burlap women? Ah so that's it said Donald. Yes possibly said Fisher Let's get a beer.

In the winter night Cambridge looked like a train derailed on a trip to nowhere. Upended, steaming, silly, jagged. Are you going to Jillian's later? said Donald. Probably said Fisher in desperation There's a place. I've never been in there. Jeez I don't know said Donald It looks pretty rough.

Two men somehow connected sat huddled against the dirty brick wall of the tavern as Fisher and Donald approached. Actually they were fighting but they were too drunk and cold to move. So they just held each other and growled. As Fisher and Donald neared the door the bigger of the two men grabbed Fisher's leg. Hey! said Fisher Let go! Grrr! said the man. What the ? said Donald. Let go now come on let go said Fisher. As if speaking to an

obstinate child. Let's get out of here said Donald. We just
got here said Fisher. Grrr! said the man shutting his eyes
and tightening his grip on Fisher's leg. He seemed to have
forgotten his quarrel with the other man for the moment.
Hey let go! said Fisher pushing gently at the man. I'm
calling a cop said Donald. Grrr! said the man grabbing
Fisher's other leg. Now see what you made him do? said
Fisher beginning to struggle in earnest. The smaller man
looked mesmerized by Fisher's voice and stared at him
glassy eyed. With a final jerk Fisher got his legs free of the
first man and nearly toppling retreated to the curb. The
man sat on his hands and knees panting and looking reproachfully at Fisher and Donald. After a minute he attacked the other man and again they locked in unmoving
combative tableau. Grrr! Mfff! Let's get out of here said
Donald. It'll be OK once we get inside said Fisher. What
will? said Donald. But they walked toward the door giving
the two men a wide berth this time. Yah! Come on! the
smaller man was shouting as the larger bumped him
against the building. The larger man clawed at Donald as
he went through the door but missed.

As they sat in a sticky booth in the smelly murk of the
tavern, Fisher, facing the door, saw it open and close,
admitting a shrill blast of cold. The patrons, more or less
the dregs of Cambridge, shuddered booed and rebuked.
A figure seemed to be making with intent for Fisher and
Donald. Well thought Fisher Now that bum who grabbed
me has summoned up his last energies before dying of
alcoholic poisoning and in some kind of blind religious
fury he's crawling in to stab me. Me, who for a second
outside had the misfortune to look like the Antichrist.
Donald was talking about his cadaver at medical school
whom he had nicknamed Jumbo. As he listened to this

sickening anecdote Fisher kept his eyes on the approaching shambler. The shambling approacher. And ya oughta see Jumbo's hands said Donald Her hands are like turnips. The man wasn't staggering drunk, he walked toward Fisher but his eyes looked slightly to the left. Donald talked on watching Fisher's face with increasing alarm as Fisher's eyes focused on ? something that was getting closer and closer to the booth. And so uh the professor said to me uh he said Demberg you'll never see nothin like this again and so he uh took his scalpel and *CHRIST!* said Donald as a dirty weathered hand grasped the edge of the table. Without noticing the yell or looking at Donald or Fisher the man from outside climbed over the table into the booth. He leaned with a groan on his elbows and stared down at the table. Motionless. Fisher looked at Donald and then spoke to the man.

Sir? Sir? said Fisher This is a private table. A private conversation. The man slowly lifted his head. He was fine featured with gray hair and dirty dark skin. He wore a filthy tie but it was a tie carefully tied. A soiled white shirt, a torn jacket, a cap. He looked as if he had dressed with great care and then thrown himself in front of a train. Private? he said What are ya talkin about private? His eyes were clear. He actually looks sober thought Fisher But it's just the adrenaline surging through him in these last moments before he knifes me. The man slowly extended his hand to Fisher who took it not knowing what else to do. My name's Frank Tauchey he said. Fisher shook the hand. Donald was pushing himself as far away in the booth as possible. My friends said the man Call me Frank of Oregon. I'm from Oregon mostly. Which parts aren't? wondered Fisher Possibly your tie which looks fresh from the Ganges. Frank of Oregon stared at Fisher.

Ah well my name is Fisher William Fisher and this is my friend Donald Demberg said Fisher. Mr Demberg! said Frank of Oregon shaking hands with the cringing Donald. I would like to join you! said Frank of Oregon loudly.

Donald was clearly unwilling to sit with Frank of Oregon But thought Fisher It may not be politic to throw out such a well mannered drunk. Fisher scanned the threatening selection of the disgruntled at the bar, noticing in particular a very big dirty drunk who stared back in antipathy. Course there's another Frank said Frank of Oregon. Oh dear said Donald. Frank of Baton Rouge said Frank of Oregon But I ain't seen im for months. He sat up and folded his hands carefully in front of him. Well ah said Fisher getting up What can I get you Frank? Of Oregon said Frank of Oregon. Ah yes just so said Fisher Frank of Oregon. Well? Whiskey said Frank of Oregon. And you? said Fisher to Donald politely. Beer said Donald in a tiny voice, hands in pockets. Fisher went to the bar. Two drafts and a whiskey he said to the bartender who rumbled off like an armored car. Fisher noticed the patrons of the bar took an interest in his wallet as he drew it out of his pocket. In the mirror over the bar he saw his wound had bled into the bandage some more. As Fisher paid the bartender a big man next to him looked straight into his wallet and winked at a companion. Not tonight boys said Fisher carrying the drinks back to the booth. Frank of Oregon was staring at Donald who looked as though he worried Frank of Oregon was going to fall over on him. Fisher sat down seeing he was being watched. What's the big deal? he thought Half the guys in here have scabs and scars and broken heads. This wasn't true but it looked as if it should have been.

Fisher slid the shot glass in front of Frank of Oregon

who sat and madly wiped at his face in a crazy way grimacing and then smiling congenially. Well thank you very much indeed Mr Fisher he said. His eyes thought Fisher Are not completely nuts, not red white and blue nuts like the eyes on the Common or the ones around the railroad tracks by the Institute. Frank of Oregon drank but did not gulp his whiskey. Fisher sipped his beer. Mm that's good gents said Frank of Oregon I knew you was all right. He finished his shot and looked at Fisher's bandage. I see you been roughed up so I knew you was OK Mr Fisher said Frank of Oregon. *Are* you OK sir? God not you too thought Fisher. Yes I'm fine he said. Now I am justifying my mental state to a bum he thought. What was it that happened? said Frank of Oregon. Just a small accident said Fisher wishing Frank of Oregon would leave if he was going to talk about the bandage. Yeah said Frank of Oregon They go right for the head these days it seems. What? said Fisher. I mean in the old days it was yer knees or yer shoulder but now it's bang on the head and good luck to you ain't it? winked Frank of Oregon. Whaddya mean? said Donald. The police Mr Demberg said Frank of Oregon Didn't you say it was the cops? he said turning to Fisher. No it wasn't the cops said Fisher. Oh said Frank of Oregon. Why would the cops hit me? said Fisher testily. Oh why would the cops hit me? said Frank of Oregon in a mocking tone Why shouldn't they ya bastard? Hey listen here I'm not a bum! said Fisher. How do you know? said Frank of Oregon Ya looks like a bum to me and ya talks crazy and angry. Like someone the cops hit on the head! Fisher stared back and forth from Frank of Oregon to Donald. Listen said Fisher This bandage has nothing to do with my behavior. What makes ya so sure of that? said Frank of Oregon I been hit on the head plenty of times and it *always* affects my behavior. Comin out from Oregon I musta got hit on the head by the bulls twenty times and I fell off the rods twice. It affects yer behavior Mr Fisher let me tell ya. Ya walks around for days kinda . . . dis-con-nected from things. Yer buddies says things to ya and ya just stares at em like yer on the damn dope. Things they say, things ya used to talk about, they don't interest ya. Fisher looked Frank of Oregon in the eye. You're right Frank he said. Of Oregon said Frank of Oregon. Yes right said Fisher Actually I feel the same way. Fisher looked at Donald who had retreated into observing medically. Well then said Frank of Oregon What's all this about ya not feelin its fects? Frank of Oregon sat back and stretched his arms over the table. Bits of dirt fell onto it. Donald stared. But ya don't look like a drinkin man to me said Frank of Oregon And I didn't think ya would come in here unless ya got conked. Well I didn't said Fisher I slipped on the ice and fell on my head. Oh even worse said Frank of Oregon. Why? said Fisher his temper rising. Cause ya must feel like a idiot! said Frank of Oregon At least I got *my* skull cracked by the *cops*. Fisher flushed and looked around the tavern. And now I gotta piss said Frank of Oregon. He blundered across Donald who winced in disgust. Frank of Oregon staggered away toward the toilet.

I can't believe I'm sitting here talking with a real bum said Donald staring owl-like at Fisher Let's go come on now's our chance while he's micturating. What? What's the matter with you? said Fisher Do you miss Jumbo? William this place is very dangerous said Donald I'm leaving, see ya, I feel the need to autoclave myself. I'm staying said Fisher in a pitiable tone as he watched Donald walk out. Observed by slitty eyes recessed in depressed faces.

Frank of Oregon crawled back into the booth. His fly was open. I want to hear more about getting hit on the head said Fisher And the alienation that results from it. Oh a-li-en-ation is it? said Frank of Oregon I guess I know something about a-li-en-ation. He sat up. He seemed to be getting more alert. Oh so you're a a a what's that word? said Frank of Oregon. What word? said Fisher. Somethin for punishment, when you want punishment said Frank of Oregon. Glutton said Fisher. No when ya can't get enough and ya keep wantin it yer a somethin for punishment said Frank of Oregon. Glutton! said Fisher. No no, but anyway you want more punishment, you're a watcha-macallit for punishment said Frank of Oregon. Fisher began to fume but said nothing. What was it you asked me? said Frank of Oregon. I want to hear about getting hit on the head! said Fisher through clenched teeth. Oh right said Frank of Oregon hunting around the table. How bout another? he said. Your round said Fisher annoyed. Aw heh heh I'm a bum Mr Fisher said Frank of Oregon Remember? Fisher got two whiskeys. I am he thought An exceedingly smelly goat. Fisher looked at Frank of Oregon's clothes. They were so dirty that from a distance of five feet or more they looked like some kind of one piece suit. It's the tie that fascinates thought Fisher picturing Frank of Oregon in an executive job and one day being literally thrown out of a high office building and landing in a slow moving coal car.

Look it is a-li-en-ation ain't it? said Frank of Oregon. The way I see it everybody's a-li-en-ated but they don know it but when a bull hits ya on the head with a reg-u-lation trun.cheon it kinda wakes ya up to the fact. Fisher pondered Frank of Oregon's figures of speech. Have you ever had a job? he asked. Sure said Frank of Oregon I was

a foreman on a oil gang an I sold cigars wholesale an I
loaded freight in Cincy an one day I was pooped as shit
an I just loaded myself under this boxcar at the end of the
day an took off. And never looked back said Fisher. Sure
I looked back said Frank of Oregon. And where did it take
you? said Fisher. *Tulsa* said Frank of Oregon Agh, what
a pit. Course after ya gets hit on the head enough times
ya lose interest in work or even where ya are. Yes yes
you're right said Fisher I'm losing interest in work. I find
nothing to embrace. See? said Frank of Oregon I told ya
it affects ya. But that doesn't look too bad Mr Fisher said
Frank of Oregon looking at Fisher's bandage. Fifteen
stitches said Fisher smugly. Stitches! yelled Frank of Oregon in lightning alcoholic rage I've never had a stitch in
my life! He seized Fisher by the lapels. *My skull looks like
Pearl Harbor* he whispered fiercely. Hence the cap he
said letting go. Bar faces looked toward them.

As Fisher sat and looked at Frank of Oregon he became aware his own shoulders were hunching. Fisher was
terrified of bad posture and thought it was contagious. If
you start to slump, life is over. He straightened up. Frank
of Oregon finished his drink. Somehow Fisher's glass had
been emptied. Another? said Fisher. Wouldn't say no Mr
Fisher said Frank of Oregon. As he ordered two whiskeys
Fisher thought I am going to get very drunk with this
bum. I wish I could take him to work to act as my spokes-
man. He could stand by my desk with a cosh. Then I could
really get something done. I could also get him to
threaten the landlady.

Where are you from in Oregon? said Fisher as they
began again to drink. Portland said Frank of Oregon But
I don't brag about it. Portland looks like a big hat. Got a
bad name too Mr Fisher specially in Montana. I worked

there awhile in the loggin and the union big shots was always showin up from Portland. Big fat jerks in Buicks. I nearly got flattened hundreds of times by those union jerks in their cars. Here at last is a man I can relate to thought Fisher. But I dodge cars every day here in Boston Frank said Fisher. Of Oregon said Frank of Oregon. Yeah Boston, Boston. It's as fat an ugly as the people in it. Yah! said Fisher But what are we doing here? I just kinda ended up here said Frank of Oregon. Me too said Fisher. For some reason Frank of Oregon went on Down in New York they say Boston's good. Lotsa cama-rada-rie among the fellas, good doss places along the north shore, lotsa deserted tracks an yards but when ya gets up here ya find out it's all crap. I ain't found one place to sleep without gettin routed out at five am by some God damn bull said Frank of Oregon. Them New York idiots says ya can sleep till noon in Boston Common. They're *dreamin.* Plenty of food in the bins. What bull shit Mr Fisher. New York is heaven Mr Fisher an so is Chicago. But the difference is Boston is *run* by bums. Guys like us we need a city where there's some good will in the government, the old fashion civic i-deals said Frank of Oregon his voice and color rising. Where they believes in repairin park benches and the drinkin fountains don't poison ya! They don't care about that stuff in Boston, they don't care about nothin cept eatin and drivin. That's all they do the big fat buggers. They get up an eat an drive their big cars to big ressraunts an eat an then drive to a donuts place an eat an then drive home an snack an sleep. Frank this is truly perceptive said Fisher. Of Oregon! said Frank of Oregon An that's another thing Mr Fisher I ain't got one free donut in one God damn donut place in Boston. In New York they'll give ya the old ones Mr Fisher an that's the

truth. Frank of Oregon settled back into the ruined uphol-
stery. He suddenly looked around in confusion. Where's
Mr Demberg? he said. He had to go said Fisher He's a
doctor. That guy's a doctor? said Frank of Oregon. Sure
said Fisher. I don't think he'd be a good doctor said Frank
of Oregon blearily He asks too many questions. Don't you
think doctors should ask questions? said Fisher. No I don't
know said Frank of Oregon It's all hooey. Everything.

Listen what's yer job o work Mr Fisher? Institute of
Science said Fisher. Yeah? said Frank of Oregon What's
that? A big grey job said Fisher Where I type and telephone and yell inwardly and outwardly if I'm in luck. I'm
an administrator. Ad-min-is-trator said Frank of Oregon.
You got a typewriter? Yes said Fisher. I need someone to
type somethin for me said Frank of Oregon. Type what?
said Fisher. Well to tell ya the truth Mr Fisher I'm startin
a union of my own. A union? said Fisher. Yah well more
of a movement said Frank of Oregon an I needs somebody
to type up our man-i-fetzo. What do you mean movement? said Fisher. Well this is the way I see it Mr Fisher
said Frank of Oregon It's like I was sayin. About a-li-en-
ation an all that. Us guys we're a-li-en-ated even though
we got nothin but when we gets hit on the head we realize
we got nothin an we're a-li-en-ated. An everyone else,
people that got somethin, they're a-li-en-ated too but
don't know it but soon they're gonna get hit on the proverbial head. The what? said Fisher. Well Mr Fisher the
way I see it said Frank of Oregon Is that the world's
runnin out of this stuff it depends on like donuts an gas an
energy an TV an plastic an sugar. Incredible thought
Fisher. So said Frank of Oregon When it runs out that's
how they're gonna get hit on the head an then they're
gonna see they're a-li-en-ated an then they're gonna be

like us, havin nothin. But they got no *trainin* in havin
nothin an they're gonna get *mad.* So I reckon we're gonna
be in charge since we got the experience. Stupendous!
said Fisher picturing the army of vagrants poised to gov-
ern America when roly poly suburbanites were flounder-
ing about the streets. Crawling over their rusting derelict
cars. Frank this is most interesting said Fisher. He rushed
to the bar. He took two more whiskeys back to the booth
nearly dropping them. Fisher was intoxicated. But Frank
of Oregon got clearer and clearer the more he drank and
spoke. As if he were honing himself on Fisher. A sort of
crapulent Demosthenes. Quite an achievement thought
Fisher imagining Frank of Oregon addressing crowds to
great effect.

Well I'd be happy to type your manifesto Frank said
Fisher. Of Oregon said Frank of Oregon. Yes yes Frank of
Oregon said Fisher Listen is it that that you consider to
be your first name? What? said Frank of Oregon. Skip it
said Fisher fuzzily. Listen he said Who was that you were
fighting with when we came in? Fightin? said Frank of
Oregon. Yeah said Fisher When we came in you were
fighting with a guy outside and you grabbed my leg. Oh
that said Frank of Oregon That was just a minor policy
discussion. You mean that guy's helping you organize it?
said Fisher. Sure, he's the sergeant at arms said Frank of
Oregon. Fisher felt very dizzy. Well where is your manifesto now? he said This really is very interesting Frank of
Oregon. Course you'll have to give up yer job Mr Fisher
said Frank of Oregon. What! said Fisher. Well yer joinin
us ain't ya? said Frank of Oregon. Well I don't know said
Fisher. Aw come on said Frank of Oregon This is the
or-gan-i-zation for guys like you. Do I have to tell you
again? said Fisher angrily I am not a bum! And I says ya

is and I says who's talkin bums anyway! said Frank of Oregon. I'm talkin dis-en-franchised Mr Fisher! A-li-en-ated! Guys like *you* and *me*.

Real interest from the bar faces. Fisher looked at the dirt on Frank of Oregon and the sad lines on his face draping down from his green eyes which flickered like two binnacle lamps. His face pointing south. Where is the manifesto? said Fisher. After a pause Frank of Oregon said Well I got it here somewhere. He looked penetratingly at Fisher. Can I trust ya Mr Fisher? Sure said Fisher immediately wishing he had said something which smacked more of sincerity. Frank of Oregon reached into a pocket which magically appeared on the surface of his dirty jacket. He put a clump of soiled papers in Fisher's hand. Hope ya can read my writin said Frank of Oregon. Fisher's eyes slid out of control over a slippery mad scrawl. Do I have to read it all now? said Fisher with a sinking feeling. Nah said Frank of Oregon But type it up soon Mr Fisher. I will said Fisher I'll get right on it. No problem. With some difficulty he put the wad in his own pocket. Probably alive with chiggers he thought But I must be calm.

Their glasses were empty. Nother drink? said Fisher. Frank of Oregon looked at him and said You gonna be OK Mr Fisher? Sure said Fisher Why wouldn't I be OK? Well I'll have another an much obliged I'm sure said Frank of Oregon. Fisher got up and fell down. He crawled to the bar and ordered two more whiskeys. You OK fellow? thundered the bartender. Yesm fine said Fisher Mbandage has nothin tdo with mhavior. The edge the bloody edge already! he thought Well that's it. Just serve me you. Fisher pivoted and danced back to the booth with the drinks. You OK Mr Fisher? said Frank of Oregon. Gdamn it said Fisher Course mright. Frank of Oregon peered at a dirty clock. I don know if I should have any more Mr Fisher It's pretty late he said. Jeez what are you? said Fisher Nineda five bum? Oh a surly drunk! said Frank of Oregon I don't need you! Gimme back my man-i-fetzo! he snarled. Sorry said Fisher. Give it back! said Frank of Oregon. No no jussedle down said Fisher. No prolm. They looked at each other. Guys who drink like you! said Frank of Oregon. Jesus thought Fisher I am completely drunk and will have to be dragged no doubt out to the gutter and even beyond by this bum who as he drinks whiskey after whiskey becomes a shining example of ? something . . . You're drunk Mr Fisher if I may say so said Frank of Oregon. Fisher opened his mouth to object but shut it. Lizzen said Fisher after a long contemplation Dya hava place tsleep? Where'sr stuff? I don know said Frank of Oregon quietly. Looking down at his glass. Fisher felt sad. Now I'm entering the sad phase he thought I am truly drunk.

THE SEVEN STAGES OF DRUNKENNESS

    I All topics found humorous
   II Linguistic play
  III Overcompensated daintiness
  IV Shouting sadness
    V Out of body experiences
  VI Severe inert reverie
 VII Passage into the epiphanic stream

Well dya wanna sleepa my house? said Fisher. I don know said Frank of Oregon eyeing Fisher The last time I crashed at a drunk's place he woke up in the middle of the night an came at me with a wrench. It's risky. Mnot drunk said Fisher. What! said Frank of Oregon. Mean, mnot *a* drunk said Fisher. Yeah said Frank of Oregon. How far is it? Fisher turned to try and look out the little window way down at the far end of Creation. An icy night. Nfar tall said Fisher smiling. In smiling Fisher suddenly felt he was smiling like his cousin, the one who always wore boating clothes. I am so drunk he thought. The out of body phase. Frank of Oregon was staring leadenly into the smoke and babble. OK Mr Fisher he said. Let's go. They gulped their drinks and got up. Hungry faces watched Fisher stagger to the door behind Frank of Oregon. The faces yelled as cold wind rushed in from outside and bit them.

Fisher had forgotten about Christmas until he saw the dirty ornaments hanging over the street. He stopped. Fisher was a poor judge of climate distance weight and time so he stared at an illuminated thermometer on a savings bank and waited for it to display the temperature. Just as a matter of interest. MERRY CHRISTMAS. HAPPY NEW YEAR. INVEST IN CAMBRIDGE. 1:17. MERRY CHRIST-MAS. HAPPY NEW YEAR. INVEST IN CAMBRIDGE. 1:18. MERRY CHRISTMAS. Oh for gossake! said Fisher They've limnated the temptre. Huh? said Frank of Oregon. No temperch said Fisher Wha kine thermom izzis? Where'd ya say yer place is Mr Fisher? said Frank of Oregon. Fisher looked around. The boulevard in the cold revealed some aspects of a former unfamiliarity. It looks so different when you're drunk he thought It looks like it did when I first came here and tentatively walked around rejoicing in things I now think are hateful. Fisher wondered if Frank of Oregon would understand this but before he could express it if in fact he could have it oozed away in the muddy stream of drunken thought.

The cold air and wind exacerbated Fisher's state and

he sat down suddenly on the curb. Aw Mr Fisher said Frank of Oregon. Oh Frangorgan said Fisher This is Cambridge! Yeah that's right Mr Fisher said Frank of Oregon. Cantabrigia! wailed Fisher. Yeah said Frank of Oregon. Well I don live Cambr said Fisher I hate it. Oh? said Frank of Oregon An where is it ya live? Bosson said Fisher Which is unfortly on thother side of Chozz Rir. I know it is said Frank of Oregon gloomily. And said Fisher Safter cartoon time so th T snot runnin. Speakin of which huffed Fisher indignantly Dya know th T wansa build nucular *reactor*? N downtown? Aw let em Mr Fisher said Frank of Oregon What difference would it make? Yer righ hiccuped Fisher Yer righ yer righ! Listen Mr Fisher said Frank of Oregon I'm pretty cold so I think I'll get goin an see ya soon. Now Frang said Fisher. Of Oregon! said Frank of Oregon shouting now with cold. Yessa course vorgan said Fisher. I am a vylinits! Are ya? said Frank of Oregon. But! said Fisher. Today mvylin was burnt up. Burned up? How'd that happen? said Frank of Oregon. Can't remem said Fisher bleakly But definite did hap today, malmost sure of it. Burnt to the ground! Listen are ya gonna be OK Mr Fisher cause I'm just gonna head on out said Frank of Oregon. Fisher looked around. Where *are* we? he said. Central Square! said Frank of Oregon Cambridge! Oh yeah. Then we do hava place stay by gosh by . . . golly said Fisher Come wif me! He attempted to stand. Uh where we goin Mr Fisher? said Frank of Oregon. To mgirlfren's house said Fisher as he bumped into a post. Aw Mr Fisher said Frank of Oregon we can't go wakin anybody up. Sall right Frangorgan said Fisher She's spectin me. But she ain't expectin ya all intoxificated is she now Mr Fisher? said Frank of Oregon. Wood yrlax? said Fisher leaning against the man Sjust blocker two or . . .

Which direction Mr Fisher? said Frank of Oregon. Good ques said Fisher looking up and down the street and recognizing it less and less. Good God he thought A bum is helping me along the street, a bum who gets properer and properer as I sink into callow stumbling. This way said Fisher.

Frank of Oregon took Fisher's arm and helped him in a cursory way. Fisher struggled to keep his eyes open in the wind the cold and the strangeness. Now Frangurgan said Fisher This smoothment of yours. Yeah great ain't it Mr Fisher? said Frank of Oregon. Ya know I think I creally tribute somth said Fisher. I'm symph with it. Yeah well if ya can type up that man-i-fetzo Mr Fisher It'd be swell said Frank of Oregon Can't ya help me a little Mr Fisher walkin I mean? Frank of Oregon had dragged Fisher most of the block. Sorry said Fisher Thizzit anyway.

Frank of Oregon stopped and Fisher fell down. He slowly turned his head and looked up at Jillian's apartment house. He groaned to his feet and grabbed the handrail of painted pipe. He crept up the steps to the front door, next to which was a panel of buttons circling kaleidoscopically before him. Fisher selected a button and began to press it in what he thought was a clever and attractive rhythm. A window opened in the night above them. What the Hell's going on? came a deep male voice. Oh God thought Fisher She's with somebody! He stumbled backward on the porch and looked up at the open window. Fisher! shouted a large white face. It was MacGillivray, Jillian's landlord. You! said Fisher. Fisher! yelled MacGillivray. What? said Fisher. Well you've pressed the wrong button again you idiot! shouted MacGillivray slamming down his window. Fisher turned and gave Frank of Oregon a sick smile. At was MacGillivray said Fisher

Shhh! Frank of Oregon looked uncomfortable. Fisher returned to the buttons and held his head in his hands to try and steady the view. At this moment the door was opened by Jillian. In dressing gown and furrowed frown.

William what is the meaning of this? she said. Jillian! said Fisher straightening up I tole ya I'd cummovr! Wonderful said Jillian looking at Frank of Oregon. I beg yer pardon ma'am but Mr Fisher's had too much to drink said Frank of Oregon. I can see that said Jillian Who are you? He's Frangurglan said Fisher. Jillian's eyes widened. I'm just seein him home said Frank of Oregon moving slowly away You OK now Mr Fisher? No no said Fisher you come in! He needs placea sleeb he said to Jillian. Mr Fisher's just drunk if I may say so said Frank of Oregon pushing Fisher at Jillian and starting down the steps. Well thanks a whole Hell of a lot said Jillian Whoever you are. He's Frankurgin, Franorklin said Fisher An he needs place *tslee*. Jillian looked at Fisher. And to think that we went to the same college she said quietly. Fisher stared at Jillian. I been thinkin! he said suddenly When ya get this drunk things look older, mean slike twas when I moved ere, mean sometimes slike it *was*. Inside he raged about the sound of his words. With a terrific sigh born of the awful historical feminine suffering she had read about Jillian yanked Fisher in the door. Get in here! she said savagely. Frank of Oregon meekly followed. You OK now Mr Fisher? he asked Because I'll just shove off now OK? Nawsense said Fisher Cmon nside. She'll calm dow in a *mint* he said in a gurgling stage whisper. Jillian flounced up the stairs followed by Fisher who was taking exaggerated tiptoe steps. Frank of Oregon cowered at the rear, afraid Fisher might pitch backwards onto him at any moment.

Jillian opened the door and held it for Fisher who was

making a laughable effort to sober up. He gave her a stentorian Thanks! as he passed her glare and went into the front room. He collapsed in a chair and watched smiling as Frank of Oregon came to the door, paused in fear of Jillian and then walked nervously into the room. Fisher thought Jillian does not want Frank of Oregon in the house but she is going to suffer it in order to use it against me later. Do you have a toilet miss? said Frank of Oregon. Of course I do snapped Jillian It's in there. Fisher tried to reconcile the disparate aspects of life he was seeing but could not and so crawled onto the floor. Ohhh said Fisher. Things went dark grey. William what is going on here? said Jillian kicking Fisher. Mmf fren of mine said Fisher. Yeah right said Jillian This is the last time you're doing this kind of shit to me. Do you hear me? Aw baby fgnt mfl said Fisher his lips caught in the rattan matting. If I sleep he thought I'll wake up and winter sunlight will be coming in the window. I'll prepare oatmeal for Frank of Oregon and everything will be all right. What am I supposed to do? said Jillian Give this guy oatmeal in the morning? Fisher began to snore. Jillian kicked him in the ribs. Stob kicking me! said Fisher sitting up. Frank of Oregon emerged from the toilet looking contrite. Don look contrite! shouted Fisher now angered. Lie down on the sofa! he said to Frank of Oregon. Frank of Oregon sat on it. Said lie! yelled Fisher God! It seems I havta take *command* whererev I go. Jillian get Frankorgan a blanket and one frme drooled Fisher. Aren't you sleeping with me? said Jillian tapping her foot. No! Sleebn righ here *baby* said Fisher. Fisher and Frank of Oregon watched Jillian go into the bedroom. In a second pillows and blankets flew out of it and then the door slammed deafeningly. Fisher felt weak. Frank of Oregon picked up a pillow and blanket and lay down on the sofa, cowed to the nines. You OK Mr Fisher? he asked. Mfine mfine said Fisher groping for his blanket.

As he rolled about on the prickly flooring he realized the ceiling light was on. Overhead light mumbled Fisher Death! He stumbled toward the wall and pawed the switch like a drugged bear. He collapsed and began to crawl back to his spot. I sure appreciate this Mr Fisher said Frank of Oregon. In spite of the drunk darkness, the sickening colors tossing against one another, Fisher felt happy. As though he were seven and had a favorite playmate staying overnight. He wanted to talk with Frank of Oregon but he was too drunk and a snoring was coming from the sofa. Think nothin of it Frankorkin slobbered Fisher Yer man after mown heart.

VI Crosbee

Just as I thought! Fisher rasped aloud when he awoke.
Winter sunlight was streaming into the hot room. The
heating in Jillian's apartment was ungovernable; MacGillivray shoveled coal like Satan in the basement. Morning
noon and night. It's just like the Institute said Fisher
When spring comes and they find the unfortunates
broiled on their radiators over the winter. Big Spring Bar-
becue. Fisher staggered toward the window. He began to
feel faint in the dizzying agony of having to figure out the
unfamiliar catch. Suddenly the window shot up and
Fisher nearly fell out. Heaving himself back inside he
turned to see that Frank of Oregon was not on the sofa.
Fisher groaned and walked into the bedroom. Jillian was
not there. The clock by her bed read 10:30. Vugh! said
Fisher.

Now in the kitchen a note written in a vicious hand
barked at him from the refrigerator.

Even without this absurd episode our relationship is
shitty. You can't treat me like this anymore. Don't you
realize I'm in Law School? We have to talk. You've

82

changed. This is ridiculous. Why don't you get a good
job?

    —J

Why don't I indeed? said Fisher. But if drinking as he had
doesn't harden a man it surely thickens him. He walked
back to the living room and reached for the telephone,
feeling sicker by the second. He dialed the Institute. Give
me Smith! he said authoritatively. The solar or the glandu-
lar? said the operator. Glands said Fisher Pardon the expression. Silence, clicking. 2197 said Smith. I'm pretty
sick said Fisher sinking down onto his knees. What! Is that
you Fisher? said Smith. I can't come in said Fisher. You
sound terrible, what's the matter? said Smith who had a
horror of ill health. I don't know . . . ohhh! said Fisher.
What do you mean you don't know? said Smith. Ohhh
groaned Fisher lying down and putting the receiver next
to his head I'm sick, calling in sick don't you get it? Well
try and come in tomorrow said Smith The report's due
you know. I will try said Fisher. Oh and another thing said
Smith Jowls is holding an inquiry into you. What? said
Fisher. An inquiry said Smith Into you, your state. Hu-
wrulggh said Fisher. What is that you vomiting? shrieked
Smith. Yeahggh said Fisher. Smith hung up. Fisher went
into the bathroom. Actually to be sick now he thought
Would be anticlimactic. Perhaps I can save it, it's important to have a potent tool for gaining sympathy always at
the ready.

   Fisher took a bath. Ahh he said Plenty of hot water
here. Where law students live. And imported soap too.
They can scrub themselves till they bleed! yelled Fisher
But their souls will still be tarnished. He pulled the plug
and thrilled at the feeling of the water draining out

around him. He got out of the tub leaving the ring for Jillian. Only ring you're ever going to get from me baby he said. He put his clothes on and looked in the mirror. The bandage aflap. Yes we did go to the same college Jillian he said But who's had the best of it? You have you *you* you! Fisher went downstairs and broke out of the house into the cold air.

So! Fisher! said MacGillivray who was rooting in the garbage cans in front of the house. So! MacGillivray! said Fisher. Going out to ring doorbells? said MacGillivray. Sorry said Fisher. If you do that once more I'm going to evict your girlfriend! said MacGillivray angrily. Do you like ventriloquists? said Fisher. What? said MacGillivray. Do you think they're courageous? said Fisher Do you think they're handsome? Get out of here! bellowed Mac-Gillivray. OK! Fisher shouted over his shoulder. He walked down the street toward Central Square. While Fisher had been more hung over than he was at present, he had never felt such impediment in moving. My spinal fluids have leaked out he thought. The perils of sleeping on rattan. I will become paralyzed rounding the corner.

Rubbish blew against him: muddy pictures torn from a pornographic magazine, snack cake wrappers, sheaves of newspaper, calendar pages, life stories smote him in the face along with the general useless passage of time. Stiffly sauntering down the busy avenue Fisher studied a pyramid of alcoholics on a bench. Comrades? He wondered where Frank of Oregon was. Fisher hesitated at the edge of a big intersection and then ran howling into the moving knot of traffic across and down into the T.

Fisher stood for twenty minutes on the Boston platform and watched five trains go past to Harvard. In all that time no trains came back. He began to fret. I know what they're doing the bastards he said under his breath It's a new policy. Now every train arriving at Harvard is dismantled and melted down and re smelted and manufactured anew and *entirely new trains* are sent down the Boston line. That would account for part of the delay.

At last a Braintree train. Fisher got on and immediately felt self conscious. The train was filled with people who had specifically boarded it to stare at his bandage. I've forgotten to see if there's any new blood on it he thought. An old woman looked at Fisher, her mouth ajar. He leered at her. Yuh thought Fisher I'm gonna follow yuh home and piss on yuh doily collection yuh huh huh. Mxptl bzzt said a voice. The doors closed. The train started up and Fisher felt dizzy. He looked down the car and saw an old man on crutches gazing wistfully at a seat occupied by three giggling girls. Fisher then caught sight of himself in the window. Bloody bandage sticking up, dark unshaven face. Rumpled slept in drunk clothing. Inspired, Fisher hunched his shoulders and began pacing the car, winking and blinking wildly and sniffing. Gawd damn Gawd damn Gawd damn! said Fisher jerking his arms up and down. He put his face up to that of a young woman in a wool suit. Beware of the vengeance of Gawd! said Fisher. She turned away. Fisher looked at the giggling girls. Gawd damn your pitiful souls to the everlasting torments of Hell said Fisher creeping toward them. Can't you see that man with CRUTCHES is dying for your seat Gawd damn you? The girls jumped up and ran screaming past Fisher to the other end of the car. Fisher turned and gestured randomly at the cripple. Now! Take this rightful seat to which Gawd himself has brung you

said Fisher May Gawd in his infinite mercy bless your soul.
The train came to a halt at Kendall and with an embarrassed look the old man got off. Fisher stared after him.
Ingrate! yelled Fisher shaking his fist Gawd damn all inhabitants of Kendall Square! Then looking around he
cackled. The doors shut. Kpzz ruptub said the voice. Everyone stared at Fisher. Gawd damn Gawd damn he
wheezed. God he thought I hope I don't blow my cover
before Park. He continued to blink and mutter. At
Charles nurses got on. Nurses! shouted Fisher jumping
and pointing. Oh Mandy look out said one nurse to another. Nurses are the angels of Gawd! said Fisher Take this
seat which Gawd himself told me to reserve for you. He
moved away, motioning them to the seat. Embarrassed,
the nurses sat down on the seat in their white uniforms.
After first checking it for disgusting bits of Fisher. Prag-
zaggn blft bzz said the voice as the doors closed. Fisher
looked about him but did not say anything. The train
rocked back and forth in a moronic lullaby. Fisher made
a face at himself in the window. Enough free entertainment he thought. At Park Street he straightened up and
walked normally out of the car. The station was cold and
noisy and every trash can was being pillaged. A green line
car came and Fisher got on it, brooding about Mr Squeaky
all the way to Copley. He got out and climbed up to the
street. He wondered if they were missing him at work.
Certainly Fisher wasn't missing them. But guilt was building and he felt he might have to give up and go in after
a few more hours. I'm too responsible thought Fisher. But
there was always the promise of Alison Mapes. *Social*
intercourse wa ha haa.
  As he turned onto Newbury Fisher wondered if the

eyes of his landlady were already upon him. He could barely see the brick cupola of his own building but he decided they were. All Fisher's landlady did in life was sneak from window to window and listen down the stairwell. If I broke down her door thought Fisher I would become entangled in telescopes and listening dishes. There's nothing that goes on in Back Bay that old bat doesn't know. Fortunately by ridding myself of possessions I have eliminated most microphone hiding places. Fisher stood in front of the house now and looked up at her drawn blinds. He silently theatrically mouthed a foul obscenity. Then he went up the steps and opened the front door. No sound from above. Heart pounding he went toward his own door. He quickly put his key in the lock opened the door and ran inside. Asylum. The apartment was dark and cold. His wet clothes were still in a pile where he had left them the night before. They stank. Fisher looked at his desk. It was littered with the detritus of his search for salvation. A pile of music books, a half completed tracing of his hand, a prosaic stump of short story about a crippled chicken he had once seen. I can't draw said Fisher crumpling up the drawing. I can't write he said tearing up the story And fortunately my violin has been destroyed because I can't play it and I can't read music! The music books were too thick to tear so he merely bit them. Then in the kitchen. The musky refrigerator. Fisher took out a beer and a box of crackers (kept there safe from insectile robbery). This is how it all began he said between mouths full. Not eating properly. When a decent meal? When my *last* meal? Even though there was a fish market around the corner Fisher never had the stamina to face the proprietor who always said Hey! You

Italian? Yuk yuk yuk thought Fisher. The telephone rang.

Hello? said Fisher. Is thawt you Fishah? came an unspeakably strong Boston Brahmin drawl. Yes said Fisher in trepidation. This is *moi* said the voice. It was Crosbee McWilliams III. Hello Crosbee said Fisher. Lissen they told me you were sick at yaw office said Crosbee Saw I decided ter call yer at home. Great said Fisher As you can see I'm here. Yes haw haw haw said Crosbee Taking a day awff? You might say that said Fisher. Wall are you interested in lunnnch? said Crosbee. Fisher looked from his crackers to the gray alleyway behind the kitchen. Lunch! he thought. Lunch . . . Yes I guess so he said Where? Mm I thought down at the Mawket said Crosbee Unless you have a prawblem with thawt. No Fisher groaned No problem. I'm *made of money* he thought Walk all over me. When can you be theah? said Crosbee. Half an hour said Fisher. Wall thawt sounds awright said Crosbee Wot are you wearing? Pink cocktail dress said Fisher annoyed If it is any of your business. Haw haw haw awl right said Crosbee See you then. Meet me in the bah. Right said Fisher. He hung up. He spent his last money on earth eating out with madmen he thought. I am insane. I will spend all my money and die. If only Death would strike as the last cent went, how perfect life would be. Fisher stared at himself in his mirror. I'm too weak to shave he thought. In the drawer he opened hundreds of ties slithered, the old ones transmitting knot grease to the younger ones that might have had a chance. He selected one already tied and in putting it on over his head he pretended it was the noose and goggled at himself in mock strangulation. Not convincing said Fisher Not convincing at all. Then stealthily creeping . . . out the door . . . cold silent fear in the hall

. . . the vestibule . . . and . . . Oh God no thought Fisher A window opening above! as he went down the steps outside. As the harangue started he broke into a run.

The bricks of Boston glowed red in the pre Christmas sunlight but neither absorbed nor reflected heat. The sun, wise deity, had indeed given up on Boston and was just giving the city light on a whim. It knew it would soon be disappearing into the awful crevice between the cheeks of The Ass. There's no cheer in this scraping redness thought Fisher trying to ignore the passersby as best he could. The gawking lanky walked mantis like to and fro; their far more numerous counterparts upholstered with pastry and fatty meats tumbled softly about the pavements of Back Bay in dewy eyed wet mouthed goglification at Christmas wares they wanted wanted wanted. I'm going to be sick thought Fisher No, I forgot, I'm saving it. What a place, to make you store up your own ejecta! As he reached the Common he saw thousands of little electric lights inexpertly strung in the trees. Hanging down in clumps. Christmas disco blared from a Park Square bar. Help! yelled Fisher. All around him a traffic of people suffering from St Botolph's disease, an unnatural swelling of the desire for more, a denial of grace, a stupefying of the senses. Some of them thought they had what they wanted. Others were still at it, beating still others to pulp. Yet others, the younger better "educated" drove relentlessly on in the professions for goals they had been told were personal. Were *individual.* Boston thought Fisher Is a beached whale of brick.

As he walked along Tremont past the Park Street T The Ass began to move in, its rumbling nearly audible. Yah! said Fisher Let's see if you can snow the whole place in. Have a good dump. The sky grew dark and a cold wind flogged the grasping populace. The corner of Tremont and Court. The intersection was clogged with a hundred barging bashing dodgems. Fisher made a break for it and ran afoul of a big oily car which nearly got him. As he stood panting in rumpled disconcertion the fierce wind invaded his clothing and sucked his scarf right out of his coat, carrying it aloft in a tremendous updraft, story after story up the face of City Hall! where it finally dropped on an inaccessible ledge. Fisher watched it go in amazement and Neanderthal fury. He shook his fist at City Hall. It's Stonehenge all over again! he shouted. The tasseled end of the scarf peeked at him from the ledge high above the plaza. It's so unAmerican said Fisher deciding to trudge. A woman glared at him. Don't worry about me lady said Fisher This bandage has nothing to do with my behavior. There ought to be a sign here, Dangerous Suction! Fisher shouted at the woman who hurried on. On they all went up and down a brick hump. On toward Quincy Market, a tangle of raging consuming, a bloody war of wanting and getting and slavering seeking three days before Christmas. Shocking! Boston's weekly papers for smart aleck BAs had trumpeted. Developers of Quincy Market Sit Back and Rake It In. Yes shocking isn't it? muttered Fisher tossed by the crowd. You call that journalism? You think they developed this place for Glory? Fisher at last reached the restaurant and elbowed his way through a crowd of tourists waiting to eat. Pardon me excuse me pardon me pardon me excuse me pardon me excuse me he said. The tourists took no notice. Careening betwixt them as if he were in a pinball machine Fisher finally fell exhausted into the bar.

Crosbee McWilliams III was a walking Yale Club, complete with awning. A hueless flabelliform body, his face flocculent flews pierced by murine eyes and (it seemed) hastily crowned with molelike hair. All at a distressingly young age. At this moment he was seated alone at the largest table in the bar, having strewn personal effects over its attendant chairs: overcoat, blue blazer, briefcase, umbrella and puffy self. Now there's a man who knows what's what thought Fisher pushing through the crowd. A real old fashioned Pig. Comes in handy I bet. Wall! droned Crosbee as Fisher reached the table Finawlly! Hell said Fisher I've been trying to get through the *lobby* for an hour. Yes haw haw haw what rabble! honked Crosbee Wall sit down Fishah. Fisher dumped Crosbee's overcoat onto another chair and sat. How's life? said Fisher How's stocks? How's bonds? How's life among high income blondes? Fack that till yow get a drink said Crosbee madly signaling a waitress who seemed to be already fed up with him. From her looks thought Fisher Crosbee's appearance alone would do it. She was ill suited to the prim uniform of the place and looked uncomfortable with the growling drunk lunchtime mob of three piece suits.

It was just like Crosbee to be quiet and reserved, to try and maintain his odd ideas of decorum after wildly waving a waitress over. Two mahtinis said Crosbee And what do *you* want Fishah? Oh so it's one of those days said Fisher. It's always one of those days kiddo said Crosbee. Just a beer Fisher said to the waitress. Then with intense self loathing he appended a Dutch name to this. The waitress looked at Fisher's bandage and then at Crosbee who frowned playfully at her. She hurried off in exasperation and disgust. She's a little ray of sunshine isn't she? said

Crosbee. Friend of yours? said Fisher. He already felt the slow decline in the quality of conversation which inevitably took place with Crosbee. Not really my type said Crosbee acidly You could have shaved Fishah. No I could not have said Fisher. I know someone who's your type he said thinking of Alison. Really? said Crosbee fluttering his eyelashes. The women of Boston were in no wise threatened by Crosbee and they acted it. He had run to unfortunate stock and bond babyfat lunching hugely every day in posh steakeries. Yes big house in Connecticut, fleet of luxury cars, Daddy has a yacht said Fisher carried off by his own fantasies of Alison about whom he knew *nothing*. Really said Crosbee grabbing a martini from the waitress before she had put her tray on the table. His hands and arms were like moray eels. She looked at Crosbee with nausea, put Fisher's beer down and stamped off. Only to be pinched on the bottom, Fisher saw, by a lunging pink faced stockbroker across the room. Who is this pehson? said Crosbee burbling in his drink. You're not interested said Fisher I suggest you keep hanging around Boston Latin. You bawsted said Crosbee. Someone I might go out with said Fisher. Really! snorted Crosbee And wheah may I awsk is Jillian these days? She stalks said Fisher. I see said Crosbee wiggling his eyebrows Wait'll she grawduates Fishah she'll sue yaw awss for something or othah. That's really very encouraging Crosbee said Fisher I'll remember that. Your table's ready upstairs said the waitress, apparently under great duress.

Crosbee made a tremendous dumb show of looking at his as yet untouched and probably thought Fisher fourth martini. Crosbee gave her the idiotic frown again. She eyed him impassively. Fisher was impressed. At this Crosbee wilted but cocked his head at Fisher and said Do you want anothah drink or ? You're deliberately torturing the waitress thought Fisher. If I say yes she'll be mad at both of us, if no I win the slobbering enmity of Crosbee for the rest of the afternoon. I just want lunch, I don't want to *become* one of them. Let's go upstairs he said. The waitress put their check down and ran away. Crosbee followed her with his eyes, his face red. Thawt bitch he said to Fisher. What's the matter? said Fisher Let's eat. I'm leaving thawt bitch a *dime* said Crosbee fumbling with coins. He could not distinguish them by sight or touch. He clattered about with his things and unsteadily followed Fisher up the stairs.

The dining room was furnished with long communal tables covered with white cloths. At which in the time honored tradition of the place the patrons were jammed together at eight inch intervals. The kitchen was out in the open, there was no carpeting, there was a terrific din of place crashing and human jabber. Shit said Crosbee It's pretty crawded. You know I suspect them of playing tape recordings of riots said Fisher I think it inflames the eating. Haw haw haw blared Crosbee. Fisher saw Crosbee was losing track of which hand held his drink and which his umbrella and briefcase and so moved toward a table which had two places open opposite each other. Fisher took the inside seat and Crosbee gracelessly banged his things around in seating himself on the outside. There was no place to put anything. They looked at each other across the table.

To one side an elderly couple were battling for their lives against prime ribs of beef three feet long. On the other hand were a young woman and a nervous looking young man. The young woman was beautiful and assured; the young man looked somehow as though his hopes had been dashed at birth. He was talking in earnest to the young woman who was presenting a markedly cool attitude toward him and what he was saying. Fisher saw that Crosbee, gnawing at his drink, was taking an interest in the conversation. Mind your manners said Fisher. Crosbee pretended to look down at his menu. I think it could be really great if you stayed Jan really said the young man. Nervous! I mean I've got the room now and we could have a lot of fun together, it could be great. Look Kevin it's nice of you but I told you I decided to go to San Francisco said the girl. I told you I'd just see you for lunch as I came through Boston. Crosbee peeked over the edge of his menu at Fisher with an evil smile. But don't you want to think about it? said the young man I mean why San Francisco? Are you sure San Francisco is right for you? San Frawncisco! said Crosbee suddenly trundling his round pink face into their conversation. What? said the man. I say you did say San Frawncisco? said Crosbee looking at the girl with actually quite a sober look thought Fisher. What knavery. Well yes said the girl not so annoyed as her companion. Great place! beamed Crosbee Been theah many times on *business*. Do you by any chawnce know the Shanghai Low restaurant on Grawnt Avenue? Oh well I'm afraid not said the girl. Oh but you must you must! said Crosbee slurping his martini Do you like Chirnese food? Listen! said the young man whose low-thyroid face had not the parrying qualities of Crosbee's. Well yes I do said the girl smiling at Crosbee's roseate fulminating. Shanghai Low, Grawnt Avenue heah I'll write it dawn faw you said Crosbee dredging his pockets. Thank you so much said the girl looking at the young man coldly. *And you?* said Crosbee turning to him *Yaw going theah too?* No I'm not the young man snapped. Well if you should *evah* get theah said Crosbee You ought ter go to this place. He was now standing burrowing in his overcoat. I'll write it dawn faw you too. The young man red in the face looked at Fisher and then at his bandage. Fisher grinned broadly. Crosbee wrote in a scrawl on the back of one of his business cards. Great place great place he said And aw yes theah's a great little Jopanese place in the Marinar district. Listen I'm afraid we're not interested said the man. Oh *come* now said Crosbee. Well Kevin if he wants to help said the young woman turning the whole situation against the young man cruelly. He's drunk out of his mind hissed the young man And that one looks like a mental case. The girl turned to look at Fisher and his bandage. Fisher smiled toothily. Crosbee was giving him a sideways smile. Suddenly Crosbee grabbed the young man's arm. Say! Didn't you go to Staunton Military Acawdemy! he bellowed. No I did not! said the man breaking loose of Crosbee's puffy pink hand. Come on Jan he said. After a theatrical hesitation the young woman got up. With a gaping smile Crosbee waved his card across the table at her. As she took it the young man grabbed it from her and tore it up, thin hands with digital watch raging. I say said Crosbee. The man grabbed the girl by the arm and towed her toward the stairs. She looked back at Fisher and Crosbee wistfully. Crosbee grinned fatly at Fisher. Only way to get any room around heah he said. He put his overcoat umbrella and briefcase on the chairs vacated by lover and beloved.

The restaurant was famed for the abusiveness of its crude hash hurling waitresses. They tempted use of the term Amazonian but the Amazons are extinct so in fact they must have been quite puny. At any rate one arrived and she was so big that Crosbee did not pull any tricks.

N'Yawk sirloin he trembled With potatoes and peas. You? said the waitress to Fisher without looking up. Here at least was one person not staring at his bandage. Yankee potroast said Fisher. She left. These waitresses said Crosbee mopping his brow. Yes said Fisher But people troop in here from all over the world to have plates of boiled food dumped in their laps and to be maligned in a Boston dialect that never really existed. Haw haw haw said Crosbee itchily looking around the corners of himself. What's the matter? said Fisher Did you lose your pen? Naw said Crosbee I thawt I had anothah drink heah somewheah. Fisher looked out the window. How many drinks did I *awdah?* said Crosbee faintly.

Half a dead steer, a sea of meaty jetsam. Fisher ordered more martinis for Crosbee and another low country beer for himself. Gawd damn yer said Crosbee Why awn't yer drinking? I am drinking said Fisher What do you call this? Awg that's nawt drinking said Crosbee. I've had enough in the past few days said Fisher. Naw such thing as enough said Crosbee spraying Fisher with meat juice as he tore into his steak. Oh yes there is said Fisher.

Fo wuffbin going ong angywaig? said Crosbee mouth full. Fisher recited without emotion. I fell on my head at Walden Pond and had to have stitches I got drenched with water at work by the fire brigade my violin was incinerated and I got drunk with a bum and he spent the night with me at Jillian's house. You meeng he followb you vere? said Crosbee plowing through a roll. No said Fisher He helped me home and he had nowhere to sleep so I told him to stay. Chrift no wongah Jillian'f unenfuftiaftig said Crosbee stuffing his mouth with ? something. His words were lost among the jostling fats. He stopped chewing for a moment and looked at Fisher's bandage.

How'g you geg thab? he said. I told you! said Fisher I fell on my head! Crosbee's eyes widened. He put a tremendous chunk of meat into his mouth and poured half a martini around it. Ogga be morg garefulg he said. Right said Fisher. Then with a tremendous effort Crosbee swallowed *the rest of his food.* He swigged the remaining cocktail. Lunch was over.

He began to feel in his pockets. Dessert? he said waving timidly at the waitress. Of course said Fisher who had not touched his potroast I'm starving! Hurry up and eat that slawp said Crosbee I got ter get moving soon. Don't kid me said Fisher You've never moved. Now hands on hips the virago listened to Crosbee order two coffees two double cognacs and two pieces of strawberry shortcake. Crosbee waited until she had gone to draw out a fat black havana which he lit with a blowtorch. A terrifying pall of smoke moved down the table and caused a family of four to choke and cry out. Sounds pretty crazy Fishah said Crosbee. Well life is only what you make it said Fisher trying not to listen to the protestations of the dying family.

I've been thinking of moving to Atlawntar or at least buying a condo theah said Crosbee leaning back bloated in creaking chair. That's a great idea Crosbee said Fisher You know who lives in Atlanta? Who? said Crosbee knitting his brows. Construction moguls said Fisher Women who suffer menopause at twenty and a million blacks repressed by the first two who would happily kill you on sight. Really? said Crosbee They say it's a boom tawn. Yes said Fisher All the white stockbrokers houses go boom. You wait and see. Wall I wasn't really interested anyway said Crosbee I like Bawston. He produced a credit card. You look like you need a free lunnnch he said. I resent that said Fisher But to deny it would be dishonest. The Amazon, bearing dessert on her shield. Can we have aw check? said Crosbee in abject politesse. She tore a sheet off her pad and stuck it in the folds of Fisher's bandage! He turned only to see her massive retreating stern heave in merriment. I love it here said Fisher. Haw haw haw said Crosbee pouring a snifter of cognac down his throat and adopting then a worldly philosophical look Fisher knew and particularly resented. Mock thought. Crosbee said Fisher If you spend every minute of your life in drunken contemplation what do you contemplate? Eh? said Crosbee. Hunting afar. I mean you must be thinking about things that happened to you before you began to drink. At age nine said Fisher. How do you get any raw data to mull over in that armchairish way? Wot *ah* you talking about you bawsted? said Crosbee. I don't know said Fisher Thanks for the lunch. It's almost recompense he thought For coming down to Quincy Market and watching you torture people. Fisher sipped at his brandy determined not to drink it all. Wall let's get going said Crosbee standing up and beginning to make a scene with his umbrella. Fine said Fisher. They went downstairs and Fisher followed Crosbee out the door as the bold financier slashed at the crowd with his umbrella and swatted them with his overcoat. The bawsteds he said to Fisher.

The cold outside braced Crosbee. Well I suppose you're going back to the "office" said Fisher. Yes haw haw haw the "awffice" said Crosbee Listen do yer want to get a drink aw what? A drink! said Fisher You've just had ten! I was recently admitted to the Havad Club said Crosbee We could go theah. Oh man said Fisher How did you manage that? Connections kiddo said Crosbee with a smile intended to be wry. It was only fat and horrible.

Fisher began to walk with Crosbee in bewilderment. He knows full well thought Fisher That if he had even applied to Harvard he would have been tied up by the admissions committee and beaten for hours.

As the two neared Faneuil Hall their attention was attracted by a disturbance. A dirty man with matted hair and bare feet was yelling at two security men. God damn you! he shouted. Sounds familiar thought Fisher. My my said Crosbee with as arch a look as he could muster with ten drinks in him. The two guards leaned against each other, awful bookends laughing at the little man. God damn you I'm comin back ere tonight an kill you God damn you! screamed the little man. Hey Petey where's ya shoos? said one of the guards. Yah huh huh huh said the other Gwan Petey! Gidaddaheer! Yuh! said the first. I never did nothin I gotta right to be here God damn you MacGillivray! shouted Petey. No wonder thought Fisher. Small world he said to Crosbee. Maybe said Crosbee Let's get going Fishah it's a little too poignant around heah faw me. Fisher looked from Petey to himself rumpled and bandaged to the puffing Crosbee. I have to telephone said Fisher. Theah's a phawn booth said Crosbee. It's a kiosk not a booth said Fisher deridingly They're called *kiosks* down here in the Boston of Tomorrow. Crosbee made a vulgar gesture. Fisher dialed. Law students union said a voice. I want to speak to Jillian Hardy said Fisher This is her lover. Just a moment I'll page said the voice. Cold wind blew through the *kiosk*. I'm sorry she's not in the building said the voice. I see said Fisher Did you know I was naked in my office yesterday? What! said the voice. Fisher hung up. Wall? said Crosbee. Not there said Fisher. Ah said Crosbee wiggling his eyebrows. Fisher felt disgusted.

The little man was being poked and prodded across the plaza. Fisher followed the waddling Crosbee onto Congress Street. Hey yaw thing's bleeding! said Crosbee suddenly. Well said Fisher That's OK. Harvard crimson eh what? Crosbee looked dubiously at Fisher. Christmas gift ideas raged at them from glittery shopwindows. I hate Christmas said Fisher. Crosbee was walking in a fog.

VII | How the Panting Died Down

Crosbee paused, hand on damnable doorhandle of Harvard Club, and looked at Fisher lugubriously. You could have shaved he said. I explained before said Fisher. Crosbee reached out and adjusted Fisher's tie. Fisher blushed. What are you doing? he said. Yaw a sight said Crosbee. You are a dried up old mother said Fisher as they stepped in.

To get to the bar they had to cross the Grand Canyon of sneer eroded into the face of the elderly attendant in the front hall. Good afternoon gentlemen he said looking at Fisher's bandage You are members of course? Of cawse said Crosbee At least I am and this is my friend. Very good sir will you be eating lunch today? No we already had lunch and innumerable drinks said Fisher Are you familiar with the meaning of innumerable? The man looked at Fisher with disdain. Haw haw haw honked Crosbee We're just going to the bah. I see said the old man Very good sir. Cold as the bricks of Boston. You awss! said Crosbee as they walked down the hall Do you want to get me thrawn out? Why not? said Fisher You don't belong here. But that's not for you to decide said Crosbee *They* think my money is sufficiently crimson. I don't doubt it said Fisher

It's bloody enough. Crosbee was about to snipe back at Fisher but at this moment they entered the bar and he was overcome with good feeling. He stopped and stood looking about, hands wedged in his slightly tight trousers. Himself more than slightly tight. Monarch of all he surveys thought Fisher.

The Harvard Club. All about Fisher were people who had gone to the big H. Slurping from tumblers of alcohol as if it were water. Crosbee beamed at Fisher, sunrise at Newport. Great bah eh? he said. It was in fact a scene of desperate misery. Crosbee what's gone wrong with the world? said Fisher These people should be reveling in handsome drinks, not dejectedly lapping it out of bowls like dogs. They should be blowing up balloons and spending their money on little rich cakes and tall perfumed women in furs. They went to *Harvard.* Yah! said Crosbee lost in something. Then he frowned at Fisher and began to plump for him to have a drink. A real drink I mean Fishah he said Cut the crawp. Oh all right said Fisher. Crosbee walked smugly to the bar and Fisher sat down at a table looking around in despair. Two businessmen at the next table eyed his bandage. Show's over gents said Fisher. Peasant! murmured one of them. Crosbee swerved up to the table with four double bourbons. Yick said Fisher Do I have to drink all of this? Don't worry said Crosbee condescendingly It's awn *moi.* That's not what I'm worried about but thank you so very much hissed Fisher. Actually it was what he was worried about. Crosbee sat down and assumed one of his studied philosophical poses. So it sounds pretty grim between you and Miss Hahdy he said. Yeah said Fisher "Miss Hardy." What do you think it is? said Crosbee lapping at the liquor in the style of the room. I think it's sex said Fisher Don't you? Eh!

choked Crosbee. I mean don't you think it all comes down to that? said Fisher. He decided to take the leash off his cruel streak and give it a good run in the twilight park of Crosbee's fleshly knowledge. Ah well I suppose so said Crosbee looking around Keep yaw voice dawn why don't you? I mean said Fisher We used to have GOOD SEX but I think she's bored with me, it was TOO EROTIC in the beginning. Jeez said Crosbee taking a good belt This is pretty pehsonal. Fisher looked around the room. At all the successful hands that could shake Jillian's hand and all the handsome lips that could kiss her. All the unsmiling eyes that could want her and the professional brains that could imagine her in their cars. His wound prickled. Then Fisher stared deep deep deep into the eyes of Crosbee and finding nothing he began to recount.

Jillian liked especially to be stroked and cooed over by the light of inexpensive scented candles. At least in the early days. I romantically and willingly went along with it. I wasn't humoring her, I liked it too. But as our love grew and I can see now there was a certain love which rose and fell early on, she told me more about what she liked and I told her what I liked and we pursued these things is that not natural Crosbee? Er said Crosbee pinkening. Including said Fisher Her possibly unusual desire to have me pretend to be a physician and examine her. It drove her to writhing yelling almost appalling orgasm which I found to be extremely exciting. Hoo! said Crosbee sweatily. Indeed said Fisher. And over the months we developed this game to its fullest. I acquired a white laboratory coat from the Institute and at times wrote her erotic "prescriptions" in deliberately poor doctor handwriting. But alas I didn't notice when she began to have her fill of it. I was caught up in the game and drove her on and on and on. Some weeks we played it every night, I feverishly drawing the curtain and taking the phone off the hook and harrumphing Now Miss Hardy what seems to be the trouble? We stopped making love normally if there is a normal way which I am beginning to doubt. But it went on. And then all of a sudden she couldn't at all. Just Boom! like that. Nothing. Oh? said Crosbee nervously. No said Fisher. I paraded through her apartment nude under the white coat but she turned her face to the wall and could not even speak. I began to worry that she had taken her fantasy a step further and was having an affair, that is to say an affair outside our affair, with a real doctor. God knows there are enough of them around, they breed like rats. Although if you really were a doctor wouldn't you find it embarrassing to walk around with your cock sticking out of your real doctor's coat which you wore to work every day? Probably nawt if you were a sahgeon said Crosbee Given the chawnce all sahgeons would walk around like thawt anyway. Yes well said Fisher I wrote on my erotic prescription pad Tell doctor what's the matter but she could only look at me in dour silence. Then a week or so later she met me on the street with Henrietta, you remember Henrietta. Uhh said Crosbee. She met me on the street with Henrietta who I never even thought of sleeping with said Fisher And then that night she said Go ahead and sleep with Henrietta, I'm no use to you anymore! Henrietta! The thought had never even crossed my mind! shouted Fisher. I was cast into deep gloom. Awg said Crosbee drinking. Then said Fisher several weeks after that I got Jillian to make love Crosbee but I had to pry her up from the mattress, she was like a pancake burnt to a griddle. She murmured Yes all right William in this tiny voice and I thought This is what it must be like with one of those rubber emergency dolls she was so unmoving. And as I neared my apogee said Fisher Tears began to roll down her cheeks and I went soft and since then everything has been sporadic and fraught with weird tension. I saw the white coat in the garbage can outside the building one day. And the next day MacGillivray was wearing it for shoveling his God damn coal! She's never enjoyed it since, we'll never enjoy it again! blubbered Fisher. Ah uh Fishah said Crosbee.

The last time said Fisher Was several nights before my accident. We argued all the way through it. She said It's ten o'clock I'm going to bed. I said Oh goody me too. Trying to make light of the situation. You don't have to she said. No no no I insist I said I want to stroke your thighs and put my thing in you. She dragged into the bathroom heaving a great sigh. Undeterred I went into the bedroom. I lit two of her scented candles. Wearing only the pathetic smile of the optimist I got into bed. As time trickled on I listened to the awesome sounds of female ablution. Running water, the toilet, the rupple of the paper roll on the door, a sort of rubbery plunging noise, more running water, the toilet, the paper roll, a long silence, then more running water and then the toilet again! I could not picture the events. She was in the bathroom so long that two hardnesses rose and subsided in me and of course when she marched into the bedroom I was drowsy and limp. She got into bed without speaking to me or touching me and curled up on her own facing the wall, every square inch of which she must know by heart. Jillian? I said. What is it? she said. I touched her shoulders. I want you I said I want to make love with you. Ha! she said. What do you mean Ha! I bellowed immediately. I have a mean bellow. I know said Crosbee. Why do you always approach me in this way? she said. What *way?* I said. When I'm dead tired I mean my God William. I *seized* her shoulders then but she would not be turned or moved. Miss Griddlecake. Look Jillian I said What's going on here anyway? I caressed her breasts Crosbee! The nipples were large and hard. Nguh said Crosbee. William she said You don't understand anything about me, we're so different. Well how do you expect me to know anything when you don't say a word to me? When you come home from school and walk around like Ms Machine and then exhaust yourself with washing and treatments and fall asleep on the stroke of eleven? All you want is sex hissed Jillian. No I said I like a little conversation with my sex. The New York Mets, poetry. Anything. Even jurisprudence. I moved my right hand down. She squeezed her legs together but I found she was wet. A HA! I bellowed again and there was some humor in the moment even if it doesn't sound like it now. At this I felt her relax slightly and I turned so that I was leaning over her. Listen I'm a human being too I said. Although I doubted it seriously I said it. Prove it! said Jillian. Nasty nasty nasty I said What's the matter with you? I added a digit. She whimpered slightly and said I'm not getting anything out of this relationship, you don't understand me, you hate my friends and you make yourself miserable sitting in that freezing apartment playing that God damn fiddle instead of trying to improve yourself said Fisher Or some shit like that. I worked my hand and rolled her breast in my other hand. I had lapidesced, I pressed it against her thigh. Wah! said Crosbee. Your friends I said Are a bunch of idiots, why can't you see that? Why do you waste your time with these professional pre-jerks? I rose above her and placed myself just outwith. I rubbed slightly in and out and she made a noise. I slowly then advanced making a noise myself with the excitement of it. I do love her Crosbee. Oh she said I suppose I should have friends like Crosbee McWilliams III?

Crosbee looked up slightly from his pool of bourbon. Foo he said in a small voice. Yeah said Fisher And then she said You never go out with me, my parents don't even know what you look like. What *I* look like? said Crosbee hazily. No no Fisher snapped *Me!* Anyway I said What does it matter what I look like? beginning to go up and down. The well known beast aborning. Oh ah ah said Jillian We're just not together anymore, we're drifting apart, we're not united. Oh baby I said pushing harder You make me sick. Mng agh oh said Jillian Why can't you just relax and enjoy life? oh oh. Mm mnnh I said You're a real idiot you know that? Oh mm mhfh? Oh William William Fisher oh oh ohh just get out of my life! UGH! AGH! OHHH! she said. Digging her nails into me and all the rest of it. Wisps of steam were playing about Crosbee's shirt collar. Then I said Ohhh baby I love you I love you! Ooog! and the inevitable happened and I thrust once more and then I retreated to the far side of the bed and looked at myself. It was tiny time. You're a real shit she said rolling over luxuriously. You're the biggest moron I ever met I said. When the panting died down we put out the candles and slept as far apart as we could. All she said at breakfast was You forgot to buy milk again and since then whenever I look at her I lapse into my favorite fantasy said Fisher Wishing I had been born to a family of thirty five in Bangladesh.

Crosbee was beet red and slumbrous. He nipped half-heartedly at his drink and shut his eyes after giving Fisher

a confused furtive look. But is it just the sex? Fisher continued Can't I divorce that from the relationship, repair
myself for her, become a Man with a Future? Zzz said
Crosbee. But as he asked this Fisher knew he could not,
his relationship with Jillian was purely sexual. And the
clinic had ruined it. That was the extent of things. Well
Hell Fisher muttered I've certainly done *my* damnedest.
Just let her put on her makeup and dress nice and go
running off to the faculty of law with whom she probably
corresponds more intimately than I dare imagine . . .

Crosbee now slept. But he still wore his expression of
benevolent concern for the misfortunate of the world.
Everyone who was over or under 28 and who did not
make at least $30,000 a year. Hands in pockets he sat with
flushed face in his chair, which began to tip backwards.
Fisher took a drink of bourbon and watched with dispas-
sionate interest. Tired after his long expiation about
which he now realized Crosbee could offer nothing Fisher
refrained from saying anything. Slowly slowly slowly,
Lord God Almighty the chair tipped backwards more and
more moving at an ant's pace but tipping tipping there
was no denying it. It paused at the moment of balance for
ten seconds. Fisher considered raising the alarm but again
chose inaction. Then a heavy snore escaped from Crosbee
and this expulsion of gas was enough to push the chair
irretrievably past the moment and Crosbee fell back onto
the carpeted floor with a soft thud. Several heads turned
but nobody moved to help. They'd seen it all. After a
moment of reflection Fisher got up and looked down at
Crosbee who had begun to snore loudly. Fisher turned to
the attendant who had quietly rushed to his side.

Anything wrong sir? said the old man. It's the strain,
the awful strain said Fisher. Strain sir? Yes the terrible

strain of course of being at the top of his profession at age twenty eight said Fisher. Ah yes sir said the man. Crosbee's feet remained immobile pointing up at the ceiling in their black pennyloafers. Poor devil said Fisher looking down at him I hate to see a man cut down in his prime. The attendant's eyes widened. But surely he's alive sir he's snoring! Eh? Oh so he is. Thank God! said Fisher Perhaps you'll assist me. They bent and Fisher taking the back of the chair and the attendant Crosbee's arms they raised him back to the table. *In situ.* When Crosbee reached the vertical he opened his eyes. As if nothing had happened he reached for his glass, took a long thoughtful drink and began working on the papal frown again. Suddenly noticing the attendant at his side he gave a violent start, splashing the old man with his drink. Good Christ wot do you want! said Crosbee. Well! said the attendant Are you all right young man? Crosbee eyed the man furiously. Of cawse I'm awl right you awld goat! This is tremendous thought Fisher He'll be the first member to be expelled before receiving his permanent card. The attendant was backing away. Get me anothah drink! shouted Crosbee. Fisher thought he was going to throw his glass at the old man but he did not. Crosbee looked at Fisher in confusion. Wot's wrong with thawt jackass? he said brushing at himself. You have misjudged him said Fisher. Awh said Crosbee I bet. What was it you wah saying Fishah? Nothing said Fisher But if you'll excuse me I have to telephone. Awhh said Crosbee staring hotly across the room.

In the course of the long regurgitation of his relationship with Jillian, Fisher had been smitten with a keen desire to telephone Miss Mapes. In the hall he saw the old man vigorously sponging at his coat. Fisher quickly went into a phone booth. He dialed the Institute and asked for the library. He thought of the Institute sitting across town. Freezing and gray under The Ass gaping like a great toilet of granite. Hello? said the wonderful musical voice. Is that you Alison? said Fisher. Yes said the voice Who is this? Oh well said Fisher This is William Fisher. Who, what? said the voice. William Fisher Fisher articulated The renowned nude administrator. Oh yes William hello said Alison. Listen I wonder said Fisher Would you like to go to the movies tonight? What a way to put it. Oh well yes that would be great William she said What's playing? Well I don't know he said Er we could discuss it over dinner if you like. The pirate! Oh well that would be fine she said Oh no there's the other phone! The *other phone* thought Fisher. Where are you? she said Can I call you back, are you in your office? Ah well no actually said Fisher I'm oh God I'm at the Harvard Club! Oh my goodness said Alison Did you go to *Harvard?* I didn't know that. Well . . . said Fisher. Well I could meet you in the square at six o'clock she said. Well yes that's fine said Fisher But I should explain . . . I've got to run William said Alison But thanks for calling and I'll see you tonight. Fisher hung up. The old Fisher style he said. Never fails. What genius. I have only two serious lies to confess to her and then our relationship will be set for blast off. I'm insane he muttered in the hall I'm mad. I'm nearly broke and I've made a date with Another Woman. Although realistically speaking there is no first woman. I'm rumpled. I'm getting drunk after I swore I wouldn't and worst of all I am unshaven in the Harvard Club. The attendant passed Fisher with a large drink on a tray. I'll take that in for you said Fisher thinking the drink was for Crosbee and swiping at it. No you don't! the old man shouted jumping out of Fisher's reach This one's for me! He glared at Fisher who shambled back to the bar.

There were two fresh bourbons on the table and a suspicious half finished one in Crosbee's hand. Jillian? said Crosbee reverting in his eyes to a veiled yet unpleasant memory of Fisher's monologue. Although all Crosbee's memories were veiled. No said Fisher The Connecticut Cutie. Haw honked Crosbee I thought you wah saving hah faw me. Fisher looked dully at Crosbee who flushed and tried for his frown again after sneaking a rabbity look at Fisher. Fisher took a swallow of bourbon and coughed. Where's yaw violar anyway? said Crosbee realizing the frown wasn't working for either of them. I told you said Fisher And it is a violin. The smaller member of the modern family of viols. Eh? said Crosbee. The next largest said Fisher being the viola followed by the violoncello and all of them badgered and smothered by the bass viol. Oh! said Crosbee. Don't mess with me boy said Fisher I'm a consort of viols. Get it? It was clear from Crosbee's walleyed expression that he did not get it nor recall being told of Mr Squeaky's end. Never joke about the arts with a stockbroker. This conversation, this afternoon is at an end thought Fisher. In a flush of self justification he made to sweep his hair back defiantly and forgetting the bandage his hand pulled cracklingly at his wound. Owaaah! screamed Fisher rising to his feet. Crosbee jumped again but this time displayed his usual uncanny ability to keep his drink in its glass. What's the mattah? he shouted. Sorry said Fisher. My bandage. Look, I have to go. Yah I oughta get back ter the awffice said Crosbee Let's have just one maw round. I mean I have to leave *now* said Fisher But you just have your *usual*. OK kiddo said Crosbee I'll tawlk to yer soon. Merry Christmas said Fisher walking away.

The carpet more deep under bourboned feet. Oh yeah Merry . . . uhh called Crosbee whose coattail caught in his chair as he tried to arise in dizzy politeness.

Fisher walked through the lobby passing the attendant. Goodbye said Fisher. Good bye you little shit said the old man, now drunk.

The Ass was threatening to exude imminently. As Fisher stepped across Federal Street he was grazed by a big noisy car. Idiot! he yelled shaking his fist. No response. He hurried to the sidewalk and stood looking up and down the street panting. He began to walk in the post lunch Christmas confusion toward the Park Street T. Perambulating agglomerations of Christmas packages under which there may have been men or women bumped into Fisher without apology.

For some reason there was a mirror in the middle of Downtown Crossing and Fisher stopped to admire himself in it. His bandage was beginning to discolor. Yah! said Fisher The terror builds. Beware the beat of the cloth wrapped feet. He walked on toward Park. Across the street a dirty man shouted slogans. With a bandage on his head! Perhaps thought Fisher I am best suited for employment with some modern day Peachum. As Fisher was looking at the dirty man he did not see a large woman who, bent over, was picking up packages she had spilled just around the corner he was turning. So he fell upon her and her items. Hey ow! Whussa idea? the woman said. Sorry said Fisher. An you another crazy one look at yo haid the woman said Ain't you got nothin bettah to do dan knocks ol wimmen around? Fisher wished he had a hat to put on indignantly. Assuming he had impacted the woman sufficiently to dislodge it from his head. Yes he said

Yes I do if only I could remember what it was. Well you bettah git at it said the woman Or I's callin de pleece. Yes ma'am said Fisher getting up. He pointedly walked across the pavement and busied himself looking in the window of a store. On display were guitars banjos dulcimers tin-whistles and Jews harps. And fiddles. ANYONE CAN MAKE FOLK MUSIC read a sign. True enough said Fisher But nobody knows what to do with it once it's made. They just stand around with it dripping all over the floor. That's the one that boy talkin to hisself the big woman was saying to a similar woman burdened in a like way with identical packages. Fisher watched the reflection of the women in the window and then shifted his gaze to the instruments again. He meditated on the Fruitlands. On Rodney stamping on Mr Squeaky. On Rachel. Fisher then had a vision of his bank account which lay in the bank blackened and shriveled like the tongue of a hanged man. A miniature emotional squall passed over his face. He went inside.

The man behind the counter was going bald although his blond hair covered his ears. His eyes looked reproachfully at Fisher from behind spectacles held together with tape and his fubsy torso was sketchily covered with a t shirt and an old vest. His pants, invisible behind the counter, were unremarkable. A large wet mustache gave him a droopy look. He looked as if war had been declared, possibly some time ago. Can I help you? he asked Fisher. Want to buy a violin said Fisher. Oh no said the man No. The guy's out who knows about them. Is he said Fisher annoyed. Yup I don't know anything about them said the man staring at a wall of fiddles. They were nasty, dry, vegetable. Well I'd still like to take a look at a few said Fisher. *Pardner* he thought. Oh all right said the man How much did ya want to spend? Less than a hundred gulped Fisher. In a huff the man began to bang fiddles against the wall searching their backs for price labels. He put a few on the counter by tossing them onto it from the wall. Jesus! cried Fisher terrified Don't you know that even *touching* a violin is like *poking somebody in the eye?* The man stopped throwing the fiddles and looked at Fisher's head. Fisher swallowed. The telephone rang. The man threw a few more onto the pile even more huffily and went to answer the telephone.

Fisher picked up a bright orange fiddle and looked at it. Bright orange violins are probably made in Guam he thought Not exactly the world violinmaking capital but actually who is to say they don't know a good violin in Guam? Just because it was bombed to rubble in World War II and is now inhabited by army men and their fat wives in muumuus thought Fisher Who says the natives haven't developed a fine violin craft out of papaya wood? Fisher almost hurled the violin against the wall. Instead he put it down and picked up another. He peered into its interior looking for the provenance. Need a miner's hat he muttered. What's that? the man said. Nothing said Fisher smiling savagely. The man turned back to the telephone. Oh all right you can bring Jason to work he was saying But for God's sake keep him in the carrier. Last time he pissed on all the mandolins. Christ thought Fisher involuntarily sniffing the violin he was holding. He picked up another and sawed his index finger across the strings like a bow. It had a sound like dark cloth which pleased him and he put it aside to consider again. Quite a few of the others were from Guam and suddenly depressed Fisher decided not to touch them. The droopy man came back to the counter. Well? he said. I wish I had a million dollars said Fisher. Sure ya don't fella? said the man again

looking at the bandage. I like this one said Fisher holding
it delicately. Well it looks like a good one said the man
grabbing it and pawing the strings Funkleaypunngk! It's
forty bucks he said Are ya sure ya can afford it? *Again* he
was looking at the bandage. Listen said Fisher This bandage has nothing to do with my behavior. Or my estate.
I had another until only yesterday said Fisher voice cracking But it was destroyed by fire. A bandage? said the man.
Violin said Fisher. That so? said the man looking evenly
at Fisher. Yes that is so said Fisher Fire in a wonderful
organic home in which you would glory. And I obtained
that one by trading in a dulcimer which I bought with real
money. Ah the dulcimer said the man suddenly brightening Now there's an instrument. The dulcimer is not an
instrument said Fisher It is a titanic pain in the butt. It is
not! said the man. It is too! said Fisher.

I went out to a wood to play it said Fisher Thinking it
was the true bucolic instrument. All that flapdoodle about
its mixolydian dorianity. It even had a picture of a tree
inside it so I thought It is to the woods I will go with my
dulcimer. I rented a foreign car, I spared no expense. So?
said the man. Bored as all get out. So said Fisher as I
snapped through the underbrush I had already forgotten
why I had bought it but it was saying Carry me to the
wood! And it suggested I sit down ostentatiously on a
boulder by a stream. I had no idea how to hold it or how
to use the noter and my strumming attracted swarms of
blackflies and wasps and batting at this pestilence my
friend shouted Say! Do you know how to play this thing?
And I could only answer Let's get out of here and the day
was further highlighted as I simultaneously stalled and
went into a skid in the Lincoln Tunnel. So to Hell with

dulcimers. That's all your own fault said the man. It is not said Fisher It's an instrument for gibbons.

To Fisher's horror the man then put his forearm out and brushed the other violins aside. As if Fisher's choosing one had made the others so much kindling. Which they were. But. Criminy thought Fisher. Need a bow? said the man. Yes said Fisher. The man reached under the counter and brought out a bow case. There were only two in it and he took one out and tightened and tightened and tightened it until it was of frightening tautness. He sighted down it and said This one's pretty straight. Yes said Fisher I'm sure it is *now.* Huh? said the man. Well *Droopy* said Fisher They're not *supposed* to be straight! He snatched at the bow in an effort to save it snapping in two and Droopy lashed at him with it and hit him on the bandage. Ow! cried Fisher What's the idea? Just watch yourself in here buddy said Droopy. Fisher rubbed his head and looked at it in a mirror behind the counter. New blood. I didn't come in here to get attacked! said Fisher. Are ya sure? said Droopy angrily.

The door opened and a small man came in carrying an ornate little banjo. Fisher continued to rub his head, carefully avoiding the bandage. Droopy held the bow and glared at him. The little man adopted an attitude of polite waiting. A case comes with it said Droopy if you're still interested. He yanked a battered black case from behind the counter and threw the violin into it. The case was demonstrably too short for the bow but this did not deter Droopy who forced it in, quickly slamming the lid and latching it. That's seventy dollars altogether Droopy said defiantly. Fisher looked at the case with quivering eyelids, afraid under the horrific tension from the bow it would lash open and kill him. He took out his checkbook and wrote on his only check. Oh God not another *check!* howled Droopy. What is the matter with you? said Fisher in a low menacing tone. Oh Hell it's all right *sir* said Droopy But I need seven IDs. Right said Fisher. Sure thing. He wrote out the check and in the memo blank he wrote YOU ARE AN UNUTTERABLY SILLY PERSON in tiny letters and handed it to Droopy who stamped it without even looking at Fisher's proffered IDs. His library card and a card declaring him a Friend of the Zoo. The only two testaments of self he now had in life. Fisher picked up the case and headed for the door. The small man with the filigreed banjo advanced to the counter. You'd better get a case for that thing buddy called Fisher Because if you don't that guy's just going to *brush it aside.* Exeunt Fisher into cold. When he was halfway down the block he POIK! heard one of the strings snap. With set jaw he tramped toward the T.

Just opposite the station Fisher was narrowly missed by a braying diesel truck which tipped around the corner against the light. Fisher and for once others yelled at the barely mammalian driver. Then he continued across Tremont feeling weighed down by the Christmas decorations suspended above him. I get it said Fisher. I know what this Yule betides. Christmas dinner with Bob Cratchit in a Chinese restaurant. Tiny Tim throwing up the cold noodles in sesame sauce. The waiter rushing up: Heya! Can't reave crutches in aisre! Endless scouring of streets and back alleys for a companion. To sit December 24th away in a freezing movie theater while all without are singing carols through the hot chestnuts lodged in their throats.

Yes to sit in a mindless violent movie and watch the silhouette of a man in the front row heave its rounded retarded looking shoulders in ? laughter or God forbid a convulsion of some kind, he may have been there for days. To think that it has come to this! cried Fisher That the grey face of a Boston hack is my wreath of smiles! My circle of lights a circular nightlong tramp of Milk Street. Unable to find the Ballydesmond and Guinness. Me! who in youth awoke year in year out to find the poor tree nearly suffocated in an avalanche of gift ideas. Some in boxes, some so large merely ribboned. From Grandma, Auntie, Mom, Dad and Santa Santa Santa. Santa! yelled Fisher. Stares from the funny faces. He caught the mumbling of a man in a doorway. A man he thought Who would find new life in a long red cap. Fisher began to sing lowly to the tune of Silver Bells

> Children
> Little children
> Flat as gingerbread men
> Soon they'll be scraped off the pavement.
> Autos screeching
> Moms beseeching . . .

Fisher went down the cold stairs into the T and in going through the turnstile banged his POIK! fiddle on it. In annoyance Fisher stood and considered whether he was sartorially fit to meet Miss Mapes. His bandage was flapping and soiled. He was rumpled. Galvanic stubble bristled on his face. He thought of trudging yes it would definitely be a trudge to his apartment and another train to Harvard. The extra stations. Economy of time and spirit won. Conquered the fleeting physical. She shall love me as I am said Fisher immediately feeling deep misgiving. He descended the RED LINE HARVARD stairs.

On this most subterranean of platforms men looked at each other in true unknowing. Cold winds howled through the tunnel of white tile. Fisher believed the center of the earth was made of ice. As a youth he had misapprehended a model in the Museum of Science and Industry, its center a black sphere which for years Fisher was sure read ICE. Disabused of this belief by angry teachers, he had however returned to it since moving to Boston. On the red line one is closer to the core he thought And it is definitely colder here than it is on Tremont.

The people on the platform had been waiting a long time and Fisher's arrival in bandage with violin afforded them new food for cold resentful speculation. You animals thought Fisher. He went and stood under a small sign that said 7. No trains. No trains. No trains. Fisher approached the only man wearing a tie on the platform. Er excuse me said Fisher But could you tell me what time it is? Jesus Christ said the man You don't ask somebody minutes away from his first appointment for *psychoanalysis* a lot of stupid fucking questions! He hit at Fisher with his newspaper. Repeatedly. Thank you stuttered Fisher backing off Thank you very much.

Ten minutes later a train rocketed into the station and jammed on its brakes at the last screaming moment. Acting upon a new resolution to protect his hearing from the ravages of the T Fisher jerked his hands to his ears and hit himself on the bandage with the violin case. BANG! POIK! Shit! Fisher exclaimed stepping into the car and surveying the passengers. They looked at Fisher in apprehension as he had a bloody bandage on his head and had just yelled an obscenity. Fisher took a seat in the middle of the car and as the train started to move he closed his eyes. He closed them tighter and tighter until colors came and he thought it possible that his fondest wish might be fulfilled. That when he got off the last stop would be not HARVARD but CEYLON where no one would ever find him.

VIII | There Was Miss Mapes

As red blooded as the bricks of Harvard University on which she stood. Fisher crawled from the T and admired her from across the street. My God he thought stepping out She is beautiful. With one sweep of the gloppy paintbrush of his imagination he pictured her childhood: lazy days on the boat of Daddy in the sound, lying in the sun dreaming of her first orgasms gained riding bareback on her favorite horse Rampager Mapes, simultaneous pleading acceptances from Smith Vassar Radcliffe Yale and Pembroke, her affaire at 16 with the heir to an Arab throne, but always her love of horses, a tan, and khaki skirts. A black sports car whipped around the corner and came at Fisher who was nearly dozing of fantasy in the middle of the street. He dashed to the sidewalk and stood next to Alison panting. Oh hello William she said his labored breathing taking her by surprise. My your bandage doesn't look too good today she said wrinkling her nose As she must Fisher thought When cooing to Rampager in his luxury stable. Don't worry said Fisher It has nothing to do with my behavior. Are you a musician? she said looking at his fiddle case. Well yes I am said Fisher shifting it to the hand away from her. To gallantly save her life should it lash open. Alison was looking Fisher up and down which thrilled him. What shall we do? he asked. Let's go to the Welles she said There's always something good there. She thinks that! thought Fisher The Welles for God's sake. Even mention of the place drove him wild with hate. But dinner . . . said Fisher in a surprising whine. We can eat after said Alison with a provoking flip of her ponytail. Great! said Fisher You're right it is an excellent theater. As they began to walk toward Mt Auburn Street she made to put her arm on his. Sensing this and to facilitate it Fisher again shifted the violin case to the other hand and fell over it. Ow! he said. Oh my gosh are you all right? she said bending down to him. Fisher got up right away. It is important to get up right away. Yes fine he said Sorry I'm a bit sleepy that's all. Sleepy? she said. I have been plied with strong Tennessee drink he said At the Harvard Club. Oh yes you called me from there said Alison I was so impressed. Oh well said Fisher I wanted to explain about that . . . Which dorm did you live in? said Alison I love them all. The little wrinkles around her nose captivated him so. Or did you live off campus? I always think it's broadening.

A great battle was commencing on the cramped and rocky field of Fisher's conscience. He looked at Alison's handbag. I could never marry a woman with a handbag like that thought Fisher So what the Hell. Always judge by the accessories. Actually both he said grieving over the immediate fluidity of his lying I lived in the dorms as a freshman and then moved into a flat. In using the word flat Fisher meant to imply he had been to Europe. And what class were you? he said casually. Oh I didn't go to

Harvard silly she said I'm a Buffalo dropout. Fisher flushed in embarrassment and rage. Why take the trouble to lie in the world of today? he thought. I know what drops out of buffalo he said I've seen it blowing across the prairies in dry cakes. Ha ha ha said Alison musically. Laugh all you want thought Fisher. They walked on down Mt Auburn past the howling Salvation Army band and through hordes of students marching relentlessly toward doctorships, judgeships, small town mayorships, automobiles and the crushing weight of unquestioning American servitude. Although for some reason they were all laughing quite a bit. Fisher felt odd with Alison's hand on his arm and he wondered what it meant. In a wave of guilt he thought of Jillian. But he thought I deserve one preppie before I go mad and am fired.

They looked up at the marquee of the Welles, a theater Fisher despised and had often wished to attend with a howitzer. LOS TIOVIVOS. CAROUSEL OF SMILES. LES CHEVAUX DE BOIS. Have you seen any of these? said Fisher. I've seen *Los Tiovivos* said Alison It's marvelous. What's it about? said Fisher looking dubiously at the poster. Small dark eyed children in unfamiliar clothing. It's a lovely lovely movie about these little Spanish children who rebuild their village after World War II all by themselves said Alison. Using their own hair and crap no doubt thought Fisher. That sounds great he said But you've seen it. What about this *Carousel of Smiles?* he said reading the poster.

A powerful documentary by supertalented young filmmaker Adam Vlemk about the lost generation of 20th century Negroes trapped as porters aboard the great

trains of the white men. For those from whom everybody
expected . . . bow . . . sleepless . . . exploitation

The stupid words swam in front of Fisher. Who *wrote*
this? he thought It's *heartless.* Oh that said Alison That's
just about *blacks.* Right said Fisher thinking that if he
were lucky Fat Leroy would come along and pick up the
Welles and Alison and heave them into the Charles. Well
that leaves this French movie said Fisher his soul crying
out No! No! Not the French movie! It looks wonderful said
Alison. I'm game said Fisher. They went in and Fisher
paid. In his mind a dollar sign spread its wings and flew
off.

Fisher looked around in dread. It's always the same he
thought Graduate owls with glasses like bottles. "Natural"
snacks that would cleave your guts if they were fresh.
Want anything to eat? he asked Alison. Well they don't
seem to have any old fashioned movie food do they? said
Alison I go for the old traditionals. The old traditionals!
said Fisher. Thank God for that he thought. He wanted to
kiss her. So I'll just have a Perrier she said. In deep resignation Fisher trudged toward the refreshment counter.
Large portions of his personality began to close up shop.
He handed Alison the paper cup. Shall we? he said. Love
to she said. As they went into the auditorium Fisher
thought I will never ever live through this. They sat down.
French films are about the only films I see anymore said
Alison. I know what you mean said Fisher. American movies are so . . . you know said Alison. Yes said Fisher. I find
them terribly shallow don't you? said Alison. Yes! said
Fisher becoming annoyed. There's no art to them said
Alison. Fisher began to choke. Already fed up dear Lord

he thought. But then he saw her legs tan and athletic showing from beneath her topcoat. They kindled him. In order to avoid having to say something he looked around the theater. Dotted as it was with the goofiest of every type of Cantabrigian. No respite. The film began.

Un film de etc. A man and a woman lying in bed. An alarm clock rang. The man reached out and turned it off. He turned to the woman and kissed her overlong. The camera traveled up and down their twining bodies. *Zut alors! Ma chérie!* said the man Time to get back! To my wife! Ha! Ha! Ha! said the woman putting on her brassiere. Music. Why do they have to have exclamation points in subtitles? said Fisher It makes the whole thing like a comic book. Damn frogs. Look whispered Alison Look at their bedroom, Europe is so tasteful. Fisher searched the arm of his seat for an ejection lever.

The film was about middle class French boors in neckties, their wives in the equivalent knit sack dresses. Great thought Fisher The modern Europeans. Who got their morality reading Kerouac sitting in the mud in some campground in Holland in the 1960s. What a great bunch. It was a charming sophisticated comedy. That is to say a lame series of clichés and trodden situations on the theme of sweaty furtive sexual intercourse outside two marriage beds. Alison loved it. But as Fisher watched he began to feel a small red insistent rising guilt, as if a minor organ the appendix or duodenum were engorged with guilty blood and poking him in a little erection of conscience. He looked at Alison who was delighting in the Parisian suburbs. I'll be right back whispered Fisher getting up. He tripped over his violin case and swore. Sh! said someone.

The owls were still perched in the lobby. They never

actually attended the films these owls. They just sat in the lobby reading the program notes and eating mice. Fisher ignored them and dialed Jillian's number in a sweat of vague culpability. As it rang and rang he felt even more guilty at the relief which suffused him. He walked back to the auditorium and sat down next to Alison with refreshed interest. A slight feeling of vindication?

Now all the French people were going for a picnic. Fisher winced in anticipation. After the French meal each Frenchman took the other's wife for a walk and more frenzied sexual acts among the shrubs. Hilarious thought Fisher. He noticed Alison wasn't laughing either but he decided she was too busy appreciating the style of things. *As an added plus, extra hilarity was included* in the form of an old French rubbish collector creeping through the bushes taking snapshots of the lovers. His only hope of beating post retirement squalor. A grating guffaw beat at Fisher. He turned around to see a young man in tortoise-shell glasses and tweeds. His mouth wide in quiche breath amusement. Yes great isn't it? said Fisher. Huh? said the man constricting his mouth slightly. Of course this kind of thing really is funny to the French said Fisher Who never signed the nonproliferation treaty . . . Shut up! said the man. And who said Fisher Still sail around detonating atomic bombs seven miles off Nantucket. Shut up! said the man. *Liberté égalité radioactivité* said Fisher. Shut up Shut up! said the man and someone else a few rows back. Fisher faced the screen in anger. What angered him was the adultery. Again thoughts of Jillian boiled up in him. Alison shifted in her seat and Fisher looked down at her legs, athletic and brown and mentioned before. He peered at the wrinkles around her nose in the darkness and thought of her taking his arm and he wondered if they would or could go to bed. He wondered if she like Jillian had ever clung to a mattress like modeling clay trod into a carpet.

But the movie. Impinging. It was so bad. Intolerably bad even for its type. Even for a French film, inexcusably bad. How little Fisher could view without succumbing to malice. He found he could only keep his eyes open for twelve seconds at a time. He shut them. He put his hands to his ears. Put ya hands down said someone loudly. In fear he faced the denouement. It occurred when the marvelously free young French professionals were engaged in coitus on a carousel and suddenly discovered each other. Then they got mad. Then! More *alarmé!* More *zut alors!* as the surprised faces bobbed up and down on the dilapidated horses. Gales of laughter from the Cantabrigians. Then a merry undraped chase through the seaside amusement park at sunset! More marvelous French sex in a fun house! Then a forgiving and an eating of dinner in a marvelous run down dive and then retiral to a lovely marvelous French country house for wine and delightful mutual sex, neckties Renaults and cheap modern art scattered all through the God damn thing.

The lights came up. Alison stretched like a cat and looked at Fisher who cocked his head and tried to smile in a worldly way but suddenly felt his neck sagging turtly tortoise neck, his teeth dentures, I look like the President! God save us. Hungry? said Fisher grasping at reality. *Starved* she said. Fisher picked up his violin and they joined the crazed chattering crowd, all remarking the marvelousness of the experience of the film, all dying for French roast coffee from white porcelain mugs. Dying for it.

Alison seemed to be heading somewhere and Fisher followed slightly behind her feeling odd with violin. Any place in mind? he said. A cold wind blew into his clothes and he wished his scarf hadn't been sucked out of himself downtown. He recalled its woolly caress. I thought we'd have a salad said Alison I love salads don't you? Looking at one of the thermometers which clutter the Cambridge horizon Fisher saw it was 18°. Yes but only in cold weather he said. They walked up Mt Auburn and entered a coven of vampire businesses all built on the chilling availability of students with bags of money.

The air conditioning was blowing a gale. The arctic conditions chilled the conversation and they stared in wintry silence at their menus. I'm not talking enough thought Fisher She thinks I hurt my brain and she's said nothing of my outburst to that tweed swathed pig in back of me. A waitress came and Fisher ordered a hamburger. He knew it was a mistake in sexual politics as well as a plain mistake to order a hamburger in a salad restaurant. They hate meat and don't want you to eat it. But they've got it all right from cows they keep in the back and slaughter sadistically slowly with billiard cues. Alison ordered a spinach salad.

How'd you like the film? said Fisher leaning back and bumping his head on the branch of a decorative tree. Oh I thought it was marvelous said Alison Are you all right? Fisher was beginning to tire remarkably at this question which it seemed had been hurled at him relentlessly since Sunday. I'm not sure anymore said Fisher wondering if she could tell it was not a jest. The waitress brought a carafe of sugary wine and Fisher poured Alison a glass.

Tell me much more about yourself she said. I can't he said You're seeing it all. This also was not a joke. What's your degree in? she said. History said Fisher. What kind? she said sipping her wine. She liked it. The big kind said Fisher The kind that starts at the beginning and ends at the end. Everything. All history. But I specialize in the jaundiced view said Fisher so I prefer not to pursue history. It's overtaken me already anyway. I prefer instead to sit in my small gray office at the Institute which is 90° summer and winter and 20° spring and fall where I can receive threatening phone calls and have scrambled documents flung at me by people who speak only mathematics. Ah said Alison Is that so you can play the violin? No said Fisher Nothing is so I can play the violin. I spend more time worrying about playing than playing. I sit in my room and make lists of sonatas and crumple them up and take them one by one to the trash in the kitchen. Then I worry some more and eat cookies and drink beer and then find myself so tired that I have to lie down on my bed and pant. It is a very great responsibility. What about you? said Fisher Do you have a library degree or something? No silly she said in tuneful derision. Fisher pictured the fireside of her parents and the possible sisters Muffy and Topsy. Tuffy and Mopsy. Mupsy . . . Toffy? I told you she said I'm a dropout. I'm just hanging around. I'm waiting for an inheritance. Aren't we all? said Fisher bitterly. So I want to get a job in public television she said. Ahhgg thought Fisher Really? he said Doing what? Oh I don't know said Alison I've been over there and they have really neat offices with plants and everything and I just thought I'd like to work there. Yes *plants* said Fisher. I met some people from there said Alison And they're really committed. Yes they ought to be said Fisher. Their stuff is excellent! he added hurriedly. Where are you from? he asked. Westport Connecticut silly she said Isn't everybody? Yes ha ha I guess so said Fisher. Oh goody said Alison Here's our food.

Fisher's hamburger was tiny and hard. The meat was black as pitch although sadly it lacked the refreshing aroma of pitch. Fisher watched Alison snap at her salad and mused on the race of women spawned in New York who ate nothing but white wine and spinach salad until they dwindled to nearly naught. Fisher contemplated establishing a clinic for them. They would be tied into bed for a week, force fed raw ground sirloin, and then be led into the ring to go seven rounds with a retired heavyweight. Everyone wearing white doctors' coats. Fisher saw his glass was almost empty. It's that Crosbee he thought I'll be drinking like a fish for days. He looked at Alison who smiled quite genuinely. Are you married? she said suddenly.

No! choked Fisher No! But you live with somebody said Alison I can tell. Perfectly naturally. Fisher found this arousing. No not that either he said As a matter of fact I'm just getting over . . . a bereavement! he said in surprise. The prevaricating cells! You mean you were going out with someone who died oh my God that's terrible it must have been terrible for you she said. Fisher did not like her unschooled bugeyed reaction. But he could not rise above the situation because he was lying. You are going straight to the Devil Fisher there is no hope he thought. As he watched Alison take a large drink of wine Fisher began to silently enumerate his sins. Covetousness, unchastity, book burning, theft of Institute pencils. What was another (that of untruth)? Hardly thought Fisher The straw to break the camel's back. More a straw thrown by a madman onto the remains of a camel so flattened so *kibbled* by his profligate naughtiness and turpitude as to be recog-

nizable only by the hump. And God is no camel thought
Fisher. He began to shake. Drink . . . sloth . . . but why
continue? At least thought Fisher I am not yet guilty of
murder. And I am ridding myself of worldly goods. I'm
. . . I'm sorry said Alison. It's OK said Fisher I'm resigned
to it.

But! I live daily with Death he thought Death! In my
little gray office. Death in my succession of wretched violins. Death in the funerary procession of objects from my
home. Death! Overhead lighting! There is no death in
Westport thought Fisher Or actually it's all Death so
what's the difference? Who cares if this particular death
is fictitious or not? I can't eat this hamburger! he said
loudly dropping it on his plate with a terrible clang. Alison
stopped eating her salad and looked at him with compassion. Well she said soothingly What we really want is dessert anyway. Yes dessert he said Is what we want. He
thought about the twists of fate which guide the lives of
girls so that some have frilly pink bedrooms and others
just think that way. Do we want it here? said Fisher beginning to fear the desserts. The inescapable tarpit of salad
restaurant frozen strawberry cheesecake. Why not? said
Alison They have excellent strawberry cheesecake.

Fisher began to wonder if he would be able to become
erect for Alison if the need ever arose, the likelihood of
which was again receding into the far reaches of the im-
probable. How to couple with one who knows not death?
You look sort of rugged said Alison Do you sail? No I don't
said Fisher gloomily. I've never been in a boat of any kind.
Silence. Fisher pondered the unacceptability of it. Alison
finished her wine. Dessert! Perfectly uniform pieces of
cake. Fisher stared at his. It will be dry on the outside and
nauseating moosh in the middle he thought. In fact he had

it backwards. Well he thought raising his fork and smiling
at Alison Maybe 1957 *was* a good year. He imagined the
ruined factory. No they ain't made cake there for years
sonny, surprised you even know about it, young fella like
you.

What happened to her? said Alison sipping her coffee.
Who? said Fisher startled out of gastric self pity. Your ah
friend who died said Alison. Again Fisher at the cross-
roads. He struck out on the high road now unafraid. It was
botulism said Fisher looking at his cake. Oh how awful
said Alison continuing to eat. Makes you swell up into a
big kelly green balloon said Fisher. Alison looked around
the room. Still life goes on she said turning a radiant smile
on him and twinkling her eyes of Columbia blue. Yes said
Fisher Still life. And now the possibility of an evil act, an
act of excitement, an act of revenge against Jillian occurred to Fisher. He decided for it. For Alison if he could.
Alison! What a haunting combination of autumn leaves,
steeples, tailgate parties and a strange down filled eroti-
cism was she. Fisher somehow thought she had dropped
out of college impregnated by a giant deaf mute ex wrestler. She was that kind of girl. Pretty and adventurous. My
kind of girl thought Fisher. But he thought I will avoid the
pitfalls. I will take and take and take this time, grab and
run, a heel to the hilt. For once!

His mind took him back to his school, dear old Third
Rate Prep. And the only Connecticut girl he had ever
dated. After their third expensive unsexual encounter
Fisher had found himself strapped to a chair in the dining
room of the family mansion, fed on wine and a "French"
dish that stuck to the roof of his mouth and later that of
his small bowel. He listened to them preen and prattle on
about BUSINESS, YACHTING, AND THE REPUBLICAN

PARTY. Yes thought Fisher following the glorious natural line from Alison's breast down her tan arm to her wafer thin gold wrist watch This could happen again. You don't get watches like that from wrestlers.

The bill was $17.80. Nice place said Fisher. He paid, pining as usual for apocalypse in the last second before the cashier's firm grip impoverished him once more. And as usual, nothing. He picked up his violin and in holding this sound producing apparatus he reflected on how sparse their conversation had been. The violin case was covered with frost. But the smile. And the legs. They went out to the street and the weather.

From the looks of things The Ass was gearing up for something dastardly. They wandered up and down the short streets of the square trying to avoid the next stage of the evening. The baring of expectations. Wanna hear some jazz? said Fisher feeling suddenly like lying down on the bricks. Alison stopped and looked at him, her hands in her pockets. Gee William I don't know it's getting late and we both have to work tomorrow. Fisher put *his* hands in *his* pockets and stared off at a thermometer. So it's like that he thought. The furniture in her bedroom again sprouted pink frills. Well may I see you home? said Fisher through chattering teeth but from winter or nerves he couldn't tell. Alison regarded him for a moment and then nodded. Where? said Fisher. Over by Radcliffe she said. Not a wrestling neighborhood thought Fisher. Careful not to stumble he shifted the violin and they walked slowly east.

Near the T they drifted apart for a moment as Fisher stopped to look in a music store and Alison went on to the window of a pretentious clothing shop. Great mumbled Fisher Recorders! The music of the ages as you drool through the wood in your wretched room, this is tyranny. As he turned to complain to Alison he saw an incredible sight. There across the street was Jillian, holding hands and entering into a warm lingering embrace with Frank of Oregon.

POIK! The last possible string snapped. Fisher opened his mouth and his brain raced to decide whether to fill it with vituperation, alarm, meaningless sound, or portions of his dinner. Jillian standing there kissing Frank of Oregon. A bum. Frank of Oregon. And Jillian. *Kissing.* She's *kissing a bum.* Fisher shut his jaw and moved back into the shadows of the doorway. Instantly clinical and coldly calculating he studied the attitude of their bodies. They have had sex. Recently. Within the hour! And then in another green shock he remembered the previous night and pictured in hateful surety the two of them wriggling like stoats while he snored in innocent drunkenness on the living room floor. She seduced Frank of Oregon thought Fisher. You lying bitch! You slut! Seducing that poor innocent man . . . aggh . . . how could he touch you . . . how could you let him! as I slobbered away in boozy sleep induced partly by your great strangeness toward me! Jillian touched Frank of Oregon's sleeve and made to get on a bus which pulled up. Fisher looked up the street and saw Alison smiling at him from the T. Unaware, innocent. He realized he must have looked odd standing staring outward in the doorway. He smiled back and after a hesitation started toward her burning raging and looking back once more to see Frank of Oregon deeply kiss the neat and attractively dressed Jillian, she getting on the bus with a satisfied smile on her evil evil face. Fisher tucked his violin under his coat for fear of recognition. Burdened in this way he waddled toward Alison and took her hand quickly. They walked across the square and out along Brattle Street.

During this walk of great anger fear and sadness in each of which Fisher felt alternately justified and ashamed he caressed Alison and put his arm around her and by the time they reached her house he had put his tongue in her ear and rubbed her breasts and she had enjoyed it and he was so angry and confused. They stood on the porch in the cold, Fisher's violin case between them. Would you like to come in? she said running her tongue around her lips. Yes said Fisher excitedly casually and although she could not know it with great vengeance. His words were brutal and mad and bewildered. For they would lead to the act. As she unlocked the door tears filled his eyes, tears he quickly wiped away as he followed her into the hall.

Everything in the front room of her apartment was the color of wheat. The walls were light wheat, the drapes heavy wheat burlap, the sofa covered in wheat muslin. Something must be done about the grain surplus thought Fisher It's beginning to affect people's minds. Alison shut the door and to Fisher's excitement and alarm locked it. Would you like some more coffee? she said. Yes said Fisher wiggling his eyebrows like Crosbee. He wondered if it would be wheat coffee but tried not to think. She went into the kitchen. Fisher sat down in the wheat. Why not sheaves and stooks instead of furniture? he muttered The country look. No one has the courage of their motifs. Drive a combine harvester to work. He looked around the room wondering when the wrestler was going to spring on him. His muscles tensed. Westport he thought A little bit of Westport in Boston. But what they want in Boston is a whole lot of Westport, they *want Westport.* But if it were airlifted in no doubt crushing my house in the process it would look little and silly even by Boston standards thought Fisher. Which is probably why they left it where it is. The bawsteds.

Alison came in with a tray, wiggling her bottom like a nurse with nothing to do. Why weren't you at work today? she said giving Fisher a cup. As I said I got mildly drunk at the Harvard Club said Fisher remembering. Listen he said About the Harvard Club . . . I like the Harvard Club she said It literally smells of power. A powerful smell indeed said Fisher. Could you have resisted? She sipped her coffee with thin marvelous lips Which thought Fisher Have kissed Daddy, Rampager, pink cuddly toys and various aspects of possibly innumerable Harvard men. Fisher felt he should be warming to the occasion, becoming excited, what with real coffee and wheat furniture but he wasn't and he began to brood about Jillian and Frank of Oregon. Jillian kissing a bum. Fisher was angry but he wanted to be angrier. His reaction was not without humor either but he wanted it to be funnier. He wanted to go wild to ransack Jillian's apartment and write J HARDY SCREWS BUMS on the wall in tomato paste. *My* tomato paste thought Fisher Bought for the spaghetti sauce I now will never create for her. Alison was looking at him. Are you thinking about . . . her? she said. Oh well yes I guess I am Fisher blushed. Alison put down her coffee and slid over to Fisher resting her head on his shoulder. I admire you she said You have tremendous courage. What a farce. Although she said It was hard to keep from laughing when the firemen sprayed you and when you were naked in your office. Typical thought Fisher forcing himself to concentrate on Alison's thigh and to ignore what she was saying. He was determined to spend the night with her. But her jaw and shoulders were bony and hard. But her legs. Tan! Athletic! But thoroughly thoroughbred and feminine. Wherever Fisher went and whatever he did his was a classic case of wanting and not wanting whatever he had, had had or might have. He was happy with everything and nothing all at once or separately. You are nothing Jillian thought Fisher Nothing Nothing Nothing. He protuberated. Mm said Alison noticing it William will you stay here tonight? Yes said Fisher. She got up and tugged at his arm. Come on she said. Fisher picked up his violin and holding it over his bulge followed her into the bedroom, bracing himself for the onslaught of the frills. There weren't any *per se.* But it was the product of a frilly pink mind. It was blue. Little boxes covered in blue print papers and blue pillows strewn about and a pad of blue notepaper on the desk.

Fisher stood, violin over abdomen, and looked at the bed. Alison grabbed him and pulled him to it. The violin fell to the floor. Oh I'm sorry she said. It's all right said Fisher It has no strings. Why's that? she said. It's God said Fisher I've been had. But never mind. Alison then pushed Fisher over and sat astride him. She grew suddenly very tense and shutting her eyes began to rub against him. !This isn't very polite thought Fisher wondering if he might wilt endeavoring to venture in the tracks of Harvard men. Oh I like you she said continuing to rub. After another minute of it during which Fisher could not think what to do she got up and motioned for him to do the same. Let's dispense with the formalities she said. Oh God said Fisher The formalities? Yes the niceties she said. She took off her cardigan and Fisher took off his overcoat. She smiled at him and took off her blouse. Fisher took off his jacket. She took off her skirt. Fisher took off his trousers. He wanted to hide his concretion behind the fiddle again but it was already buried under the clothes. She took off her stockings. Fisher took off his socks. She took off her bra. Fisher waited, having no equal. She took off her scanties, what a word, there is no better, and stood facing him. Then she turned off the light.

Moonlight was coming through the window and in it she turned back the bedclothes and looked at him. Fisher took off his shirt and shorts. He admired her form in the moonlight and pictured her riding Rampager naked through the Connecticut woods only a stone's throw from the unknowing fat men driving their cars up and down the turnpike. He went to her and they rubbed each other. Adultery! thought Fisher But how stupid, you're not married, it's only unchastity. He thought of the camel. Ooh said Alison getting into bed. Something crackled. Flames of Hell or the starched blue sheets? Fisher paused to look at the bookshelf by the bed but not wishing to be rude all he had time to note were *Siddharta, The Women's Room,* and *Winnie the Pooh.* He crawled on top of Alison and they rubbed each other some more.

Ooh said Alison. Mm mm mm said Fisher reminding himself of Fat Leroy and quickly trying to forget him. They continued in this way for some minutes. Alison said Ooh regularly. Unchangingly. Fisher wondered if headway was being made as he was finding it hard to contain himself. Ooh said Alison as before. Fisher moved back and looked at her. She was upset. What's the matter? said Fisher surprised. Oh I'm sorry I'm sorry she said. Tears in her eyes! What's the matter? What is it? said Fisher. Well

I can't come she said. You can't? said Fisher Not at all? His opinion of Rampager plummeted. No she said I can't unless . . . Unless what? said Fisher with apprehension. Well I don't know you very well I'm so embarrassed said Alison. What *is* it? said Fisher. Well said Alison I can't unless you ah you unless you scold me. Scold you! said Fisher What for? Please don't be upset please you're so nice said Alison But I can't come unless you pretend to be my teacher and scold me for turning in a paper on *Wuthering Heights* two weeks late. *Wuthering Heights!?* thought Fisher. Is that all? he said matter of factly. Well yes she said Do you mind? Why not at all said Fisher a great wave of unreality carrying him off. It's quite common. It is? she said getting up. Yes it happens all the time said Fisher Where are you going? To get something for you she said. Fisher watched her bottom flex as she rummaged in a bureau drawer. *Wuthering Heights* he thought. Alison came back to the bed and put something in Fisher's hand. What's this? he said holding it nearer the window. A red marking pen. You have to hold that it makes you a teacher said Alison getting under him and wiggling. Fisher looked out the window at the Cambridge sky and wondered if he would ever turn to religion. I'm glad I live in Boston he thought Cambridge is madness.

So they began again. Hold the pen where I can see it she said. Right said Fisher. Scold me she said. Ah well said Fisher Miss Mapes this is unforgivable. Mmm she said. I uh think this is a terribly sloppy paper and what's more it's a week late. Two weeks! hissed Alison. Ah just so said Fisher Two weeks late. I'm going to have to write a note to your parents. Ngg said Alison slapping against Fisher who was warming to his task. I see you refer to Heathcliff as an Iago figure Miss Mapes now what's the point of that?

If I didn't know better I would suspect you of cribbing this from someone of lower intelligence than yourself. Say how late it is! whined Alison. And it's three weeks late! shouted Fisher struggling. *Two weeks* said Alison Oooo squeezing Fisher with a set of muscles Known he thought Only to members of Connecticut riding clubs. More more she said. Uh this kind of thing will not be allowed gasped Fisher I run a tight ship ng mn oh as punishment you will be required to write an additional paper on *Barchester Towers.* Mmm! said Alison Ohh. Please refrain from inappropriate allusion grunted Fisher And stick to a standard thematic analysis of . . . UGH! AGH! OHHH! said Alison suddenly swooping on Fisher and squeezing him terribly. Yipe! said Fisher. She squeezed him again and then turned.

They started again feverishly now obverse to obverse. She looked at him pleadingly. Oh and this sort of thing can only result in a lowering of your gruggbf said Fisher. No no it's OK now said Alison slapping a hand over his mouth. Fisher let go of the pen and worked in earnest. This is *crazy* he thought *Why* am I here? It's my accident. I wish I had died on the pond. What do I want with this woman? he thought Oog ahh oog ahh he said I love you I love you! Ooooog! He reached his vanishing point. He fell across her.

You're silly she said after a while. But nice. *I'm* silly he thought. He laid his head on her chest. They were both drowsy. Before he drifted into deep sleep Fisher murmured I love you and groggily kissed his own arm. A cringing Jonah in the brick whale.

IX | The Jowls of Jowls

The breakfast looked like a photograph of a breakfast. Berries biscuits cream cheese juice and coffee. Fisher stared at it and wondered what impulse buried in the heart of antiquity caused women to put a bowl on a saucer on a plate. All the plates matched, the blue checked tablecloth was clean. It made Fisher uncomfortable although in a different way from the Fruitlands. Alison kissed him on the forehead and made no mention of their activities. She sat down and smiled at him. Fisher smiled back and knocked over his juice reaching for coffee. Sorry he said. It's OK said Alison wiping it up with a tremendously clean rag which she then threw away. Would you like to go out to dinner tonight? she said I want to show you off to my friends from public television. Fisher tried to swallow. Well yes fine that sounds just great he said. He finished the berries and tried to lay the spoon by the bowl photogenically but he could not think how. So he just put it down but it did not look right and Fisher was secretly ashamed. Do you want a ride to work? she said. Fisher felt his face. A hedgerow. I should shave he said. I like you like that said Alison. Ah I see said Fisher And would you like me to smell of cigars and beer and sweat and leather and gun-powder and dust and cattle? Ooh yes she said. Hm! said Fisher. I'm rumpled he said suddenly. I love it said Alison. You don't understand the horrid inner meaning of it said Fisher.

They drove smoothly through the crazed morning traffic in her luxury car. In the big lobby of the Institute she turned toward him for a kiss. He kissed her with great embarrassment. She was looking around to see if anyone she knew saw it. I'll call you she said and skipped off toward the library. Fisher elected to trudge. Through the long cold corridors and up the stairs to his office. He was not exactly sure why he was trudging but he knew he should be. As he neared his door his steps became slower and slower and he briefly hoped he would never reach it. But alas at last he did.

Smith was standing there rummaging through Fisher's desk. Morning said Fisher. Fisher! said Smith Where's your report? I haven't done it said Fisher And anyway it's going to be very short this month. Oh and why's that? said Smith. I have a feeling said Fisher. Well sleepyhead said Smith with a sneer It's due today. In truth Smith did not give a brown hoot about the monthly reports and Fisher knew it. And another thing said Smith retreating toward the partition Jowls is coming in for the inquiry today. What? said Fisher. The *inquiry* said Smith So try and act with some degree of normalcy if you possibly can and start typing the God damn report. He slammed the door. His little door. I can't write it until you tell me how much uranium you've used called Fisher. Oh Hell came the reply I don't know, make it up! Well *about* how much?

said Fisher with rising petulance. Smith opened his desk drawer. Well I had some in here he said But how am I supposed to know who all has been at it? Great said Fisher Don't you know it's supposed to be kept in the vault in the lab? Don't tell me my business! screamed Smith Just write the report and for God's sake shut up and leave me alone! OK! said Fisher. He sat down businesslike at his desk and stared at his calendar for an hour.

The next sensation was that of something in his pocket. It was his hand, feeling about. Fisher took it out and looked at it. It clutched the loose pile of grime that constituted Frank of Oregon's manifesto. As soon as he saw it Fisher recalled the man soulfully kissing Jillian at the bus stop in the square. In disgust he moved to throw the bundle in the trash, but holding it over the basket Fisher began to read the document which smelled like the old socks of a thousand putrefied mummies.

Briefly described the manifesto was seventeen sheets of various materials. The 1st leaf was a yellow handbill promoting amateur wrestling at a Philadelphia gymnasium. The menacing face of an idiot wrestler showed faintly through Frank of Oregon's stirring scrawled preamble. The 2nd leaf was a small brown paper bag with ? something in it. The 3rd leaf was the final page of somebody's copy of *A Farewell to Arms;* the 4th leaf was a pasteboard cigarette advertisement stolen from the T or a bus; the 5th leaf was a handbill advertising the Mystic Delites Massage Parlor and Ye Olde Publick House in Groton Connecticut; the 6th leaf was a piece of purple suede; the 7th leaf was a sheet torn from a copy of *Awake!* magazine ("God Guides Your Dentist's Hands"); the 8th leaf was the racing page of the New York *Daily News* of

2 August 1978; the 9th leaf was an empty white envelope
addressed to Occupant, 477 Western Avenue, (indeci-
pherable) NY; the 10th leaf was a 1969 seasonal scorecard
for the Baltimore Orioles; the 11th was the bottom of a
doughnut box; the 12th was a plain piece of paper; the
13th was a hall pass from Astoria High School, Astoria,
Oregon; the 14th a page from a mimeographed treatise
on herbal medicine; the 15th a smearily printed appeal
from an Indian family for aid to their failing pharmacist
father; the 16th a sheet of aluminum foil and the 17th leaf
was a potato chip bag split lengthwise and opened up.
Frank of Oregon had been able to procure tools appropriate for writing on each surface; that portion written on
the potato chip bag was in crayon, the suede had been
scribed with marking pen. And so on.

The text revealed Frank of Oregon's impression of the
general Rot and Hell bound direction of American society. He felt things were bad and getting worse due to
GASOLINE (and a lack thereof), PLASTIC (which he asserted
is made from gasoline) and LACK OF DONUTS which he
blamed on complications arising from the first two and in
which he saw symbolized a great many grievances and
sorrows. The style was childish yet somehow arresting and
Fisher read the manifesto holding it all in his hands the
while for fear it might befoul his desk. He was taken by
the basic reason of a particular argument:

> And who amung us has not experiensed the dilema of
> wanting a cup of the joe? But yer siting in a cold dorway
> and its erly morning and you need a cup of the joe befour
> you can go hunt up a cup of the joe. And it gets two the
> point of you need a cup of the joe befour you can think

eny more bout howe you need a cup of the joe befour you can go hunt upp a cup of the joe. I say joe to evrybody joe in the donut shopps. Joe H Y D R A N T S for all Travling Pilosefers.

The manifesto democratically updated the idea of the philosopher-king with that of traveling philosophers, men like Frank of Oregon "in toon with howe the planit ~~funtiuns~~ ~~punksouns~~ works" poised to take over when capitalism and western culture bought the farm. Frank of Oregon asserted America would soon be done out of its previously uninterrupted supply of gasoline and doughnuts by "Arabiens" and by "the greed we the Travling Pfilosepers see itched on the faeces of blubbry peple living in the bluber belt of Bosten." The only people competent to run society were people who walked for months in one pair of shoes and no socks. "When the Rushens come men with no sokcs can figt them but fat Bosten men like tois who have just run out of gass will bee ovirrun." It was Malthus revised by J. Edgar Hoover. Fisher found himself nodding, transported back to the seedy tavern where he had found his spirit kin to Frank of Oregon's. He considered his rage against the man for having Jillian. He thought of Alison. This led nowhere. So Fisher began to type the manifesto, a convert, using it also as a weapon against the unbegun monthly report.

Fisher had typed most of the manifesto but when trying to decipher a murky passage written with burnt bark on aluminum foil (the 16th leaf) he left for the toilet. There he looked at himself in the mirror. He was rumpled. His bandage was caked with blood and he was disreputably unshaven, not attractively unshaven as Alison had claimed. He looked as if he were hanging around waiting to kill someone.

Often when looking in mirrors Fisher would pretend to have a Picturephone conversation with his father. I don't know Dad he said aloud Things are really odd here but it's not my fault. It's just bad luck Dad. I know you're proud of me. Administrator! But it's not like you think. Not like when the survivors were all smiles after the war and technical industry snapped you all right up and the mortgage rate was .01% of course what do I care about the bleeding mortgage rate! shouted Fisher turning slightly and blanching to see Dr Jowls standing in back of him with open mouth. Gug said Fisher.

Fisher! bellowed Jowls Come back to your office with me this instant! Yes Dr Jowls said Fisher examining his fly and then following the big man out into the hall. What the Devil do you think you're doing? said Jowls You must be mad son. Don't you know only insane people talk to themselves? Do you realize that while looking for you I had to answer your telephone myself? Who was it? said Fisher. What do you think this is? said Jowls Cartoon time? This is the *Institute* Fisher. Institute of Science said Fisher. Damn right said Jowls This is technology. Yes Dr Jowls said Fisher feeling queasy. I think our little panel said Jowls Will be very interested to hear of the condition in which I found you. He pushed open the office door.

Smith was sitting there fidgeting next to old Dr Shaker from the health service. Come on Jowls said Smith This is a complete waste of time, as you can see Fisher's back at work. Huh! said Jowls You may be interested to know *Smith* that I just surprised Fisher talking to himself in the john. Smith glared at Fisher. Dr Shaker stared at the floor and breathed in and out in a labored rattle.

Fisher sat down at his desk. Jowls planted himself belliger-
ently between Smith and Dr Shaker. The inquiry. It
should be stated that Jowls had his own problems. His wife
was frigid and spent every day on a divan reading the
Bible. He had lusted for a new car for three years. Jowls
had a habit of long standing of making a tremendous issue
out of everything. This was why Mrs Jowls was unrespon-
sive to his brutish caresses and why he was one of the
great administrators of the day. Vice President of the
Institute of Science. Jowls was the kind of burly fellow
who if he apprehended you grappling with one of his
sainted blond daughters would club you to death with his
hairy elbows and heavy gold watch.

Now listen Fisher said Jowls We want you to go for
tests. You administer a research program involving radioactive materials and we can't have you unstable. You ask
him Timothy said Jowls to Dr Shaker Couch it clinically.
Eh oh all right trembled Dr Shaker. With apparently
great effort he raised his veined plotchy cabbage of a head
and looked at Fisher with eggy eyes. How do you feel son?
he quavered. Fisher shot a glance at Smith in whom he
thought he might have a partial ally but at this moment
was met with an unkindly look. I am fine said Fisher.
Where were you yesterday? said Jowls. I was sick said
Fisher. But *what kind of sickness?* said Jowls leaning forward. Bodily sickness said Fisher It had nothing to do with
my accident. So you assert said Jowls. He threw up on the
phone! said Smith of a sudden. Good God said Jowls eyeing the instrument on Fisher's desk with disgust. No no
said Smith He called me from home yesterday and while
I was giving him instructions on the monthly report he
became ill. Oh said Jowls. Disappointed. And suddenly:
AND IS THIS THE REPORT? said Jowls *gathering up the*

sheets of the manifesto. Sweet God thought Fisher.

The jowls of Jowls puffed in and out and rippled reddening from time to time as the eyes of Jowls scanned the pages of the manifesto and the brain of Jowls processed the text. Pretty efficiently too. To Fisher's surprise Jowls said nothing until he had read the complete document, that is as much as Fisher had typed. Fisher saw Smith looking at Jowls without interest. Smith thought it was the report. Dr Shaker was again examining the floor or perhaps his shoes. But Jowls as he neared the end of the typewriting began to foam and sputter. This this this! he said. Heavens thought Fisher. This this is *outrageous!* spat Jowls God's Bones! Do you think we pay you to sit here and incite revolution and riot? No said Fisher. What are you talking about? said Smith. What am I talking about! howled Jowls This is what I'm talking about! What a showman. He threw the papers at Smith and turned on Fisher. Listen you are very ill young man he said. I can explain said Fisher. You'd better and in a very great hurry said Jowls. Dr Shaker was smiling to himself still looking down. That is not a real document said Fisher I mean it is fictional, it is a work of fiction. I don't believe you! cried Jowls It is so real, I think you are a terribly sick little revolutionary boy. You're wrong said Fisher looking to Smith who was paging lifelessly through the manifesto. What crap said Smith Oh how can you take this seriously Jowls? Just what I've always suspected of you Fisher said Smith A retributive fantasizer! He slapped the pile down on the desk. Just *do the job* Fisher said Smith. Find another outlet. Jowls blinked at Smith. Right! said Fisher jumping up. Another coup. Ohh-hm-bmm! hummed Dr Shaker moving his head back and forth to some tune he was recalling. Jowls had now to shift the basis of his anger.

This made him sad but he was gallant about it. We don't pay you to type avant garde fiction! shouted Jowls This is the Institute. He tried to pound the desk but was too far away from it. Right said Fisher I apologize for that. I have been caught out in a series of events designed by fate to enrage and embarrass me, I'm sure it's happened to you at times! He was shouting at Jowls *again* he thought, *shouting* at the Vice President of the Institute at the top of his voice. But Jowls took it for some reason, suddenly oddly deflated. Perhaps he knew Smith kept rare earths in his desk drawers. Yes yes it has said Jowls catching for the first time a whiff of the manifesto MS and retreating even further.

The telephone rang. Grabbing at it in his haste to appear competent Fisher knocked over Smith's cup of coffee. God damn it he said into the mouthpiece brushing at the hot wet coffee on his lap. It's Alison said the earpiece. No! said Fisher I can't talk. William I'm all alone in my office said Alison Scold me a little. Oog said Fisher looking at Smith and Jowls. Come on, just for a minute! she said. God not now you don't understand squealed Fisher hanging up. What was that all about? said Jowls. Nothing said Fisher It was a wrong number. Smith was getting red in the face, longing to get back to his as yet untwisted genes. Jowls looked at Smith and Dr Shaker in a disappointed way and then at Fisher. He loved inquiries. This one had been grossly unsatisfying. Do you give me your word you are fit to continue? he said That you feel as you did one week ago? Yes said Fisher with a remarkable warble born of phlegm. We should continue to trust you with confidential information about radioactive substances? said Jowls. You bet said Fisher. The telephone rang again. Fisher picked it up but said nothing. Come on

William come on said Alison breathily. Hell! said Fisher
Bad girl bad girl! It's two weeks late! It's no good! I can't
accept it! Bad! Bad! He hung up. You see said Smith He
knows what he's doing, people listen to him. Smith stood
up. I'm fed up with this Jowls he said Fisher's OK in my
book. He went behind his partition and slammed the
door. Jowls stared hard at Fisher. I'm going to keep an eye
on you he said. Fine said Fisher And while you're at it why
not keep an eye on the fire brigade? The fire brigade? said
Jowls. They're the ones who started all this said Fisher
thinking nonetheless it was all Thoreau's fault. Why was
I not taken to goose heaven right there? thought Fisher.
Jowls got up and went out followed by Dr Shaker who
shuffled and waved. He always wore bedroom slippers to
work, he was that old. Fisher put his head down in the
pool of coffee uncaring. Then refreshed he sat up and
finished typing the manifesto. He picked up the smelly
leaves and ran down the hallway to the wheeled recepta-
cle the janitors loved to push around. With a sigh of relief
he dumped Frank of Oregon's manuscript into it. He
went back to the office and took out the form for the
monthly report.

THE UNITED STATES OF AMERICA

DEPARTMENT OF THE INTERIOR

ATOMIC ENERGY COMMISSION

OFFICE OF NUCLEAR FUELS & WASTES

INSPECTION DIVISION

MATERIALS REPORT FOR GENETIC ENGINEERING PROJECT:

027SR/IS/Smith-Brown-Jones "Third Arm" Study.

(1) NUCLEAR FUELS CONSUMPTION: A mere handful as dictated in Project Directive 027SR/IS/345-T (revised).

(2) RESIDUAL CONSUMPTION: Leftovers used as joke favors at project cocktail party (see Cocktail Party Directive K85RR).

(3) NUCLEAR MATERIALS SUPERVISOR'S SUMMARY: As far as I know we haven't lost any more to "mice" but today under severe stress I wanted to take some and climb to the top of the big dome of the Institute and threaten certain people with it. Due to an accident in which I sustained lacerations of my brain case and its associated covering of skin and hair I have been sorely pressed by top level management for assurances of my moral fiber. But despite the aforementioned lapses I can now assure them fully on this point. There is little cause for alarm.

(4) PROJECTED USE OF NUCLEAR MATERIALS IN NEXT MONTHLY PERIOD (PURSUANT TO TRUTH IN LENDING OF NUCLEAR WASTES ACT 1979): Wouldn't you like to know?

(5) SECURITY OF PROJECT NUCLEAR MATERIALS STORAGE: It's in Smith's desk drawer and he doesn't know where it goes. But I know Where It Goes.

(6) VARIATION IN SECURITY CLEARANCES (DEFINED IN PROJECT DIRECTIVE): Huge fistfuls of U-235 happily doled

out to visiting Russians and Chinese . . . uncountable!

(7) SIGNATURE OF NUCLEAR MATERIALS SUPERVISOR:

A Lincoln

Fisher read over the report chuckling. Shut up! said a
voice from behind the partition. Sorry called Fisher. He
was momentarily sorry but Hell he thought. Hell either
way. Fisher put the report in its special government envelope and ran before he had time to reconsider down the
hall and posted it. He walked back to the office slowly.
Flushing freezing worrying and thrilling. He put his head
down on the desk. Someone had cleaned up the coffee. He
found this suspicious. He shut his eyes. The telephone
rang. What? he said into it. William it's me said Alison Can
you talk? You! barked Fisher Do you realize I was being
interrogated by Victor Jowls when you called me? What
do you think this is, cartoon time? What? said Alison. This
is the Institute of Science Miss Mapes. William it was great
when you scolded me said Alison. Happy to be of service
said Fisher gloomily. William you are coming out to dinner with me tonight aren't you? said Alison. Yes said
Fisher But where? It's a surprise said Alison. A surprise
thought Fisher. Meet me in the square at 6:30 she said.
OK said Fisher. Bye! she chirped. Fisher hung up. Bad girl
he said. Shut up! said Smith.

Fisher looked at the typed manifesto. He folded it and
though he felt resentment rise he put it in his pocket. He
hoped he would run into Frank of Oregon soon. But ?
why? Fisher fell asleep at his desk.

But he was shaken awake by Smith. Fisher! he said Are

you all right? Fisher looked up clearheaded but instead of answering Smith chose to stare at him like a raven. It's five o'clock said Smith Why don't you go home? Have you ever seen my home? said Fisher. Where's the report? said Smith. In the mail said Fisher. Fine! See you later growled Smith stamping off down the hall. How can a man inventing ways of sprouting extra limbs on people be so foul tempered? said Fisher in the empty office. I'd be on cloud nine.

Fisher picked up his violin case from under the desk. It was stained with coffee. He put on his overcoat and bumped down the stairs and across the wide lobby. Buffeted by cruel winds Fisher forged his way across the Harvard bridge, he and his violin battering itself and himself with each other and the spiked railings along the footpath. The Ass was producing voluminously. Fisher was aware of feeling terribly hurt in some way he could not completely connect with the weather. His fist shook autonomically at the blind pilots of roaring motorcars. Muttering and crouching against the gusts Fisher slowly got on toward the Evening Star.

X Too Full for Sound and Foam

If one thing is wrong then everything is wrong. If you have a bad day you cannot retreat into a good beer. It will be a short flat beer because there is no real escape to be had and things just get worse and worse and worse all the time through all the geologic ages. The whole history of Everything is only slow deterioration which is best spotted in the decay of manners but nonetheless is occurring in strata of rock and in temples and in the decreasing availability of interesting high grade blends of pipe tobacco thought Fisher sitting on a stool with a spring that poked his bottom.

The Evening Star was packed out. Fisher had had to elbow and violin case swipe his way to the bar for which he had received the grumbled damnation of the clientele, particularly dirty and scowly that evening. The approach of Christmas had them all in a panic of sourness. The bartender, a stoic, had refused to be caught by Fisher's eye. Why should he? thought Fisher I'm so rumpled he may not even recognize me. Fisher looked at himself in the mirror behind the bar and turned away in moral distaste. I should get on a plane thought Fisher And go crawl under the bed of my youth and refuse to come out until

I am either younger or older. Finally the barman jerked his head at Fisher. Guinness! said Fisher. And under his breath: You idiot, you know what I want, you know me. But perhaps he doesn't want to anymore thought Fisher who often became depressed when people he had a nodding acquaintance with suddenly turned curt. And in the barman's haste the Guinness was short and in a surprising lapse of standards it was flat and this had led Fisher to muse on decay. Then looking up over the rim of his glass he saw Frank of Oregon. Signaling. In the back.

Fisher did not know what to do but after a few seconds of making sure he was not going to suffer panperistalsis he got up and slowly made his way toward Frank of Oregon, his mind a rush of grasping calculation. The one thing I will not do thought Fisher Is pick a fight or pour my Guinness over Frank of Oregon even though it is short and tastes like the tubes were last cleaned on V-J Day. I will not fight I don't want to fight Fisher continued to think as he drew nearer through the haze to the smiling beckoning Frank of Oregon. I wonder if he's killed men thought Fisher It's a tough life riding the rods. Jesus! thought Fisher continuing to walk but thinking suddenly of Jillian again but still walking toward Frank of Oregon. Who had had her! Never had Fisher felt such anger except when his plastic woodpecker kit was crushed by a fifth grader. He was almost at Frank of Oregon's side now after the battle with the crowd I won't fight thought Fisher smiling at Frank of Oregon, reaching out and touching him now in an odd gesture he himself did not fully understand.

Hiya Mr Fisher said Frank of Oregon making room for Fisher on the bench by routing a little man away with his rump. Yip! said the little man dribbling beer. Sorry mate said Frank of Oregon. Hiya Mr Fisher. Again he says it thought Fisher who began to tremble. He gripped his glass of stout hard. Oh man I could just pour it all over you you stinking bum thought Fisher And hurl the glass into your face! Your teeth bloody teeth scattering against the mirror! But without a word Fisher sat down next to Frank of Oregon in the narrow space provided. Hello said Fisher. How are ya Mr Fisher? said Frank of Oregon in a basso betraying a disturbing degree of self control. Fisher looked deep into the eyes of Frank of Oregon. Unlike most of the eyes he had looked into lately they had in them at least a suggestion of reason, of thought, of knowledge risen out of the barm of experience however awful or sordid or smelly.

Frank said Fisher in a wet red rush I saw you with Jillian last night. He looked hotly at Frank of Oregon and his hand trembled again on the glass I won't become violent! he thought. But already the impulse to cry out was rising in Fisher as Frank of Oregon was looking back at him with a terrible evenness and taking so long to reply. Of Oregon said Frank of Oregon reaching in his coat for cigarettes. His usual correction! And cigarettes thought Fisher Which no doubt Jillian has bought for you. Fisher grabbed Frank of Oregon's sleeve. What's going on! he hissed. The brown hand that immediately clutched Fisher's was calm, strong, friendly, tough. Aw come on Mr Fisher said Frank of Oregon shaking Fisher's hand off I saw you with a girlie last night too.

Fisher tensed all over and then relaxed and then tensed again. Already proven a hypocrite he thought. Did Jillian see me? he said quietly. Nah said Frank of Oregon An I kept it to myself Mr Fisher. Well anyway that has nothing to do with it said Fisher catching himself and deciding as usual to explore dangerous new territory in midstream. You should see Fisher play chess. Is that so? said Frank of Oregon. Mr Fisher yer always sayin things don have nothin to do with anythin but they do. Ya got clyped on the head an went around actin crazy an ya said it had nothin to do with it. Well at some point Mr Fisher somethin's got somethin to do with *somethin.* I think anyways. Some point. Everythin's not on its own forever said Frank of Oregon his eyes narrowing horribly. When I saw ya comin in here tonight Mr Fisher I thought He's gonna give me holy Hell for takin his girl out an even though he took another girl out he'll say it had nothin to do with it. Really? said Fisher ever fascinated by assessments of himself however dreary. Yah said Frank of Oregon. Yer full of shit Mr Fisher I mean almost completely. If I may say so. Frank of Oregon took a large gulp of whiskey.

Fisher sat in homeostasis. Thinking pure thought. Suddenly he felt a great deal of his anger slip away, unfounded. He struggled to retain it. Fisher had a famous capacity for retaining unfounded unjustified anger but it failed him. He saw himself a mammoth blunderer. The maker of all the mistakes throughout time. I feel unfortunate and victimized thought Fisher And I am convinced at the same time this is all my own doing (suddenly) (somehow) and now I am filled with remorse. Remorse! after just warring to keep myself from violence. The turns life can take. And me with no headlights.

Fisher looked at Frank of Oregon who was smoking a cigarette. Honestly. Openly. Fisher considered what to say.

1 Well Frank of Oregon I was just so surprised what with Jillian being a middle class law student inviting

you to her bed while I the only other middle class person in the house was allowed to rot in my puddle on the floor. And not just the once but exactly how many times have you coupled and etc.?

2 Well Frank of Oregon I have hit my head and in fact it does very much have something to do with my behavior I must be honest I really can't think things out at all if indeed I ever could. I really must plead inability to see connections between one thing and another etc.

3 Well Frank of Oregon even though I unfairly condemn you I have a right to do so as I am an administrator at the Institute of Science and a violinist and you in comparison are draff, slops etc.

4 Well Frank of Oregon you see I am filled with repressed hate, the bits of my broken woodpecker kit etc.

5 Well Frank of Oregon I have drunk too much etc.

6 Well Frank of Oregon I have not drunk enough etc.

None of these was any good. Fisher was becoming embarrassed as the honest face of Frank of Oregon deserved a reply but he had to sit and think it out. Staring at his Guinness Fisher began to feel relief albeit an indefinable unacknowledgeable relief (everything is indefinite if interrelated). He felt even a kind of joy. It was energy, a new or old energy he wanted to thank Frank of Oregon for just as soon as he thought it out. But the embarrassment was mounting. Fisher felt the talk in the Evening Star was quieting in anticipation of what he would say next. Waves of confusion went up and down his arms.

I'm sorry! said Fisher but this immediately seemed inappropriate and tears filled his eyes. Frank of Oregon punched Fisher's arm playfully. Aw come on now Mr Fisher There's no hard feelins. Fisher began to stream and gurgle Oh Frank of Oregon it's just everything. Right said Frank of Oregon It is just everything Mr Fisher. No said Fisher I mean falling down on the ice and getting drunk and my landlady yelling and Jillian yelling and Jowls yelling and I was squirted with water and had to eat natural food and see a French movie and talk with video people and my violin in flames! It just hasn't been a good week, there's no such thing anymore. Yeah said Frank of Oregon looking around with some embarrassment as the patchwork of sympathies and comprehension in the Evening Star turned toward the blubbering Fisher. I'm a normal person Frank of Oregon sobbed Fisher I mean I used to be. I was *born* normal. I've seen the certificate. Things like this upset me so. Fisher put his head down on the table.

But shortly he raised his head enough to look into the glass of stout. A watery layer of tears floated on top. And beyond the glass Fisher saw Frank of Oregon barging through the crowd and getting two large whiskeys from the bar and bringing them back. Oh Frank of Oregon I can't drink that snuffled Fisher I have a sexual obligation to go out to dinner later. Oh aye I see said Frank of Oregon. But said Fisher looking at the layer of tears I will have another Guinness. Frank of Oregon kicked and punched his way to the bar returning with a black glass. Thank yugg said Fisher gulping. He felt cheered but then in another wave guilty for feeling cheered. In truth he wanted to storm on for days. It was his way and old ways die hard especially when they give so much pleasure.

But Fisher sat up in an effort at self composition. With a long curving swipe he decorated his sleeve with a snail trail of mucus. Snuk! said Fisher. Mr Fisher should I get ya some hankies? said Frank of Oregon. Hankies? said Fisher No no I'm all right. The parts of it that are me are not the parts I wish to blame any longer. Huh? said Frank of Oregon. Hankies! thought Fisher The very idea. Nonetheless Fisher was prompted to feel in his pocket. The manifesto's clean bulk. Frank of Oregon! said Fisher I typed your thing. Yeah? said Frank of Oregon Let's have a look.

As Frank of Oregon read the typed version of his own opinions Fisher looked at the curve of his back, the angles of his arms, the general beaten boniness of him and in his mind stripped him and put him in Jillian's bed and began to feel sick again. Alone. Recovering, seeing the sense and doesn't matterness of it but sick all the same. Pretty sick and worried at least in waves. Frank said Fisher. Of Oregon said Frank of Oregon not looking up. Of Oregon said Fisher Listen I want to know. Was she like you thought? Or like I thought or like I thought you would think? Mm said Frank of Oregon shuffling the pages. He was falling in love with them. Frank of Oregon! said Fisher banging his glass down. What! said Frank of Oregon. About Jillian said Fisher. What about er? said Frank of Oregon. Well yes thought Fisher *What* about her? Well ah did you enjoy it? said Fisher feeling sick again. The price of directness. Oh to be sure said Frank of Oregon. Fisher ruefully looked him over again. Just tell me one thing said Fisher. What is it? said Frank of Oregon his eyes twitching, *desperate* for the manifesto! Did she er call you anything? said Fisher hoarsely. Well now that's pretty personal Mr Fisher said Frank of Oregon. Please said Fisher I'm through with her, she's through with me, it's all over, just tell me. The right eye of Frank of Oregon twinkled (the left was unobserved thank God) and he said Well come to think of it Mr Fisher she did call me darlin. Darling said Fisher. And she called me her cute little bum said Frank of Oregon. Cute little bum said Fisher. His hand tight on his glass. Did she said Fisher At any time call you Doctor? Doctor? said Frank of Oregon slowly Naw Mr Fisher why would she call me that? She wouldn't said Fisher I was just wondering. Frank of Oregon escaped into the manifesto again.

So! thought Fisher She can manage with somebody not masquerading as a physician! Fisher wanted to crush his glass in his hand but on a test squeeze found they gave Claude Rains very thin glasses. I suppose it's me he thought I guess she really wanted me to be a doctor or other professional and that was her subtle way of breaking me in to the idea. Suddenly he boiled over fleckily foamily like hot milk and you in the other room. Did she make you wear a white coat! Fisher shouted at Frank of Oregon snatching the sheets from him. What! said Frank of Oregon grabbing them back Whatza matter with ya Mr Fisher? She didn't call me nothin cept darlin and my cute little bum an we wore *nothin,* it were *nude sex* Mr Fisher! He said it viciously but not too viciously. Fisher shut his eyes. Then he blundered to the bar and got another Guinness and another whiskey.

But while Fisher calmed at the bar Frank of Oregon had become angry at the table. You better stop askin me these personal questions Mr Fisher he said I don think you got any reason to complain. What do you mean? said Fisher halting on the road to complacency. I'm talkin about that snooty lookin bitch you was with snapped

Frank of Oregon as the whiskey took a bite out of him. Yah! said Frank of Oregon She looks pretty well set up to me. And to think I thought I could trust ya in the movement Mr Fisher. Listen said Fisher If you only knew. Yah! said Frank of Oregon She looks fine! You disgusting bum said Fisher Not only do you steal my girlfriend but you make disparaging remarks about my affaires. Ah said Frank of Oregon Now it comes out Mr Fisher! He seized Fisher's hand. I jus makes love with em till they throws me out said Frank of Oregon quietly. They all decides I'm a bum sooner or later. Fisher looked at him. They decide that about all of us sooner or later Frank of Oregon he said. But that's what I'm *tellin* ya said Frank of Oregon. The trick is to *take yer cues* Mr Fisher. Oh said Fisher. Right.

But I wouldn't mind settlin down Mr Fisher I really wouldn't said Frank of Oregon. What! You? said Fisher sinking into confusion again. Naw said Frank of Oregon Lectric appliances, minicher golf, I pine for it sometimes Mr Fisher. After bein with one of *their* women. Yes? said Fisher. It's powerful said Frank of Oregon bolting his whiskey. With an odd resigned look at Fisher he resumed his examination of the manifesto. Yes said Fisher It is, you're right. It is very powerful. He stared around the Evening Star. He felt he was in an aquarium that was being filled and he wasn't sure he was a fish or not.

Well Mr Fisher this is jim dandy said Frank of Oregon. I'm glad you think so Frank of Oregon said Fisher I really am. So if you'll excuse me. But Frank of Oregon jumped to his feet! And cleared his throat!

Scuse me! Scuse me! he said. Heads turned reluctantly from glasses. Mouths opened dumbly. A general dirty deepening of awareness. Small scuffles had been going on

in the corners but they ceased. Men! said Frank of Oregon
What I have to say takes just a minute. RHUBARB RHUbarb
rhubarb rhubarb rhu barb rbrb rr r. The bartender looked
at Frank of Oregon and Fisher in annoyance. Men there's
goin to be a meetin said Frank of Oregon Of concerned
citizens at the Fanul Hall downtown. I say we are dis-en-
franchised an we gotta band together. We are the rightful
in-her-itors of a great tradition. The tradition men of com-
pleteness! Wool! Glasses made of glass an everythin work-
in right in genral. So I want ya all to come to the meetin
to hear about it. Now this here said Frank of Oregon Is Mr
William Fisher who has helped me write up a list of our
un-ne-gotiable demans. Our man-i-fetzo. What ya talkin
about? growled a big man at the bar who had lined up five
boilermakers before his gigantic tattooed arms. Nothing!
shouted Fisher He doesn't mean anything, ignore it! Aw
now Mr Fisher said Frank of Oregon. And then to the big
man: You of all people Lennie! Who was done out of a job
in the biggest mill in Lynnfield. Arrggh! said the man
slamming his fists down on the bar I told you never to
mention that Frank of Oregon. I'm dead thought Fisher.
An you Terry said Frank of Oregon to a man with strange
ears Con-taminated and then fired from the nucular reactor! Well that's right Mr Oregon said the man looking
down. *Jesus* thought Fisher. Woody! Tom! shouted Frank
of Oregon Ernie! Dave! Phil! You all know what I'm talkin
about! Wull yuh I guess so said a voice. Mr Fisher here is
a breath of fresh air to us men! said Frank of Oregon. God
damn it said Fisher clutching at Frank of Oregon Stop
pointing me out. Aw come on Mr Fisher it's great said
Frank of Oregon. Men! A buzz had already arisen. Men!
We stands for the America that was an is comin again!
When all these Boston fat guys is fightin with each other

over gas an the last donuts on earth or dead of boredom in their big ugly cars! Then we take over! Don't ya see men? We been livin this way for a purpose! Jus wait an the whole country's gonna fall inter our laps! Who wants it? called somebody. Why we do men said Frank of Oregon Cause only by runnin things ourselves will human life be in harmony with e-cology! It's true thought Fisher He's really worked it out. A guy with a design for living. Covered with dirt. So I wants ya all to come down to Fanul Hall tonight said Frank of Oregon. Thanks gents. He sat down. The noise shot up to deafening. The men were talking about Frank of Oregon and Fisher and spine chilling glances were thrown at them.

Frank of Oregon beamed at Fisher. They liked it Mr Fisher he said. They did? said Fisher. Yes sir said Frank of Oregon They'll be there to hear your i-dea. Just what is this idea? said Fisher testily. You know Mr Fisher About us bein the only ones livin right and that. I thought that was *your* idea said Fisher. Naw naw Mr Fisher said Frank of Oregon I just kinda expressed it for ya. Ar-tic-ulated it. Really? said Fisher desperately. He couldn't remember. He felt a part of absolutely nothing. He looked around the Evening Star and imagined its inhabitants viceroys in the new order. After nuclear holocaust. He couldn't picture his own apartment or the Institute surviving atomic attack. Or the Fruitlands. But the Evening Star looked as if it had already borne the brunt of one and could stand another.

Suddenly a scraping high pitched voice. THAT MAN IS RIGHT YOU GOD DAMNNN SCUMMM! YOU LOUSY STINKING SCUMMM GOD DAMNNN! It was the little man earlier uprooted by Frank of Oregon. He stood on the bar. Unshaven, dried up, ? drunk? Hard to tell. GOD DAMNNN IT

LOOK AT YOUUU! he wailed. YOU ARE THE NEXT AMEEERI-
CANS THAT MANNN IS RIGHT GOD DAMNNN HIMMM! He
waved a cigarette. AND I SAY TO YOU GO WITH THIS
MANNN GOD DAMNNN YOUR SOULS! GET YE AWAY FROM
THE GOD DAMNNN MASTERS! DO SOMETHING TO SAVE
YOUR GOD DAMNNN STINKING GOD DAMNNN SELVES!
THAT MANNN HAS SHOWED YOU THE WAYYY! howled the
little man. He shrank to a third of his size by the end of
each exhalation. That's the way to get their attention said
Frank of Oregon nudging Fisher. Yo Spunkeh! came the
great black voice of Fat Leroy What yo sayin? OHHH YOU
ESPECIALLY LEEEROYYY! whined Spunky trying to see
Fat Leroy who incredibly had managed to hide himself in
the hazy crowd. OF ALLL THE SOULLLS IN THIS BAR
YOURRRS IS THE GOD DAMNNNEDEST! Now now said the
bartender clawing at the little man Get down from there
Spunky. AND YOUUU CLARY! cried the small prophet FILL-
ING US WITH YOUR *GOD* DAMNNN WHISKEY! YOU WILL
TAKE YOUR PROFIT TO THE GOD DAMNNN DEVILLL! The
bartender suddenly grabbed the little man's trousers and
pulled him off the bar to wild applause.

Well Mr Fisher Let's get goin now said Frank of Oregon. What? said Fisher. We gotta go to other places Mr
Fisher an tell people bout the meetin. Wait a minute said
Fisher I'm supposed to dine out, don't you realize? Frank
of Oregon looked hurt. We have to spread the word Mr
Fisher. I'd like you to spread the word. Damnation Frank
of Oregon! said Fisher I don't want any part of it anymore.
Oh yeah? said Frank of Oregon Where ya gonna eat in
that coat anyways Mr Fisher? Fisher looked down at himself. Stained with coffee, rumpled, strange. Good question
thought Fisher Where *am* I going like this? But while he
could not lie figuratively speaking among the pink frills of

Alison's bedroom neither could Fisher find it in himself to embrace the dirty enthusiasm of Spunky. It's a surprise said Fisher. Eh? said Frank of Oregon. Where I'm eating said Fisher. A surprise. Come on with me Mr Fisher said Frank of Oregon. No! said Fisher rising in panic *Where can I get changed? Where are my clean clothes?* In a trice the thundering babble died. They were all looking at him. Frank of Oregon in the slow swirl of smoke. I thought ya had passed that stage Mr Fisher he said lowly. Fisher grabbed his violin and made for the door.

Will ya just wait a minute Mr Fisher? said Frank of Oregon walking directly behind him. Fisher was stumbling toward the square. Frank of Oregon grabbed him by the seat of the pants. Fisher stopped of necessity. I want ya to come along tonight OK Mr Fisher? What *time* is it? said Fisher without turning around. Search me said Frank of Oregon. Fisher started up the avenue again and Frank of Oregon followed right behind. They crossed Prospect Street and Fisher found himself waiting for a traffic light on a cement island populated by little cold men. They were sharing a bottle and one of them saluted Frank of Oregon.

Fragk ugh Oregugh he said. He had no teeth although his gums were magnificent. Hiya Dan hi Rudy said Frank of Oregon. He acknowledged the others with nods. Fisher moved to the edge of the island. That's Mr Fisher said Frank of Oregon He's OK take it from me. Fisher looked around and glared at Frank of Oregon. Mr Fisher's organized a big meetin for guys like us downtown at the Fanul Hall tonight said Frank of Oregon Can you boys make it? Jesus Christ thought Fisher looking at Frank of Oregon who in the light of signals and vapor lamps suddenly appeared young, earnest. But this quality which Fisher found naive and depressing arrested the attention of even the drunkest of the men in the little pile. They all looked at Frank of Oregon with bright pink eyes. Shit it's cold said one. What kina meetin? said another. A po-litical meetin said Frank of Oregon Since we're dis-en-fran-chised. Any freshment? said Rudy. Oh I think so men said Frank of Oregon But the point is to be there. Disinter-ested yuhs. They didn't know what anybody was talking about. Need some freshments they murmured together like a lake. Frank of Oregon walked over to Fisher who had missed the light and was deep in analyzing the com-plexities of his position. What's the idea? said Fisher Am I supposed to provide cocktails as well? If ya got a dollar or two it might go a ways said Frank of Oregon. For the men Mr Fisher. The men! said Fisher What am I, a gen-eral? Just a couple o winter warmers said Frank of Ore-gon. His earnestness was beginning to nauseate Fisher. In his own way Frank of Oregon was as dogged as Jillian. They're made for each other thought Fisher. He gave Frank of Oregon two dollars. Frank of Oregon began to scan the horizon for a liquor store. You wait here with the men Mr Fisher he said. Listen said Fisher I'm not standing here with them, I have to go to *Harvard Square.* Oh yeah *Harvard Square* said Frank of Oregon With that snooty pooch! *Here's* where your friends are Mr Fisher. Why don't you come with us? Why don't ya do somethin for once instead of drinking and broodin?

Is this helping me or not? thought Fisher. In two days I befriend a bum who *rapes* my girlfriend and plunges me into a sea of dirty men. He takes my money for liquor and then lectures me on what is right for me and also on what is morally correct although it's true I agree with him. But he is the lover of Jillian Hardy! At this moment Alison pulled up in her car. Oh ho *ho* said Frank of Oregon savagely jabbing Fisher with his elbow. Alison waved at Fisher merrily. Frank of Oregon and the men waved back at Alison merrily. Her smile began to fade. You pig said Fisher You can't have her too! Aw now Mr Fisher said Frank of Oregon. Fisher got in the car. Frank of Oregon leaned on the windshield cupped his hands and screamed Now come along tonight Mr Fisher! Why's he doing that? said Alison. He thinks we can't hear him said Fisher. Remember! yelled Frank of Oregon No gas! Arabians! Wool! They jerked forward depositing Frank of Oregon in the gutter. Christ said Fisher. Hello said Alison putting her lips up to Fisher's. Fisher turned to look back in the direction of Frank of Oregon. He was waving and gesticulating in the distance from a prone position. I hope we didn't hurt him said Fisher. William said Alison putting the lips up again. I mean he's really an all right sort said Fisher. During this ride Fisher and Alison became estranged.

In annoyance Alison said Who is he? He's a bum said Fisher. The word made his wound prickle. My God William you mean a real bum with no house or job or anything? said Alison. Well he has none of those things said Fisher. But something, something he thought. Jillian Hardy! This soured Fisher. What happened to your clothes? said Alison. Fisher looked down at his rumpled caffeinated beguinnessed attire. I had a meeting he said. Oh William said Alison And we don't have time for you to change. No time to change thought Fisher. Er what does that matter? he said shifting in his seat. Well we *are* going out to dinner said Alison. We *are* thought Fisher We *are* going. But where in the square? he said. Wheat said Alison. Oh God not Wheat thought Fisher Ohh Lordy not

Wheat. Listen he said not daring to look at her I don't think I can make it tonight Alison. What do you mean make it? said Alison You didn't have any trouble last night. Eh? said Fisher. His mind had wandered as Alison was beginning to drive in a very fast pout. I mean I can't make it for dinner said Fisher I've been meaning to tell you. Oh? said Alison coldly. The car darted frighteningly through the traffic and Fisher sank down so that his violin case blocked his view of the street.

Is it your coat? she said not without compassion. That and my brain said Fisher. Don't worry it looks all right to me said Alison zooming into the square. How do *you* know? said Fisher The stitches aren't loose are they? Your *coat* said Alison. Another stoplight at which she had difficulty stopping. Fisher pressed against the dash and his knuckle cracked. So he said I just can't tonight. They started up. Of course you can darling said Alison I want to show you off and then take you home and enjoy you.

Fisher did not like to be in a car with a woman who said Of course you can darling and did not mean to stop and let him out. He started to feel for the door handle. Alison put her hand high on his inseam. I like you she said. The feeling is mutual said Fisher But . . . I think you could do great things said Alison. Like taking a shower once in a while. Another commedienne! But this morning said Fisher you applauded my perspiry masculinity. Silence. But the hand was a powerful persuader. After two more blocks had flashed by Fisher knew he was going. Going to Wheat.

Alison parked on a luxury side street. Fisher picked up his violin and got out of the car. He slammed his door and stood on the sidewalk thinking the things one thinks when waiting for someone who irritates. After fifty seconds

Fisher realized Alison was still sitting behind the wheel expecting him to open the door for her. This isn't the American Girl Book of First Date Stories he said under his breath. What? said Alison as he held the door. I said These early American houses often have several stories said Fisher. Alison looked at him. Severely. Yes they do she said. They walked without touching toward the bright vapid hoity toity of Mt Auburn Street.

XI In the Ant Farm

It was a deathly precious restaurant, lurking in a courtyard surrounded by new office buildings in the middle of
the square. Everybody who was anybody who ate ate
there. Fisher began to lose his nerve and his walk slowed
to a crawl. It's called Wheat for God's sake he whined as
Alison began to drag him toward the door. So? she said.
Alison was becoming suddenly very tired of Fisher and
was trying to think of ways to get him in hand. She undid
the clasps that held her snide tone raging in the lead lined
canvas tote bag of her heart. What does the *name* matter
William? she said sensing it did matter. In Fisher's mind
a huge flapping torah of wrongdoings burst open the door
of an ark which had her name on it.

As they entered the place Fisher looked around in
dread. He looked into the bar. A slim tan bartender
among tan slim bottles, a look of divorce and forced casu-
alness about him. It did not look to Fisher as if there would
be anything there for him. Foo he thought. Alison pulled
him toward the dining room. You could have shaved she
said in a tone reminiscent of Crosbee's. No I could not
have said Fisher I already explained. What? she said. To
someone else, excuse me said Fisher. To another one of

you he thought. There they are! said Alison waving at a group of people.

The dining room had been designed to give the impression of space. Low terraces. Small three sided bays with tables in them. The only impression it gave was of the dismal failure of someone desperate for space. Patrons stuck out of the bays like toys out of a Christmas stocking. Or an ant farm at dinnertime thought Fisher The food dragged up and down the sandy tunnels. Alison pulled at him. Come on William she said They're all good people. Good people! thought Fisher dragging his heels Hi! Hi good people Hi!

Fisher found himself standing with Alison on the lip of one of the platforms. He was being introduced to two men and two women whose names he was not catching. The men shook his hand in turn. Fisher clattered about with his violin to annoyed looks from the group. They all looked at his bandage. But they were either too stupid or too polite to say anything about it. Fisher sat down hoping he had squeezed the hands hard enough. Nothing like a manly handshake thought Fisher recalling the gelid piscine grip of the family minister. He had once to run around behind the church to throw up after receiving it. Fisher stared out at the center of the room, already unable to look at Alison or any of the people at the table. He occupied himself trying to recall the events of the afternoon. Then Alison poked him. William she said Darryl's asking you something. Fisher turned to look at the man Darryl across the table and tried to put on a pleasant interested look. It was difficult as the man was guffawing in Fisher's face. Ha ha ha what I said was What do you do? the man said. His dark hair was cut very short. Institute of Science said Fisher coldly. Oh then you must know

Ruth Kane in patents? said Darryl jangling a large linked bracelet. No I'm afraid not said Fisher. Well what exactly do you do there? said Darryl. I clean toilets said Fisher. William! said Alison. Oh er uh said Darryl. What kind of toilet does your friend have? said Fisher Perhaps I can recall her by her toilet. Well I don't know I'm sure said Darryl blushing. The two women were looking from Fisher to Alison. Fisher decided to throw them a bone and smile. Just kidding he said I dole out money to research projects. Oh! Thank heavens I thought for a moment you were serious *William* said Darryl looking down at his lap and brushing at it as if he were wearing a skirt. Fisher stared sullenly. The other man, Drew or another cowboy name, was tonguing a big drink and the veins on the sides of his head and the cords in his neck were pounding. TV coronary exec thought Fisher. The man was avoiding Fisher at any rate. Darryl was looking at Fisher in a sickly penetrating way. What do you do fella? said Fisher. It's *Darryl* said Darryl. Darryl's Assistant Program Director said Alison proudly. Darryl looked away and swigged from his glass of white wine in modesty. Listen said Fisher How come whenever I turn on public television there's some program with Baroque music about how the insides of wristwatches as we know them are a direct result of farming upheavals during the Guelf-Ghibelline disturbances? The group looked at Fisher in silence. William! said Alison. Aw skip it said Fisher. He threw them the smile again. His famous winning smile. The two women held a whispered conference about him. The one with black hair thought he was drunk, the blonde merely rude but interesting. How wrong could they get? Darryl was still looking at Fisher in an unwholesome way. We're looking for creative people said Darryl. What for? said Fisher. Alison, thoroughly embarrassed, understanding and not, rising above it and not, broke in with a quacking question about *policy* and from then on Fisher was exempt from the conversation. And from awareness of them except for Darryl who although he was listening to Alison kept looking and grinning at Fisher. I'll be right back said Fisher getting up and meeting Alison's irritated eye. It's just through the bar said Darryl. What is? said Fisher. Er the men's room said Darryl again searching his lap for the longed after skirt. Well I'm not going to THE MEN'S ROOM Darryl said Fisher loudly. Heads turned to see Darryl reddening and Fisher walking down the steps with his violin.

He was going to the men's room though. He rested his violin next to the urinal and wondered if it would become covered with an undetectable mist which would later cause disgust or rot. Fisher held himself and in satisfaction stared directly ahead at the wall. But even though he had triumphed over Darryl for the moment he was having difficulty. And he was alone! Fisher looked down and quickly looked up again as he heard another man come in and stand at the urinal beside him. Fisher pictured garden hoses, Bridal Veil Falls, the Hoover Dam hydroelectric station. Nothing. It was the other television producer, the one with pounding arteries. Nice place he said to Fisher. What is? said Fisher Wheat? Cambridge? Massachusetts? The men's room? The urinal *alcove?* His prostate languished. Chip on your shoulder fella? said the man. Although unhealthy in a gin and sunburn way the man was well dressed glamorous and obviously urinated with ease, the key to success in media and business. Fisher found he was able to urinate only by filling himself with hate for the man. It happened. However to Fisher's disgust it went in several directions, the end of him being slightly adhered with dry spawn. They stood at the washbasins together. That Alison's a sharp one said the man. Depends said Fisher oversoaping. She'd make a good gal friday the man said. Yeccch said Fisher What terms you use. Takes all kinds said the man with a rehearsed cock of the head. The voice too tired of inexperience and of the admitting it to the self. He left. He had used the last towel.

Instead of returning to the ant farm Fisher turned right and went into the bar upon emerging with dripping hands from the men's room. The bartender studied Fisher's bandage and then his head vibrated in a short spasm, Californian for Can I help you? Want whiskey said Fisher. The man reached for a bottle. No said Fisher I want special whiskey. I want to buy a whole bottle and sit here and drink it, perhaps wearing a borsalino if someone would bring me one. Yeah? said the bartender. Interested? said Fisher. Not really the man said. Then he peered under the bar and with great difficulty uttered the name of a highland glen. I'll take it said Fisher. Twenty two bucks said the man not moving until Fisher's pay envelope appeared and began to disgorge. Not that it was any too capable of disgorging. It was more the dry heaves of the dying. As Fisher handed the bills over and his hands dripped on the bar he pictured begging Smith for an advance. What happened to ya head? said the bartender. Just a slight scrape said Fisher Incurred from foolish misuse of a croquet lawn mowing machine. Jeez said the man. He gave Fisher the bottle and a glass. Are ya on yer own? he said. For the moment said Fisher Although there are people of my acquaintance in the dining room. Ah said the bartender. Not that it matters said Fisher. No said the bartender. Are ya gonna drink the whole thing fella? No no no said Fisher What do you take me for? Without answering the bartender moved off and polished glasses. Thanks MacGillivray thought Fisher. He leaned his violin against a bar stool and sat. He opened the bottle and began to drink. Not rapidly or heavily but efficiently.

Soon he was under a carapace of stars, his personal empyrean of constellations. Savoring the warming malt like a child its cocoa Fisher remembered his fondness for the Crab Nebula and stewing on his stool wandered among the Magellanic Clouds. He had taken a canter on Cetus and tipped his starry hat to the Man with the Watering Pot when he looked up and beheld her. Cassiopeia! mumbled Fisher. You OK fella? said the bartender. Great! said Fisher throwing him the smile. The jerk's bone the beef jerky thought Fisher alarmed at the ragged turn his thoughts were taking. Dear God he thought Already past the stage of linguistic play. Fisher turned awkwardly and surveyed the bar through the firmament. Two business students stood admiring and touching each other's ties. Christ mumbled Fisher. He turned and looked back at the girl. She was alone, sitting regally in her chair with a vermouth in hand. Excuse me but is that Harris tweed? said Fisher sloppily indicating her jacket. What? Oh yeah. No. I don't know said the girl. Embarrassed. Thank you very much Cassie said Fisher. You OK? said the bartender. He was unused to trouble of any kind. All who drank in Wheat were too full of themselves to cause trouble. And the seductions which occurred there were discreetly whispered exchanges of advanced degrees and expected salaries. The *God* damnnn masters said Fisher under his breath. The bartender set down the glass he was polishing and glared at Fisher. An incompetent kindergarten teacher. Fisher resented the chain of events developing in the bar. He lashed the bartender with the smile. Then the galaxies wheeled as Cassie was joined by a Jupiter of blue wool khaki and rugby muscle. Fisher gave up. He sipped primly from his tumbler. The dainty phase he thought. He felt a tapping on his shoulder. More of a knocking he thought. It was Alison.

William what are you doing? she said pink in the face. Her tinge of anger lent a warm glow to the sharp lines of her classic American tailoring. Having a cocktail said Fisher The service was so bad in the men's. Very funny said Alison Perhaps you're forgetting we have company in the other room. Company! said Fisher. Maybe for you. I don't understand William said Alison Why are you acting this way? Fisher looked at her. Bad day he said Very bad day. Metaphysically bad. Terminally. Mesozoically. Come with me right now William said Alison You're making me very unhappy. Fisher turned to the bartender who had been watching them. I'm making her unhappy he said. Yuh said the bartender. Fisher arose with bottle and violin and followed Alison to the door. Put that back! said Alison. No no said Fisher It's mine, I paid for it. Alison looked around Fisher at the bartender who nodded. Oh the reluctant bottle holder thought Fisher.

Fisher and Alison ascended the platforms toward their table. The bounteous table of fruits thought Fisher *Gradus ad persimmon.* Alison sat down but Fisher stood holding his possessions to his heart. He beamed at the assembled opinionmakers. I see where you've been chirped Darryl trying in his own way to make the best of the situation. That's right Darryl said Fisher I've been to Scotland. He sat down, his things in his arms like babies. William why don't you look at the menu? said Alison. Why

I'd be glad to *darlin* said Fisher nudging Darryl slyly in the ribs and noisily planting his bottle in the center of the table. The executive urinator was drinking heavily and silently. The two women spoke quietly between themselves or sometimes to Alison. Alison shot quill-like glances at Fisher; Darryl kept looking at him and alternately around the room, examining slim men. Fisher picked up his menu.

He could not focus on it. Not that he wanted to, all it had to impart was horror. But his eyes wandered across the type like two warring tribes. Fisher felt Alison tapping his foot with hers under the table. What! he said irritably. She looked up from her menu. What William? she said. What do you want! Fisher demanded. She looked at him questioningly. Want? Why were you tapping my foot? said Fisher. Alison looked at him queerly and then with a nervous smile at the group said I think I'll have the scallops. Ooh do you think they're good? said Darryl. Beware! said Fisher Scallops in places like this are often manta ray cut to look like scallops! The two women especially stared again. Devil fish! said Fisher And I also understand that the quiche is shit. Silence again except of course for the neighing and crowing coming from everybody else in the place. I see said the black haired woman And what are you going to have? Er said Fisher still unable to read the menu I haven't decided. I'll have what the executive has he thought Good for the kidneys. Well here's the waitress said Alison. I'll have the quiche on the dinner said the executive. Darryl and the women all ordered scallops. I'll have the quiche said Fisher. I thought you said it was shit said black hair. It is said Fisher. The waitress blushed. See? She knows I'm right said Fisher. Not knowing what to do, she left.

But only to return almost immediately with their food! Fisher raged. A restaurant he said clumsily unfurling his napkin Which reheats by microwave and charges you $7.85 for a piece of quiche made and frozen by robots ought at least to have the decency to *pretend* to be cooking it! But no one was paying attention to Fisher anymore. He picked up a leaden roll. Wholemeal Parker House rolls William said Alison encouragingly. Was that what she thought of him? Fisher smiled at Darryl with his mouth full of dough. The others *relished* their food, bleating and squealing about it. Alison's scallops were not scallops or manta ray or possibly even of oceanic origin; they had the smooth Romanesque color of pasta. The cold heart of Fisher's quiche put him in mind of Jillian and of the inedible cheese preparations which sailed through the air of the dining room at Third Rate Prep. Fisher began to fail. He watched the executive glory in his quiche. It's drink thought Fisher. Drink has ruined me. He sat back in depression. Oh no he thought Reverie. Not long until I get in my little boat and sail into the stream. The gurgling drone of ideas for public television. Nothingness rioted before his eyes. When an end? he thought When a real end?

In looking forlornly toward the door Fisher was surprised to see the bartender's back, muscles under tapered shirt flexed in struggle. Fisher stopped chewing his quiche and stared. The bartender's back appeared and disappeared. It was as if he were dancing a tango but there were too many violent movements. And a kind of rustling and squawking. Suddenly he lunged and vanished from sight; the next appearance in the doorway was by his long unseen partner. Not a rose biting señorita but Frank of Oregon in his horrid raincoat.

Excuse me! said Fisher jumping up. Darryl grabbed his arm. Let go! said Fisher. He barged down the platforms to the door. He looked back to see Alison staring at him. Woebegone, angry, confused, bitchy. It was quite a look and contemplating it Fisher walked into the wall just to the right of the door. He's drunk I think said the man at that table. Yes said his female friend angrily. That's manta ray you know said Fisher pointing at their scallops.

Frank of Oregon was holding his own against the Californian. The bartender's slim tan belied inner weakness. You fucker grumbled Frank of Oregon. Get out of here, this is no place for you sir said the bartender. Stop calling me sir you scumbag said Frank of Oregon tussling. The bartender looked up and seeing Fisher coming toward them became more worried. Just a minute here said Fisher. He noticed some normal people standing by the hostess's table looking toward him in hope. Let go of this man said Fisher to the bartender. The bartender and Frank of Oregon froze. They looked at each other suspiciously. This man is a friend of mine said Fisher And you are not to wrestle with him unless I give specific persimmon. Permission! He tried to be authoritative but a terrible smile was already cracking his features. The bartender took a stab at reasoning with Fisher but his face showed he had little hope of success. In a confidential tone he said Look sir this guy's a bum, he's got no money. He's with me Fisher affirmed. Aw sir said the bartender. And stop calling *me* sir said Fisher. Slowly the bartender released Frank of Oregon. With a grim look he turned and went back into the bar. Fisher assumed a benevolent posture for the benefit of the citizens still huddled in fear near the entrance. Frank! he said. Of Oregon said Frank of Oregon. Yes yes said Fisher Come and join us!

Oh God said Alison under her breath. I want you all to meet Frank of Oregon said Fisher taking a chair from an adjoining platform and viciously making room for it by banging it between the chairs of Alison's friends until they moved. Frank of Oregon sat down, nervously pawing his rancid raincoat and rubbing his stubbled chin. I want you to meet the collective brains of the mass media said Fisher Names aren't important. Pleaseda meetcha I'm sure said Frank of Oregon looking around the table. Everyone looked at Fisher with rising deep rooted hate. Have a drink Frank of Oregon said Fisher opening his bottle and pouring two five ounce drinks. What are you doing here anyway? Well uh I don like ter say Mr Fisher said Frank of Oregon But I'm sorry about the dis-a-greement. Oh that guy is a known ass! said Fisher loudly Don't give it a second thought. Uh OK Mr Fisher said Frank of Oregon smiling and winking at the woman with black hair.

Alison was staring cuirasses at Fisher. And just what again does Mr Oregon do? she said. Ahhh said Fisher gulping his drink Frank of Oregon is unemployed. Yup said Frank of Oregon. He is said Fisher An indigent, a solivagant, a traveling philosopher. Sad but true eh? Frank of Oregon grinned at Alison. Frank of Oregon had roused the soused executive out of mortgage musing. Now at least the table was united. In suspicion of Frank of Oregon and visceral dislike of Fisher.

But Frank of Oregon what are you doing here? said Fisher. Well to tell the truth Mr Fisher . . . said Frank of Oregon. Frank of Oregon's a great guy for the truth! said Fisher loudly to Alison. I'm shouting he thought It's the beginning of the end but at least thank God the end of the beginning. Well I came lookin for ya Mr Fisher said Frank of Oregon I really need ya to come with me down to the market tonight. Alison threw down her napkin. Anyone hungry enough could have scrambled an egg on her beautifully formed forehead. But their tummies were full. Ah yes the ? market said Fisher Uh what was it . . . ? The *meetin* Mr Fisher said Frank of Oregon. Ah yes the ? meeting said Fisher. He drank deeply. Nobody knew what to do.

May I call you Frank? lilted Darryl out of the pastel blue. Of Oregon said Frank of Oregon eyeing Darryl. Oh yes well said Darryl Frank of Oregon then. I'd like to hear about riding the rods! Darryl then broke into a convulsive spittly laugh. Yeah that white wine's a killer ain't it? thought Fisher. But the others saw the ? humor of it and tittered. And in the aftermath of the tittering the silk serpent of Darryl's voice: *Tell me is there much homosexuality among vagrants?* Fisher overturned the table.

You outrageous faggot! he screamed. The table crashed off the platform shedding glasses cutlery stoneware and wholemeal Parker House rolls. Alison and the women jumped back, three fists in three mouths in three expressions of shock learned from the same three movies. The tan pissant remained in his chair wondering what to do with his hands. Fisher and Frank of Oregon were standing, Frank of Oregon with fists clenched in childish excitement, his mouth a dot of joy; Fisher was immobile in a pose out of socialist realism. Darryl was under the table, pinned to the edge of the platform. Slowly in the now utterly silent dining room the butter dish slid down the incline of the table and shattered against his head. Little birds and planets.

Fisher looked about. He found the atmosphere unpromising. He cleared his throat. Ladies and gentlemen said

Fisher. There is a big meeting tonight at Faneuil Hall in Boston for everybody here who is fed up to the back teeth with this kind of nonsense. Thank you. Fisher picked his violin and overcoat out of the rubble. Let's get out of here he said to Frank of Oregon. Yer the boss said Frank of Oregon leaping over the table. William Fisher you come back here! screamed Alison. Pandemonium ensued however nobody moved to do anything. It was seated pandemonium. You are inhuman! Alison yelled as the shadows of Frank of Oregon and Fisher disappeared on the lobby wall. Somebody call my wife said the executive.

The edges of the snow were molars in the mouth of night. Hard shiny biting at them from the edges of their blundering progress up the slippery dirty red brick tongue of Mt Auburn Street. Fisher was unhappy to see Frank of Oregon had only his raincoat and sweatshirt. What is more the raincoat had only one button although it was a sturdy one. This Frank of Oregon duly buttoned. Mighty cold Mr Fisher he said. Fisher regarded him as soberly as he could. The temperature would soon ruin his investment in malt whiskey. I will go with you Frank of Oregon he said. Really? said Frank of Oregon That's swell Mr Fisher I'm gladta hear ya say that. But first Frank of Oregon said Fisher We need a cup of the joe, speaking for myself I need several. Like in the man-i-fetzo? said Frank of Oregon. Just so said Fisher. They began to walk north.

The Ass was producing a light covering. Of what it would be hard and ungentlemanly to say. But it was falling. Cold, dark, miserable. Wazzat guy a fairy Mr Fisher? said Frank of Oregon He was rubbin my leg under the table. Fisher stopped and stared at Frank of Oregon. So that was it! He rub yers too Mr Fisher? said Frank of

Oregon. They carried on. Yes said Fisher red in the face And he sent his buddy to watch me take a whizz. No kiddin said Frank of Oregon You can always tell em. To emphasize his worldliness Frank of Oregon unbuttoned and rebuttoned his button. Zat girl yer honey Mr Fisher? he said. I don't think so said Fisher grabbing his stomach Listen Frank of Oregon have you ever had coffee from a French plunger type pot? I don bleeve so said Frank of Oregon looking around. Then come with me said Fisher. It's all the rage. They entered a brick café specializing in the corrosive the overpriced and the sweet. As they did so Fisher reflected bitterly that his bottle of whiskey had been abandoned in the seething interior of the ant farm. You're getting the grand tour tonight Frank of Oregon he said All the places you never wanted to go.

The waitress gave them a long look which lingered on Fisher's bandage. But she kept her pencil on the pad which was all that mattered. Sumatra for six groaned Fisher. She went away. Whazzat? said Frank of Oregon. Kind of coffee said Fisher. He kept his head on the table in case the police should come by and also because he could not lift it. The café was not helping his churning senses. It was a dessert version of the ant farm. At a repeated irritating little sound Fisher managed to put an eye over his arm and look at Frank of Oregon. He was trying to light a sodden cigarette with a succession of damp matches. He struck one and as the head sputtered out before he could raise it to the cigarette he threw it to the floor and tried again. And again. And again. Frank of Oregon! shouted Fisher. Sorry Mr Fisher said Frank of Oregon. He gave up and returned to buttoning and unbuttoning his button. The waitress brought the beaker and two cups. Coffee Frank of Oregon! said Fisher raising himself in sick eloquence. First hailed as a wonder drug, then vilified as a poison. So is every new substance adjudged by civilization. Yuh said Frank of Oregon. Now said Fisher The balm to oil that civilization's sweaty brow and the prime cause of the perspiration in the first place. ? Yuh said Frank of Oregon. Fisher looked at the apparatus which though simple always daunted him. You do the honors said Fisher. Uh the honors Mr Fisher? said Frank of Oregon. You push the plunger down and it makes the coffee said Fisher. Sure thing Mr Fisher said Frank of Oregon. With no sense of the subtle he stood up and grabbed the pot. He gave the plunger a mighty downward thrust and Fisher rose from his chair bleating *No-o-o!* Unsteady as he was he grabbed his violin in leaping away from the table. A dark geyser of scalding coffee rose into the air and rained searing death down around them. It was The Ass in reverse. Fisher had retreated to the counter where he stood panting and watching clouds of vapor rise from the chair in which he had been seated a moment before. Frank of Oregon stood at the table, hand on empty pot, an expression of surprise and unrest on his face. The waitress ran over to him. Oh my God are you OK? she said. For once somebody else gets asked thought Fisher. Frank of Oregon made no sound. She held out a towel to him. He brushed it away. But then to the dismay of everyone (although they knew it was coming, the cowards) Frank of Oregon threw his head back and emitted the most bloodcurdling scream Fisher had ever heard. He seemed to be parboiling within his clothing. When it was over, some twenty seconds later, Fisher went over to him. Are you all right Frank of Oregon? said Fisher. Yeah said Frank of Oregon *Now.* Everyone was looking at him in fear and compassion. Wouldja like another pot? said the waitress. No said Fisher I think we'll run along. They left untheatrically.

Outside it was colder than when they went in if that is possible. What with all the screaming and freezing Fisher felt quite ill. They stood on a brick walk under the Harvard dormitories. Fisher looked up and through the clean windows glimpsed a decorative life. As an undergraduate Fisher had been made to live in an unheated Quonset hut on the bank of a foul river. You God damn Harvard punks! he yelled I hate your guts! and in a wave of emotion he bent over and began to retch loudly. A window opened. Please be quiet! came a voice We are trying to study! Fisher raised his head and shook it in resignation at Frank of Oregon. Let's go he said. They walked across the street toward the T. Where I saw you with Jillian thought Fisher. A car suddenly came at them. Fisher tripped on the curb as he reached it and fell heavily on his violin case. Frank of Oregon helped him up. I don't feel good said Fisher.

They had just enough change for the T. Standing on the platform Fisher tried to get hold of himself. First physically but his overcoat was too thick. Then mentally but it was just the same old dim lights in the distance. On the train waves of faintness swept over Fisher. At the conclusion of the journey Fisher was relieved of his overcoat by a machine.

He followed Frank of Oregon off the green line at Government Center onto the long escalator to the plaza above. Standing on the escalator Fisher felt a severe tide of nausea fatigue and fear of the unknown. He slumped. The tail of his overcoat caught in metal teeth. Aaagh said Fisher. Frank of Oregon turned and seeing Fisher in distress ran to him against the direction of the escalator which jarred him considerably. They stood, approaching the top, tugging at the coat. It was stuck. When they were ten feet from the summit, Frank of Oregon grabbed Fisher's violin and ran back up saying Yer on yer own Mr Fisher! Grrr said Fisher pulling frantically at the coat. Three feet from the top he saw it was no use and in a last fit freed himself and landed with a yelp at Frank of Oregon's feet. Then before their eyes the coat was shredded and began to disappear under the floor in ribbons. At last a sleeve waved goodbye. Goodbye said Fisher waving. Now Fisher had only his jacket against the brutal assault of The Ass. Frank of Oregon looked at Fisher and buttoned his button. He gave the violin back to Fisher and they walked out across the plaza where the day before Fisher's scarf had been sucked out of his coat. The coat now destroyed. He looked up and was annoyed to see the scarf peeking at him from its hiding place high on City Hall. Fisher and Frank of Oregon walked up over the brick rise and down toward Faneuil Hall atop which a golden locust gleamed in floodlight for some reason everyone in Boston had forgot.

XII Imbroglio

While Fisher had been wallowing in alcohol, approxima-
tions of sex and self pity, Frank of Oregon had been very
busy. Indeed his reserve and calm were those of a man
satisfied with his day's work. Frank of Oregon's particular
genius was an ability to remember minutiae pertaining to
every indigent man in Boston. He remembered that Roaring Ronald, normally found in a crumpled condition in
the doorway of the Hi Fi bar, Roxbury, was born in a
sharecropper's shack in South Carolina. He knew that a
small man called Teddie who orated constantly to no one
in particular in the Public Garden was a connoisseur of
fine wool clothing gleaned from the night garbage cans of
Beacon Hill. He recalled that Henley, a kind of British
man who lived in a wooden barrel in the Swampscott yard
of the Boston & Maine, was concerned enough with the
quality of life to wear a fresh flower every day in the
buttonhole of his reeking jacket. Frank of Oregon remembered these traits and had enterprisingly used them in the
space of two days to interest all these men and in a like
manner all the men he knew in a mass meeting. Where
his movement, his union of traveling philosophers, would
be born. And now all these men he had seen, coerced,

cajoled and bribed had come, and brought their companions, wheedled in more animal ways. They trickled into the forecourt of Faneuil Hall like the rusty water that appears from nowhere and collects in pools on subway platforms.

Frank of Oregon! whispered Fisher It's happening! Sure thing Mr Fisher said Frank of Oregon. They sat together on a cement planter. Men were arriving and despite their inappropriate aspect (it was after all Quincy Market at Christmas) they remained shy and inconspicuous for the moment. Me for a cup of the joe Mr Fisher said Frank of Oregon. That's a good idea said Fisher seeing the brown stains on Frank of Oregon's raincoat and remembering. I'll just get us some said Frank of Oregon. He got up from the planter and walked toward the market. Fisher saw him beg on the way from a group of pink sweatered high heeled suburban kittens on their way to a disco. They gave him some coins and Frank of Oregon turned and happily waved at Fisher. Fisher waved back and sat on the planter in expectation. But Frank of Oregon did not return. And just to spare you worrying, he did not return throughout the balance of the narrative.

Fisher however, fool that he was, was still expecting him forty minutes later. He was longing for coffee and Frank of Oregon equally. Probably met some of the men thought Fisher. The men! More and more of them pressed into the plaza and the more Fisher looked for Frank of Oregon the more disheartened he became. After an hour had passed Fisher felt something was wrong. The courtyard was filled with pungent men. Bottles of economy whiskey fruity carbonated wines and various cordials (not to mention cooking sherry mint extracts and several flagons of solvent) were being passed around by the men who were in a convivial preconference mood. Ripples of sound which Fisher kept hoping were anticipation or recognition of Frank of Oregon rose and fell. A restlessness was born. Fisher held his violin against his jacket and shivered.

Finally some kind of definite commotion broke out and Fisher still holding out hope Frank of Oregon would return heard his named bruited. An awesome booming noise grew near and finally materialized in the great bulk of Fat Leroy. Yo Fisheh! What is it Leroy? said Fisher finding he had one supercilious smile left. Yo mah man said Leroy It don look to me like Frank o Orgin gonna be comin here in de mediate future. He's here said Fisher desperately Don't worry Leroy. But ah be freezin mah butt off said Fat Leroy We all wants to get goin an heah from you Fisheh. These were the words almost exactly which Fisher had been shuddering, eyes shut, about. No Leroy he said softly I don't . . . Don't we? shouted Fat Leroy turning to the men Don't we wants to be hearin Mr Fisheh? Collective agreement was wheezed out. Fisher was despondent. It had been an hour and a half. There was nothing to do but get up. With a grimace at Fat Leroy, Fisher climbed up on the planter still holding his violin and with his other hand clenching his jacket shut against the knifing breezes which sliced at him from Congress Street and ultimately The Ass.

Music! said a raspy voice. Fisher shut his eyes. It was an idea. It was something. He imagined playing to the group. The scraping might draw Frank of Oregon out from wherever he was hiding. Fisher put up a finger for time and knelt down in the planter. As he opened the case he was of course reminded there were no strings on his damn violin. But there on top of it was the typed copy of the manifesto with the penciled addition

> Your wright Mr.Ficher. You got to do it.
> Its me and Jillyan for the rode. I got
> someone else to conseder now.
> > Frank of Orgeon

Oh *fine!* said Fisher under his breath Peachy! His attention was suddenly completely absorbed and attracted by fear, a scorpion on his stomach. Fat Leroy lapped at the edge of the planter, a sea of black pudding. Yo what is it Fisheh? Nothing nothing at all Leroy said Fisher snapping the case shut. In one hand he held the manifesto. In the other the mute violin, transformed now completely to security object. To huggy bear. For once Fisher had made a decision and although it was very wrong it was at least a decision. He stood up and cleared his throat. Close to the planter he saw several of the big men who had thrown him out of the Evening Star. One of them pointed at his violin. Not a note! he said menacingly Or we'll trepan your cranium immediately. No strings! said Fisher See? The men squinted at the fiddle and then nodded at each other in grave satisfaction. They folded their arms and stepped back into the crowd. Fisher again cleared his throat and opened his mouth.

You men! he said Aaaahh! Here he fell to the ground, having experienced the worst nausea yet. The silence of the men was succeeded by a mumble of concern. Fat Leroy and another helped Fisher back up to the planter. Men! said Fisher (upright again but for how long? he thought) I have here a document, a statement from Frank of Oregon whom we all know and respect and who is apparently tied up with urgent business. Fisher's vision misted slightly. I have been elected by default to read it to you he said. By who? said someone. Frank of Oregon said Fisher. He looked about the plaza. It was filled with a large assortment of the dis-en-franchised. Some bag carrying women had started fires in trash baskets. The flickering light bathed the assembly in the noble aspect of pre electric history. They were Covenanters, Althingmen. Sooners! Ghibellines! thought Fisher. A parliament of fouls. Fisher began to read the manifesto.

And so they were addressed. Reading the garbled yet rousing document Fisher referred the men to the city of Boston which suddenly appeared around them. Many looked and saw the tops of buildings for the first time. The manifesto enjoined them to stop looking in the gutter. Quincy Market was treated and with a sweep of the hand Fisher seemed to make it rise behind him. It sneered at the men, symbol of all they could not get, a hive of haves looming behind Faneuil Hall. They were children in a planetarium. Fisher read on, dizzy and hoarse. The men had never paid attention as close as they paid Fisher. Everything in the manifesto seized them. No matter how unclear. Its assertions came together, catalyzed their feelings. More so however for them than for Fisher who upon his third reading of the manifesto found it made barely any sense at all. Still somehow it was exciting. Free, you will be free to begin a new America of wool and iron and fresh vegetables if only you band together. Who cares what it really said?

Shouts of agreement and fever rose to meet each statement. Right! Yah! Whoa! echoing in the plaza. The stream of suburbanites going to the market, an assembly line of rubber tubs, quickened, afraid, disgusted.

And so in conclusion said Fisher wondering when the

police were going to arrive I say assail Quincy Market, the defiled former cornucopia of fresh fish and vegetables! Raid the disco! Smash the tools of hypnotism and punish those with $18 haircuts! Enlighten them! Bury them! They know not the way. Smash! Punch! Smash! Punch! Punch! Punch! Punch! he read, spit streaming from his lips. Now a slowly rising mumble grumble rant and shout came from the crowd of men. They had been ignited by a document which they only partially understood. Twas ever thus.

The group suddenly stiffened and swayed in the firelight like a field of tall scraggly weeds. Then shouting and yelling, some of them in imitation of Indians, others merely screaming as best they could through vocal cords sanded by years of whiskey, they began to jog then trot then they were running around Faneuil Hall toward the canvas canopy of the south market. Perhaps fortunately for Fisher the first stone cast in the cause, whatever it was, caught him directly between the eyes and sent him unconscious down into the planter.

Fisher was shaken back to a fuzzy consciousness. People loved to shake him awake. His shoulders were made for it. Jillian told him his right shoulder was always dawning perfectly over the sheets when she awoke. Ready for shaking. But in this case it was an old lady. Fisher gradually understood he was in the planter, mouth full of peat, lying on top of his violin. Are you all right young man? said the old lady I thought you might have been hurt by those awful *bums.* Fisher sat up abruptly. Mglfh he said. In the distance, shouts sirens breaking glass and the crackling of flame. Ptoo oh my God he said What time is it? He sprang out of the planter and ran toward the south market, jamming the fiddle into its case as he ran. Nine thirty! screamed the old lady.

Quincy Market was being wrecked by a sizable army of traveling philosophers. It was mayhem. Deafening bedlam. Rout. Boom and bust. Everywhere glass shattering metal bending men shouting. Fisher looked up to see Spunky clinging to the weather vane on the dome of the south market. In waving at Fisher he nearly fell. Fisher waved back. He began a tour of the zone of battle using his violin case as a shield from flying objects.

And they were numerous. Uncountable. From the windows of a perverse shop which only sold objects shaped like bears came a steady stream of the things. The bears beat against Fisher and his violin. There were so many fires about that the market was actually warm. For the first time in weeks Fisher relaxed all the muscles he tensed against the cold. In the part of the south market previously covered by the canopy (now tatters and ash) a squad of men was busy overturning the painted carts of vendors who in the guise of craftsmen sold large cookies, mugs printed with names, and peanut brittle. The merchants of candy apples cheap belts and rag dolls jointed with sharp wires. Near the rotunda fevered consumption was occurring at what had been a fudge counter. A group of traveling philosophers led by Fat Leroy had smashed open the cupboards and was sharing out industrial size blocks of fudge. Yo Fisheh! said Fat Leroy through a mouth of sweet mud Theah yo is! Wheah yo been? A nap said Fisher I needed a nap. He declined the slab of chocolate proffered him by Fat Leroy and walked on. Of the ogling Christmas crowd which had filled the place two hours before there appeared to be no survivors. No doubt gone home complaining in their big cars thought Fisher.

Gone home to complain and slam each other about in front of the tube. The ion massage that soothes all care.

Now Fisher happened on a most striking scene. Twenty philosophers had formed a gauntlet through which polyester decked expensively coiffed suburban disco kings and queens were being made to pass as they were ejected with great force by more philosophers marauding the dance floor. A separate battalion was smashing the hypnotism equipment. Phonograph records flew out the door like angry bats. As the squealing teens were pushed through the line the men punched, kicked, clawed, spanked and besmirched them. One fat old fellow was even managing to regurgitate a little on each, his tools a big block of the fudge and a bottle of sweet wine. Crunch, swig, barf. Crunch, swig, barf. He had it all worked out. Ah! a man and his system thought Fisher.

He looked across to the north market, up to the restaurant where he had watched Crosbee eat the day before. It seemed years. The air was filled with volleys of corn bread, prime rib, dishes and bottles of beer. The old-fashioned lamps hanging from the ceiling were being knocked this way and that by missiles fired from both sides of the dining room. Traveling Philosophers vs. Amazonian Waitresses. True to legend the girls were holding their own. As Fisher looked around him he felt excited but empty. Most of the rioters he saw were looting to their own ends, striking senselessly at the mausoleum of the consumer stratum which held them in check. This is not what you wanted Frank of Oregon! Fisher sighed. You foresaw a great new beginning. Perhaps Frank of Oregon had known. Had seen at the last moment the time was wrong. And now he was on some road traveling to somewhere with Jillian. Who had given up her bright future to be with the man she loved. Fisher was beat at his own idealistic romantic game. In the midst of the chaos he cackled.

He then heard an Irish voice blare through a megaphone. It was the police but in laughably small number. They called out like mice at the end of a telescope turned the wrong way. Hearing the angry Celtic accent Fisher began to thirst for Guinness. He recalled the Ballydesmond was just around the corner. Hoping it was under siege and dispensing free stout Fisher ran the length of the plaza, dodging bears, bottles, fashions and stunned disco kings.

The Ballydesmond was a curious bar, more curiously located. It was quite old although situated on the edge of the dirty hoopla of the market it had been obliged to make itself look new. It had gone respectable with "pints," flocked wallpaper and old engravings of nobodies and noplaces illuminated with art lamps. Its customers however were largely still Irish dockmen. Occasionally on a Sunday there would be a battle between regulars and turtlenecked ones strayed from the market looking for a combination of breakfast and lunch. Fisher had been to the Ballydesmond but barging through the market often tried him. More than once he had given up and fled back to the T.

The Ballydesmond had indeed been liberated. It was the eye of the storm without. Several men stood at attention behind the bar. The cigarette machine had been ransacked. Packs neatly stacked on the bar for the taking. It looked like HQ. One of the men nodded at Fisher and poured him a Guinness. He pointed at Fisher's violin case. Don play at in ere Mr Fisher he said All due respec. Christ word gets around fast thought Fisher. He took the glass and retreated as far into the back of the place as he could go. He sat at a table and taking a mouthful of stout considered his position. I am he thought either the leader of a new revolutionary group or as Jowls said a little sick boy. A young alcoholic who has whipped up a bunch of bums out of sheer boredom and happenstance and who will be relentlessly hunted down and charged with a thousand counts of mayhem. Even though I was only reading Frank of Oregon's manifesto! said Fisher I'll probably lose my job. He found himself picturing his office with insane nostalgia: a wing armchair, a fireplace, tea, a cat. Shaking this off he gulped stout and imagined with horror his imprisonment and trial. His cell! Thousands of disco kings gathering outside daily to chant threatening dirges written especially by famous pop groups. They would tap their parents, amass an enormous fund for renowned attorneys while he would be defended by a paralegal trainee. The attorneys waving the manifesto. You typed this didn't you? It's been typed on *your* typewriter.

SECOND RATE EPIPHANY

Fisher stared into the Guinness. The richness of his personal vision of Ireland rose again. It called him on, reminded him there were other shores, concerns other than the immediate. No matter how petty, they beckoned. Still life goes on. In its rich loamy color the Guinness was at that moment Fisher's only connection with life, biology, the history of the earth, the ice in the center. He silently worshiped the black beer. This he thought Is the greatest achievement of man, being the most natural, the most deserving to endure. Fisher sat and stared and sipped until he felt that he knew he no longer cared, until he no longer cared that he did not feel he knew, until he knew no care that he felt not. He was an idiot.

He finished the Guinness and got up. His decision or realization, to put too fine names on it, concealed in his pocket like a weapon. He nodded to the men coming in to refresh themselves and walked out again into the boiling fracas.

In the plaza Fisher was met by a strange sight. A detachment of men had imprisoned a large number of policemen in a dumpster. Various police extremities protruded from it and wiggled. A strong brogue called from within: You're all under arrest! Every stinking one of you by God! Give up! But all the men did was to caress and tickle the exposed arms and legs of the constabulary in a variety of inventive and (sad to report) obscene ways. Fisher walked on. Most of the police and fire brigades of the commonwealth were battling their ways into Quincy Market but so many men had come to destroy it that just tearing them out of the way would take hours. Hours. Oh well, they like a good battle, it's their lifeblood. The market buildings were a loss. The shouting had given way to the merry singing that so often accompanies long awaited pillage. Fisher began to whistle. He headed back toward Faneuil Hall. Philosophers waved to him no matter how odious or difficult their particular act of vengeance. The noise! Roaring flame stampeding feet and raucous song. In front of Faneuil Hall a vicious unit had tied Saint Nicholas and the Quincy Market Children's Clown to a post. Fisher walked around to the back of the building. To the forecourt. Where it had all begun. A block away on Union Street a savage fight was taking place between fifty policemen and a steady stream of men. They're still *arriving* thought Fisher. He rested his violin on the planter and wondered what time it was. Out of the corner of his eye he apprehended a figure running toward him. When Fisher turned, perhaps too late, it was Crosbee McWilliams III. Trench coat afly, hair touseled, face pink, although from exertion rather than inebriation. Or so Fisher thought.

Jesus *Christ* wot the Hell's going on heah? said Crosbee. Big clambake said Fisher And what are you doing here? I saw yer on television you awss said Crosbee And let me tell yer something kiddo he panted The fellows at the club are getting togethah their *awn ahmy* to put a stop to this. What! said Fisher The Harvard Club? That's right said Crosbee I came right ovah, I almost spilled my drink. What do you mean army? said Fisher. I mean said Crosbee They're massing theah Cawdillacs and rifle collections on Federal and they're coming up heah ter help the police and the fiah brigade. Dear me said Fisher. Crosbee looked around. Fishah dawn't you think you're going to be in a lot of trouble? Yes said Fisher I do, suddenly. This isn't my fault Crosbee. Oh? said Crosbee They seem ter think it is on television. Television! said Fisher What do *they* know? Yaw name faw one thing said Crosbee. I hadn't counted on war said Fisher It's just that it's been a very bad day. Jeez said Crosbee. Fisher and Crosbee looked at the great orange glow in the sky over the market. Their appreciation of the scene was interrupted by an angry cry.

THERE HE IS! The cry, so feminine, came from the corner of Faneuil Hall. Fisher and Crosbee turned to see Alison Mapes flanked by two policemen. *YOU NEVER WENT TO HARVARD!* she screamed. Is she talking ter *me?* gulped Crosbee blushing deep red. No said Fisher To me and we'd better be toddling along. IS YOUR NAME WIL-

LIAM FISHER? yelled one of the policemen. NO! called
Fisher waving at the man. Where is thy car? he said to
Crosbee. On Tremont said Crosbee transfixed by the sight
of police running toward him with drawn guns. Let's go,
let us go said Fisher breaking into a run. Fisher feared the
unmaneuverable Crosbee would fall into the hands of the
police who seemed to be coming across the courtyard
very quickly indeed. If tortured thought Fisher That is
given no martinis he will confess. But Crosbee surprised
Fisher. Although attired in underwear, a shirt with ex-
traordinarily long tails, a three piece wool suit, a heavy
topcoat and the slippery but de rigueur pennyloafers he
kept up with Fisher as they bolted up the steps to City
Hall. The two policemen followed as best they could,
pushing through the crowd shouting imprecations and
illegal threats.

Fisher and Crosbee sprinted across the plaza to Tremont. The car was parked at a strange angle. Crosbee
began to fumble in his topcoat and Fisher looked about
nervously in the crazy traffic. Dimwits had come from far
and wide to watch Quincy Market burn. As Fisher's fears
mounted, Crosbee's fumbling slackened, then stopped.
Fisher realized Crosbee was horribly drunk. The exertion
of attaining the plaza had infused the scary number of
martinis he had consumed at the Harvard Club into his
bloodstream at once. Crosbee! yelled Fisher. Crosbee
pawed ineffectually at his clothing. My keys! he gurgled.
With horror Fisher saw the two policemen appear on the
plaza. He leaned Crosbee against the car and violently
searched him. Hey bustah that's a Brooks Brothahs cawt
said Crosbee wrenching himself free of Fisher and falling
onto the pavement. Fisher bent and found the keys in
Crosbee's front pocket and then pulled the great mass of

him upright. Ya bawsted mumbled Crosbee. Wise up said Fisher.

He unlocked the door and thrusting Crosbee into the driver's seat he ran to the other side of the car. He banged on the door with the violin case until Crosbee, momentarily comatose, was awakened and unlocked it. Fisher got in and sat watching Crosbee try to put the ignition key in the cigarette lighter until he could bear it no more. The policemen were running toward them. Fisher grabbed Crosbee's hand and brutally forced it toward the lock. Owww said Crosbee.

Somehow at the last elegant moment the motor was started and first gear engaged. It may have been a statistical accident. The car moved malignantly out into Tremont Street. I'll get thawse pigs burbled Crosbee. Fisher grabbed the wheel. Idiot! Ignore them! he cried Just get us out of here! Right! said Crosbee suddenly wide eyed. He pressed his foot firmly down on the accelerator.

XIII | A Daring Escape by Sail

For reasons differing slightly from the usual ones Fisher declined to comment on Crosbee's driving. At the best of times it was capricious; at the worst, it bore a strange relation to the works of Dante. Fisher held his violin tightly between his knees and concentrated on the appalling right of way unfolding before him. You gonna be OK? said Fisher. Cawse said Crosbee Er wheah ah we?

The car bearing Fisher and Crosbee took the following route at the approximate speeds indicated:

A Up Tremont to Park Street (45 mph)

B Across the sidewalk between the two entrances to the T (50 mph)

C Across the Common, slowing momentarily to shear off a portion of the bandstand, then across the south edge of the frog pond and on toward Beacon Street (50-10-40 mph)

D Up a hillock and through a fence onto Beacon in front of the State House (50 mph)

E Left on Beacon to Charles (60 mph)

F Right on Charles scattering pederasts and pedestrians and damaging a salad restaurant (just as well! thought Fisher) (65 mph)

G Into the rotary at the intersection of Charles and Cambridge streets at the edge of the river (70 mph)

Here they circled at 70 mph. Crosbee had a terrible fear of rotaries which Fisher now recalled in dread. Other traffic fled and the two men circled alone in the crumpled luxury car. After ten revolutions Fisher began to feel sick. Bracing himself for the worst, he felt he must criticize. Crosbee he said dryly We will have to come out of this sooner or later. Jesus I hate these things! said Crosbee his voice tremulous. I know I know said Fisher soothingly But it hardly advances our cause. Around and around, no exit no exit! said Crosbee. Come now said Fisher There are plenty of exits, just take one, any one please. He saw Crosbee's hands tense on the wheel and he shut his eyes.

At a moment just past the optimum they bumped across a cement island and the car whipped along the embankment. Thank you very much said Fisher. But he noticed the brick face of a dead end looming ahead. A siren wailed in the distance. Jesus said Crosbee stopping centimeters in front of the wall. Someone called from an apartment above You punks! Crosbee rolled down his window. Fack you ya bawsted! he cried. Crosbee please don't bother about that now said Fisher. A squealing reverse and they bumped across the veldt of the embankment again. Fisher looked for rhino. Then it was over. The car approached the large wooden doors of the boating pavilion. Crosbee did nothing. Perhaps in the dimness he took it for a tunnel. The car exploded into the place and came to rest in a morass of sails and rope. Fisher realized his long avoided introduction to water travel was about to be had. He rolled his window down and climbed out with his violin. He grimly went around to Crosbee and opened the door. Come on said Fisher Let's go. Anchors aweigh. Yo ho ho. Eh? said Crosbee.

Dragging a snarled assortment of canvas and tackle Fisher and Crosbee hurried down the pier. A hundred little boats bobbed up and down. The cold moonlight. Suddenly Crosbee tripped and fell into a small boat. This one he said Awl numbah twenny seven. In erecting the sail, which he did from one of his dimmest memories, Crosbee suggested an unwholesome representation of the once popular Iwo Jima tableau. Fisher danced about in fear on the dock. When do I get in? he said. The siren was getting louder and louder. Anytime you want you awss said Crosbee fumbling with the lines. Even with things as they were Fisher had difficulty summoning courage. But a screech of rubber and siren from the opposite side of the boathouse decided him. Cast awff! shouted Crosbee from under the sail. Fisher jumped into the bow and nearly upset the boat. By standing up and twirling around, Crosbee was able to wrap some line around his head and partly hoist the sail. He looked as though he had been lashed to the mast. Gagh! he said. Fisher fell to his stomach in the bottom of the boat. Foul water entered his nose and mouth and the centerboard box crushed his rib cage. The Ass supplied a zephyr which drew the boat across the lagoon. Shouts from the dock! Fisher peered over the gunwale to see three policemen gesturing. There they are Crosbee he said. Jesus Christ said Crosbee. He was entangled in a kilometer of rope. The boat was sucked out into the river. Come back! commanded an amplified paternal voice. Fack you ya bawsteds! screamed Crosbee. He attempted to wave impudently but only involved himself deeper in his Gordian knot. The boat picked up speed in the icy black water. Where are we going? bubbled Fisher from his prone position. Shat up said Crosbee. He was as good with a boat as a full martini.

The wind broke plenteous now from the unseen cheeks of The Ass, the stars its raging pimples. The boat plunged back and forth. Fisher lay in the stinking ice water trying to guess which way they were headed. No sound save the waves rippling against the hull and the wind and Fisher's snorkeling. No sound of steering or pulleys. No sound! Fisher looked up. Crosbee had passed out. Slumped against the mast. Crosbee! said Fisher getting to his knees and slapping him in the face. Whaaa! said Crosbee. Christ! he said looking around. Fisher pulled him partly free of the ropes. Listen said Fisher Are you in control? Are you competent? If not I am going to swim for Newbury Street. Prepeah to come about! shrieked Crosbee. Fisher frowned. Stop using these nautical . . . But at this moment the mainsail swooped and hammered into his head. ♪ Ohh! said Fisher as the boom swept him out of the boat into the freezing water.

Even as he plunged into the black deep Fisher's lips moved slightly in vile condemnation of Crosbee's driving and sailing abilities. But he had been struck very hard indeed. Heah! Grawb this! Crosbee called. With his free hand he threw Fisher's violin and struck Fisher on the head. As the frantic Crosbee again became bound to his ship burial Fisher lost consciousness and flowed down toward the Harvard bridge.

XIV | Redoubt

Fisher opened his eyes and in that moment thought: ?—
Oh yes — Market — Car — Boat — Water! Drowned?
Dead?

No. He decided his afterlife would not be to lie tucked
up in a bed in a clean room. Natural light, from a window
Fisher supposed behind him. Great waves of pain crashed
down on Fisher when he tried to turn his head. He stared
at the ceiling light. As he usually did when he stared at a
ceiling Fisher began to wish he could walk on it. That the
room were upside down. And the best thing he thought
Is that all the lamps would rise from the floor like balloons
and there would be no overhead light.

Fisher returned to the problem of his location. Its
smell. Not my house. Not Crosbee's house. Not hospital.
Suddenly the soft clean smell seemed familiar. Shadow
images began to form in his groggy pain swept T of a
mind. It was the smell of a place where there are never
strong odors. A place where the inhabitants do not drink
to excess and spew up. Where no tobacco is smoked.
Where the strongest smells are bread abake and God's
gentlest vegetables asteam. He was in the Fruitlands.

Fisher convulsed in a yell. It hurt him so much he

convulsed and yelled again. And a third time. Then, fatigued with the monotony of it, he rested. In convulsing he had attained semicircularity on the bed and so was afforded a new view of the room. On a table next to the bed was a ravaged looking piece of stoneware. Function unknowable. Fruitlands all right thought Fisher. At the foot of the bed Fisher's violin case sat dully. Fisher thought he recognized his clothes on a chair in a pile too neat to be of his own making. On his second yell he had heard noises in another part of the house. Now feet. Feet of normal size to judge from the sound thought Fisher So it's not Rodney. Pounding up the stairs. Feet driven to pound by madness or some forbidden lust. No no thought Fisher tossing. The door opened. Sound of feet approaching. Fisher stiffened but could not look. William? said Rachel Are you awake? Nug said Fisher. She began to chafe his temples. Longer and more languorously than is strictly necessary thought Fisher. He opened an eye. Snow clouds darkened the sky outside. Are you OK? she said. The question of a lifetime. Truly she was concerned. But she was also Rachel. Videotaper of the unfortunate. A maker of charts. Don't tape me said Fisher thickly No Foley! Do you want something to eat? she said. Fisher nodded which caused him great pain and he yelped again. Only after she had gone downstairs did he realize he had asked for food at the Fruitlands.

She brought him a tray. On this tray was a plate and on the plate was a multicolored hot mass. It was not stew, it was not salad, it was just food. Lump food. Yum thought Fisher I wonder what color code this got? Code blue, do not resuscitate. Fisher picked up his fork and with quickly decreasing appetite studied the round clump. He poked it. It hissed and subsided by several inches. He tugged a piece free with the fork and put it into his mouth. Ten minutes went by. He was still chewing. He was desperate. For the first minute the food had had an agreeable taste but now it was a flavorless rubbery ball which stuck limpetlike to the roof of his mouth and seemed to be slowly expanding. No doubt it lives on the fluids of others thought Fisher. He was reduced to slowly scraping it off his palate with the fork. Exhausted by the ordeal of one mouthful he dropped the fork and fell asleep.

He woke a few hours later. The light in the room was just disappearing, the awesome cheeks sliding over the bowl above them all, getting set for a thumper. Snow was predicted but Fisher was indifferent to the guises of excreta. Rain, snow, hail, sleet . . . to him they were all the same shameful opprobrium from on high. And so often were they the only topic of conversation. He turned to look out the window. The bare branches of the apple tree which stood in the garden of the Fruitlands scratched the window, spooky bony hands.

He sat in the desperately cozy kitchen. Rachel sat across the table, tentatively admiring him with furtive yet unmistakable looks. She had given him a robe. A wheat colored kimono. For this he was grateful. She has lustrous hair and has given me a robe thought Fisher But the systems. And the ? socks. She had clothed Fisher's legs in knee length tubes of wool secured at the tops with drawstrings and little silver bells. Hopelessly cheery patterns. They're Icelandic socks said Rachel Lapps wear them. Then how can they be Icelandic? Fisher said. The stiff wool scratched him horribly. Sure they're not for reindeer? said Fisher. But she did not reply. The main topic of conversation although as yet unbroached was the copy

of the *Boston Globe* which lay in front of her. Fisher could
see his name yipping and yapping at him from various
locations on the front page.

Parley. So—harrumph!—said Fisher Now you know
what I was doing last night. Yeah said Rachel dreamily.
Fisher looked around the kitchen. Such a tidy house could
only be run by people in league with the police. Are you
going to turn me in? he said swallowing. Oh no oh no man
no said Rachel breaking into a frightening smile Oh man
William how could you think that? I think it's great! she
said. Fisher stared at her. You do? he said. Oh man I think
it's fantastic she said. She certainly was looking peculiar.
I beg the favor said Fisher Of being told how I got here.
Do you want some tea? she said. Again the smile. Something is happening he thought. Yes all right he said
quickly adding What kinds do you have? Camomile, rose
hip, mint, spearmint, lemon, strawberry, caraway, sage,
cinnamon, smoked orchid and eelgrass she said proudly.
Don't you have any tea? said Fisher I mean real tea? From
China? Oh no man said Rachel Tea is really bad for you.
Fisher sighed. Strawberry.

Snow blew against the windows. Fisher slurped his
strawberry tea from an unglazed cup which tore at his
lips. In front of him, a plate of untouched cakes like dis-
carded gaskets. Now said Fisher Tell all. Well said Rachel
We saw the riot on TV, it interrupted this show on re-
storing we always watch. And so we were sitting there
watching it you know and then like they said your name.
Television! said Fisher I'll get them for this. And said
Rachel They said you started it. That's not true said
Fisher. Anyway said Rachel We decided we'd help you.
Help me? said Fisher. Yeah we all hated that place said
Rachel It's so plastic and phony. But Rodney eats there in

three piece suits! said Fisher. Rachel stared at him. He does? she said. Yes said Fisher I've seen it. Rachel looked out the kitchen door and up the stairs. Her gaze the spirit of the new age, gliding silently up to the bedroom of Rodney to damn him, to exorcise his crassness from the sanctuary. Anyway said Fisher. Oh well anyway said Rachel We got in the car and went down there. Only we couldn't get there, there was a tremendous traffic jam on the bridge. Fisher was trying to recollect his movements. The end of his memory dangled like his scarf on City Hall. Yes? he said. Well said Rachel We were like stuck on the bridge and I looked down and saw you and this other guy on this little boat and then he attacked you and you fell out. He attacked me? said Fisher That worm! Yeah or something anyway that's what it looked like said Rachel So then we drove back to the Cambridge side and Rodney and I climbed down the piling and pulled you out. It seemed to Fisher symbolic and ignominious in the extreme that his body had drifted to the Cambridge side. He colored. And you brought me here? he said. No said Rachel We decided to get you some dry clothes so we took you home. Home! said Fisher You mean Newbury Street? Yeah said Rachel And let me tell you your landlady is really uncool. My landlady! said Fisher. Yeah man said Rachel See when we dragged you in she thought you were drunk man. When you dragged me in said Fisher. Yeah said Rachel She said she was going to *evict* you in the morning man. Meaning this morning said Fisher. Yeah said Rachel. So I'm evicted said Fisher. Yeah said Rachel She was really steamed up. I'll bet said Fisher You couldn't have left me in the car and brought my clothes out? Uhhh said Rachel. Christ said Fisher. Don't worry man said Rachel We destroyed your personal effects man.

Eh? said Fisher. Your effects man said Rachel Your address book and papers and stuff. Fisher stared at her. I suppose you were right to he said slowly. Yeah man said Rachel We want to protect you. A damp feeling of lostness and entrapment began to envelop Fisher. Well what happened to Crosbee? he said. Who? said Rachel. The other guy in the boat! said Fisher. Oh I don't know man shrugged Rachel It went way down the river. What! said Fisher. Well we just had to rescue you said Rachel. She looked as if she might slobber. Yes I see said Fisher seeing the desire in her plans and her eyes. May I see the paper? he said. He was too dizzy to read properly and the Globular account of things swirled in front of him unrealistically.

QUINCY MARKET DESTROYED BY MOB . . . POLICE AND NATIONAL GUARD BATTLE 2,000 . . . BIGGEST RIOT IN HISTORY OF BOSTON . . . Situation Now "Under Control" Says Mayor . . . Christmas Shopping Terror . . . revolutionary speaker . . . inflamed . . . 9:30 . . . south market . . . north market . . . burning . . . million dollars . . . courageous waitresses . . . chaos . . . disco horror gauntlet . . . rubbish bins . . . alcoholics . . . FBI . . . William Fisher . . . bloody bandage . . . unshaven . . . rumpled . . . Institute of Science . . . insane says vice president . . . guitar case . . . accomplice . . . Charles St . . . boating pavilion . . . million dollars . . . escape . . . car explodes . . . dynamite suspected . . . boat found sunk . . . Soldiers Field . . . million dollars . . . market will rise . . . ashes . . . developer . . . million dollars . . .

Jesus thought Fisher He drowned at *Harvard.* God bless him. He raged at the inaccuracies and editorializing in the story which had been co written by a Dolan a Schwartz and a Bacigalupo. All Boston viewpoints. He

looked at the snow dancing on the panes and heaved a
deep sigh. There was no turning back. Wanted! A police
cordon around his parents' house. He felt sorry for his
mother. Interpol agents screaming at her in Esperanto
and ringing the doorbell to use the bathroom every five
minutes. He tried to frame an elegant apology that would
be accepted by the people of Boston, the mayor, the developer of Quincy Market, the children's clown, his landlady, and Crosbee's mother. She would be looking for him
soon with the bill for the car. It was impossible. He would
have to hide in thickets and snowy burrows. Walden?

Do you want some more tea? said Rachel. Fisher held
out his mug with a grunt. As she began to pour she stroked
his hand. Yog! he said pulling away in surprise and splat-
tering hot tea on his hand Yip! in response to this and then
Yeow! to the skeletal pains his jerkings had caused him.
Man William sit down! said Rachel. Fisher sat and looked
at her. William she said in a sudden purr I've always
thought you were really neat. Fisher slurped wide eyed
from his cup. And you he thought I have always thought
you a mad anal retentive harridan. Fisher didn't know
where to look. To his dismay his brain told him to look at
her directly. Mr Honest. He did so and realized it was too
direct and she brightening misunderstood it. He looked at
the wall which conveyed nothing to either of them and he
found himself back where he started. Stay here she said
quietly. Now Fisher looked her full in the face and said
What! Stay here with me, I'll protect you she said. So!
thought Fisher It's blackmail, this *is* Hell, I *am* dead! He
stood up. What are you talking about? he said. There was
lust in her eyes. William I think what you did was fantastic. I hated that place said Rachel I hated the plastic people who went there. They're going to rebuild said Fisher

beginning to panic. I want you to stay here with me said Rachel And we'll build a new kind of lifestyle. Eh! said Fisher loudly stalling for time. William think what Quincy Market could be said Rachel also standing up We could make it into a fabulous environment. *Environment?* said Fisher taking a step back. Yeah man said Rachel We could fill it with food co ops and day care centers and granaries and craft shops. No said Fisher taking another step backwards. Potteries! said Rachel Weaving studios! Leather shops! No no said Fisher. Just think said Rachel now in her stride Plants! An inspirational center of alternative lifestyles man! Video! William! You started it by destroying it now we must build build she said advancing on Fisher around the table I want you, I love you! I'm just a drunk! said Fisher retreating backwards circling the table I didn't know what I was doing! William stay here with me she said resorting to her bargaining point I'll protect you from the police, we'll wear clothes we make ourselves! Yiii! said Fisher in pain as she pursued him faster and faster around the table. His back and legs ached and the Icelandic socks ripped his flesh as he tottered around. We'll grow our own food, we'll start a movement she panted. I don't want to be in a movement said Fisher. I'll protect you man said Rachel You'll be mine and you can repay me in the way I've always wanted. They ran faster. The one at, the other from. Circling the table in the hot kitchen. I'll cook for you! said Rachel and at this Fisher's heart jumped into his throat. Or perhaps it was the bite of lump food. He broke the circle and ran from the room. Aw William come on man called Rachel running after him through the craft filled house.

After skidding crazily on the polished wooden floor in the Icelandic socks, Fisher ran at full speed into the dark living room. He traversed it and was almost to the porch door when he caught his absurd long woolly foot on a huge pillow and went cartwheeling into a giant loom. With a terrific creaking crash ancillary snaps and accompanying sproings he was instantly tangled in hundreds of pieces of doweling string and wire. He was immobile, a fly in a singing web. A coil of yarn poised on the crossbar Fumped! down on his head. To struggle he thought Would be pathetic. Would be illustrative. Dowels jabbed at his ribs but he stayed motionless. Rachel turned on the light. Ms Nice Guy no more. Oh man William she said You're really in trouble now man. Now? said Fisher from under his turban of wool. That loom cost five hundred *dollars* man said Rachel It's *Sandra's* man and you just wrecked her tapestry. Her fabric art man. Fisher felt unrepentant until he realized this gave her yet another lever against him. He started to try to wriggle out. Let me help you said Rachel. No said Fisher I can do it. He put his weight on the crossbar which intentionally gave way with a loud crack and sent him farther into the loom's satanic workings. He felt he was leaving the world, crawling through a harp to the next. He felt a trickle of blood at his side. Are you OK William? said Rachel her tone incredibly creeping again toward that of desire. I'll be out said Fisher When it has finished writing GUILTY on me. Huh? said Rachel. With a great effort Fisher raged out of the loom. He took the ball of wool off his head. He looked at Rachel and started edging toward the door. William she said following. No said Fisher bolting No a thousand times no! He ran around the corner and up the stairs. William! she panted behind him. Fisher ran into the bedroom in which he had earlier achieved consciousness. He slammed the door and locked it. Rachel immediately beat her fists against it. You're a hero she cried I want you! Go away please said Fisher You don't know what you're talking about. He looked around the room for a blunt instrument. William William let me in cried Rachel. The fists! I'm a drunk said Fisher wishing it were so. You don't need to drink if you have a great woman! said Rachel pounding. And what do you know about it? said Fisher It was when I was possessed of a "great" woman that I was obliged to start drinking! Let me in! said Rachel I saved your life! You saved my body is all! howled Fisher. He sealed his ears with his hands. The fists, the fists.

After ten minutes of incessant mad timpanizing they stopped. Fisher took his hands from his ears and heard her going downstairs. He lifted his robe and looked at his side. A small gash decorated with tufts of wool. I wonder if I can be invisibly rewoven he grumbled. He was faint. He crawled into bed and in the dark he began to sleep and then to dream.

A tremendous courtroom. Everyone Fisher had ever known or even laid eyes on had assembled to unanimously condemn him. The judge was his college roommate, a law student Fisher always suspected of having it in for him. The judge blew a pitch pipe. Guilty! he sang. Guilty! sang everyone. Guilty! sang the judge a third lower. Guilty! chorused humanity. Guilty! crooned the judge. Really quite a fine baritone thought Fisher. Guilty! sang Creation in all harmonies, medieval classical romantic and twelve tone all blending magically. Fisher held out his violin and the judge began to bang it with a sledgehammer. Fisher was then taken off but instead of being incarcerated

He found himself on a lonely road by a sea. He was

riding a bicycle. He was dressed in a suit of dark brown tweed with a waistcoat and a collarless white shirt. Heavy brown brogues on his feet. On his face a pair of novelty glasses with large rubber nose. A sweet bun hung from the handlebars in a kerchief. And pedaling in the dream Fisher realized sub subconsciously where he could go. Away from Boston. Away from Rachel. Away from Smith, Jowls, his landlady. He rode on. After he had gone a mile he turned to look at the sea and then turned

to his right to his partner at the dinner party who was Jillian. Jillian as she was when they had loved. Her wonderful hair. Her sweet lips. Her law briefs unattended in the corner, her briefs attended by Fisher under the table. A dinner party. Her favorite kind of party. The guests were big fish from the ocean who preferred when on land to eat fruit only. The conversation was divine, the fish contributing some very fresh seagoing anecdotes. Then the party was over and Fisher and Jillian began to make love.

Fisher rarely had erotic dreams and when he did they were usually frustrating and vague. A glimpse of delights and some kind of racket going on in the background. But this thought Fisher sub sub subconsciously This is so richly textured. So fleshy and fruity. It was wonderful. Just as it had been. A truly erotic union and a very passionate one before the pad and the white coat and MacGillivray. Fisher could almost believe he was really having her as she had been. Her quick little breaths. Her neck turned for his mouth. The eager squeeze of her

YEOW! Fisher screamed awake jabbing Rachel lying naked next him in the ribs. Oof! she said releasing her grip on Fisher's priapus. Fisher jumped up in shock and anger, seeing he owed his dream of Jillian to the sordid caresses of Rachel. What are you doing! shrieked Fisher. I want you I want you! said Rachel.. And then! She *grabbed* Fisher and *forced* him under her and herself onto him. Jesus she's strong thought Fisher. She began to move up and down, up and down, blah blah blah.

What a flood of conflicting ideas emotions pains and pleasures coursed through Fisher! While he had thought he would subside in the face of intercourse with this madwoman who dreamt only of a society ordered on yeast and photosynthesis, Fisher discovered his privates and abdomen were enjoying the experience, the brigands! And it seemed the enjoyment would spread if he allowed it. Rachel moved feverishly. I love you I love you William she said. Fisher looked up at her dark hair, flashing eyes, her neck thrown back, her skin glistening in the dimness. Nonetheless he thought I must fight back. It isn't right. He tried to lift her off him, he grunted. But in grabbing her thighs he only increased her pleasure and fervor. She is so strong thought Fisher. He decided on insult. Get off me you! he said tensely. Rachel merely moaned and undulated more quickly. It felt absolutely wonderful. But still Fisher struggled for freedom. But there had never been a mortise like this! It was perfect. For all her faults! This was the cradle, the alley (call it what you like, crudity will not be brooked) he had been molded for. The cul de sac? The Fond du Lac? The *estuary?* Yet he struggled for a moral foothold. Bran eater! he grunted. Sure you ugh like it like this? Sure you don't unnh want to be bound with Aran wool? Oog ahh. Smeared with tofu? Urrgh! She really was good. No William she shivered All I want is you. Oh oh oh. Fisher gave up. He began to move with her. To push against her. Imagine! Wuff wuff said Fisher. Ooh ooh ooh said Rachel. Great. But far behind all the ecstasy

Fisher heard a high sound. An alarm. A ringing of the ears from the excitement of it all? No an alarm. Not an alarm. A siren. A ringing. No a siren. A siren! Then Fisher reacted. Agh ulh the police! he moaned. Rachel whimpered and slammed up and down on him. Ooh stay with me here she said I'll protect you William baby ooh. Fisher began to panic. But it was the best. He put all of himself into it. With a terrific exertion he pushed Rachel over and quivered on top of her. Largo, lento, presto! Prestissimo! They chorused together in short Orff-like passages. The siren contributed, approaching. Louder louder wailing. Oh ah ah said Rachel. All woman. Grrr rowf! said Fisher. What a guy. At this moment Fisher understood Rachel was his natural mate. So right he began to quail at the thought of it. She wanted him. She felt wonderful. Not arid not expansive not slothful. One in a thousand. Million dollars. I had thought Fisher The wrong right woman before. A blinking pinkish light began to fill the room. At first Fisher thought it elation but no. Police were driving up to the Fruitlands. Fear pushed Fisher over the brink. He threw himself up and down. Rasp! Rasp! went the Icelandic socks. UGH! AGH! OHHH! said Rachel. I love you I love you! said Fisher. They experienced it together. Tadaaa. Whatever it was. But in a flash Fisher tore himself from her and dove for the pile of his clothes. Rachel continued to writhe on the bed. A banging noise came from downstairs. Fisher put his bare feet in his shoes without tying them. Already he felt empty, a deep loss not touching Rachel, not lying against her. It horrified him. He yanked on his trousers. Open up! said a voice This is the police! "*These are* the police" thought Fisher correcting the man as he pulled on his sweater Or "This is a policeman" or possibly "Here we are, members of the police."

He grabbed his jacket and violin and lunged for the door without a glance at the still undulating Rachel. He raced down the back stairs, grappling with the jacket. Out the back door, across the organic victory garden of Rodney. Flap! Floop! toward open fields in driving snow. The Ass never gives you a break. Fisher noticed he was still erect as he jumped a low fence. He stumbled down a small heavily drifted hill and crossed a field at a fast walk Fump! Fump! Fump! heading south. Not looking back. Just a guy and his violin in the snow.

XV I Was a Fugitive from a Tofu Farm

The sea returning day by day
　　Restores the world-wide mart;
So let each dweller on the Bay
　　Fold Boston in his heart,
　　Till these echoes be choked with snows
　　Or over the town blue ocean flows.

Emerson, "Boston"

Close to the center of town the fields and matronly back-yards of Concord were enclosed with higher and higher fences. Fisher clambered up and down them and slogged across the drifted expanses without care, depressed beyond measure. In the very heart of town paranoia and fences ran so high Fisher was obliged to heave his violin up and over them and then from a running start vault them in a scrabble. Dogs barked. Lights went on. But Fisher was too stealthy. He had however to keep off the streets. Streets of Christmas Eve.

He pushed on. He knew where he was going. More or less. Now he was nearing Walden. Snow blew all over him and filled the forest with flurries. In the dim moonlight Fisher saw figures on the pond. For a moment he had the feeling they were doing something which pertained to him. If he marched out on the ice, where his troubles had begun on Sunday, he would get involved with these figures and somehow things would be altered. Again. But the snow was deep between the road and the pond and a queer feeling enveloped Fisher. For once and once only he decided to stick with his original plan. Not his original original plan, for that was to become a professional drummer. But his original plan of the evening (excluding the one to brain Rachel with the stoneware) and that was to make the journey he had set out on.

Fisher thought he could make up time lost away from roads by cutting across frozen ponds. This he did with some success and had there been passers by any of those ponds that night they would have seen him. A small figure wild of hair, bespectacled, sportjacketed picking its way across the ice with a violin, talking to itself. A long journey ahead of him, Fisher decided to muse mull and worry. He would have liked to trudge but the snow was making him trudge. Which he resented. So in the spirit of trudging he tried with all his might not to trudge. First he considered the cold and with it The Ass. The cold Fisher thought Of my apartment, of Brattle Street, of Quincy Market. The heart of Jillian. Fisher didn't consider aspects of these things other than their cold. And so they were all connected by their iciness, what a crude thinker, animals think that way. And they were connected to his sockless feet which already were numb wood in his shoes. His legs three feet deep in snow. Several times Fisher talking to himself and so not noticing slowly entered a very deep drift and was gradually forced to halt. Down down down finding himself completely buried. He had then to retrace his steps, no easy matter since they were invisible. But still he got on.

Three hours later Fisher felt he was in a place beginning with N. Newton? Needham? Nonantum? Nnn thought Fisher. He found railroad tracks which led south. He began to walk along them. N! N! N Nnnn! A train came and went on the other track honking and whipping Fisher with more snow. Perhaps it was Nobscot. Now walking the tracks the ties of which afforded more opportunity for horizontal progress Fisher felt he could think cogently within the geometric confines of the rails. Clickety clack.

First he thought of Rachel. His tumescence had long since vanished in the snow but thinking of her warmed him. Not at all like I thought said Fisher It just goes to show you how wrong you can be. Yeah right! But he began to ache for her. Or at least he ached and he told himself it was for her so that his subconscious might warm him more. Then Fisher tried in his mind to separate what in his life was due to accident, what to poor planning, what to The Ass and what to women. Especially in his life since Sunday and in events previous to Sunday but directly bearing upon it. To amuse himself he first heaped it all on women. Very neatly he blamed his insistence on going in his damaged state to the Fruitlands on Jillian, his flight to the seedy bar where he met Frank of Oregon on Rachel. His confused wanderings in Boston on Alison, the riot on all three of them. But he tired of this because he felt differently about Rachel now. Aloud he pictured sharing a seaside cottage with her. But the image of the broken loom intruded. She'll wake up said Fisher True love is larval until all the bills are paid. How complicated it all is he said pursing his lips like several people he knew. He seemed on the lonely walk to be flooded with the attitudes and habitual actions and verbal expressions of so many. He shifted the violin to the other hand and pressed down the snowy tracks. A sudden increase of sloppy cold outfall from above. This suggested to Fisher he contemplate The Ass's role. It was possible to work out quite a nice little system wherein The Ass caused everything. Medievally beautiful. The Ass shat all over the pond and made Sunday cold which brought out the God damn skaters said Fisher Who made piles of ice on which I slipped and hit my head and in the ensuing weather I could not of course recuperate swiftly. The Ass! called Fisher. After a brief silence to warm his teeth which were buzzing with cold he considered for the next few miles a combination of women and The Ass. This package was extremely attractive. During particularly good parts of it he whistled. He could not however fix much if any blame on Rachel for long. And he warmed whenever he relieved her of blame. He experimented in moments when the snow did not blow coldest against him with recalling what he did not like about Rachel. Her filed teeth. Crafts! But these did not chill him as they once did. He was chilled to the bone but thinking of Rachel warmed his marrow. So why didn't I stay in the house! Fisher shouted. A rabbit ran from under the ties into a wood.

Fisher thought of Jillian. And what was the point? he said feeling sheepish however as he recalled his dream of her (though also remembering it was precipitated by Rachel). Their short autumn of love. Fisher and Hardy. Laurel and Hardy said Fisher But at what point did our paths really diverge? He screwed up his face in terrible pondering. It was probably the day she said I'm going to *law*

school and I said A panorifice stuffing to you. Yes said
Fisher The honeymoon was over on that day as shortly
thereafter my smoking things were bumped off the little
table by her bed to make way for the huge ugly blue
casebooks. That was it. Fisher was very cold now thinking
of Jillian so he switched to Alison. Now there was a mistake if there ever was one. A revenge affair of startling
spontaneity and decrepitude. Nearly simultaneously wax-
ing and waning. Although! he said warming slightly It was
she pursued me. This had excited him at the time. But! he
shouted shaking the violin in the windy snow and momentarily losing his balance Pursued me to Wheat! And in-
formed on me to the police! Fisher chilled rapidly.

He walked on in the hazy moonlight and counted ties
for a while. The Ass supplied a steady abrasive element
against his face. Now as the tracks veered more to what
he supposed was due south Fisher timidly tried putting
everything on himself. Just for a lark. But where to start?
he said Boston? College? 12th, 11th, 10th, 9th, 8th! 7th,
6th, 5th, 4th, 3rd, 2nd, 1st grade? Kindergarten? Super-
vised play area? *Birth?* No! I am blameless. If for no other
reason than that my initial error can't be pinpointed.
Whose can be? Fisher shut his mouth for a while as he was
gradually overcome with an old fear. That of all his misfor-
tunes owing to his complete ignorance of the multiplica-
tion table. But with great courage he dismissed it. For
once and for all. So in the end bobbing along the railway
Fisher was able to work out a heartrending explanation
for everything that had happened based mainly on inter-
sections of fate, with strong measures of women and The
Ass thrown in. Even Rachel, a little, in moments when he
didn't need to be warm. He walked on down the tracks.
Clickety clack.

Fisher's hands were so cold they would not open or close. They were stiff half open curls. To transfer the violin case from one hand to the other he had to bend forward slightly as he walked and bump his hands together. Two steam shovels in love. He thought of Rachel. Her head thrown back . . . Ah well catch as cas can said Fisher. The phrase had always been thus to him. There is no explanation for *cas* other than dyslexia or tumor. But it had always sounded right to Fisher who spent the winter of 1973–74 hunting it up in dictionaries. They were unyielding. But Fisher found when he said Catch as cas can people nodded and smiled. So there is a cas and so there are many things. It has an inner reason said Fisher. He came upon a large open area. Several sidings. Here Fisher walked properly through a switch as though he were a train and joined the main line to the south. Clickety clack.

In its own good time The Ass raised one of its cheeks slightly on the seat of the bowl to allow New England its infinitesimal daily allotment of heat and light. Two or three footcandles. It was all they deserved. But this meant day would break soon for Fisher. Christmas Day. Nothing changed in the sky. Its darkness persisted. Its exuviae. But Fisher sensed the darkness *was* persisting, resisting some awful change which could never be an improvement but was coming. Rachel! said Fisher Your tawny velvet skin against mine own! This heated him and he pushed on. All life is escape. Life at its best anyway he thought. Back through the grades. Blameless but an escapist. But escaping what? Mathematics? Probability? *Birth?* Not again! howled Fisher. The only thing my kind can do he said Is escape. Escape! Escape Spunky. Escape Alison. Escape

French films, Institutes, luxury, whiskey, landladies, objects, the T. But the escape is the fun of it. The only thing that makes life livable for my type. Escape to escape, everything being escape. No matter what you do it is escape. You can't escape that! Even if you volunteer, campaign, crusade, it's as much escape as withdrawing posturing and belittling or spending eating prospering and driving. And self denial wheezed Fisher Is the greatest escape of them all. No objects is no excuse. Living Minimalism! Ha ha ha! Fisher got a mouthful of snow. He walked on.

In the muffled predawn Fisher tramped the ties through Ponkapoag, Squamscutt, Massaponsett, Ponkaponsett, Squampoag, Massascutt, Ponkascutt, Squamponsett, Massapoag, Poagponka, Scuttsquam, Ponsettmassa, Poagmassa, Scuttponka, Ponsettsquam, Poagsquam, Scuttmassa, Ponsettponka, Ponkapoagwam, Squamscuttonet, Massaponsettquoddy, Ponkapoagquoddy, Squamscuttwam, Massaponsettonet, Ponkapoagonet, Squamscuttquoddy, Massaponsettwam, Ponkaponsettwam, Squampoagonet, Massascuttquoddy, Ponkaponsettquoddy, Squampoagwam, Massascuttonet, Ponkaponsettonet, Squampoagquoddy, Massascuttwam, Squamponsettonet, Massapoagquoddy, Ponkascuttquoddy, Squamponsettwam, Massapoagonet, Ponkascuttonet, Squamponsettquoddy and Massapoagwam. NEW ENGLAND! Even though Fisher passed through these places in the dark he was aware of each one and became riled. The names flew at him in the snow and he batted at them with the violin case to clear his way. A regular trail of tears said Fisher The Indians paved their own way to oblivion with these God damn names!

In shifting around The Ass had disturbed itself and now gave vent to a high foul wind which whipped Fisher for several hours. What do you want! he cried You already got my scarf and your buddy Fate got my overcoat! Fisher felt he was being summoned back to Boston by the forces of nature. He thought if he looked back he would be overtaken by the weather, that he would have to know it. No no said Fisher Not this boy. In the distance the headlamp of a train flashed and Fisher stumbled down the embankment out of its way. As he stood and watched it pass he remembered Fat Leroy claimed to have walked the tracks to Boston from Virginia in 1958. I's too substantial fo de *rods* baby. When Fisher had regained the tracks he saw the sky was growing light. On he walked. South foreverward. He plodded past telephone poles, signal boxes, rusty junky backyards of dead or dying businesses which once needed a railroad. He passed through sleeping towns which showed him nothing but the smashed windows of dead mills. For a game Fisher tried to reconstruct the whole of each piece of garbage that blew against him. In another hour he found himself in the flat almost midwestern fields strewn with scrap iron and dune grass where the Commonwealth of Massachusetts gives characteristically grudging way to the State of Rhode Island and Providence Plantations.

In time Fisher neared Providence. The place not the divine gift. He knew this because of the increasing number of switchyards. The winds of The Ass still howled and Fisher repeatedly fell on flanges hidden under the snow. His trousers were slashed and his knees bled. Forgetting the magic of Rachel for the moment Fisher felt quite cold and alone. Head bandage stringless viol pants without knees Jesus Christ! he shouted.

Fisher wondered if he should stay on the tracks

through Providence or get off and sneak along the streets. He felt this was too dangerous yet when he found himself walking through Union Station he regretted his choice. People waiting on the New York platform for an early train stared at Fisher as he carried his violin through on the southbound track, bandage flapping. He caught the eye of a well dressed young woman. Huffa chuffa huffa chuffa woo woo! he said. She turned away. A bored-looking black man stood in a uniform next to a steaming metal box. Amfood. Fisher winced. He stopped briefly staring at the box but then went on. Yo what you doin down dere? called the man. Huffa chuffa said Fisher not looking back. You a train? the man called. Fisher did not reply.

He hurried out of the terminal and over a spine-chilling trestle and soon got shut of Providence. What a name for that place! The day was turning bright and even colder. Fisher wondered if he was still under The Ass or if the bite of the weather in Rhode Island was due to its being just out from under the monstrous left buttock of the thing. Or the right buttock thought Fisher It must be the right. Because that would mean the being sits looking out to sea and who wouldn't? And when it spies good weather coming it leans hard to the left and voids heavily on Boston but yields a crack over the southern lip of the bowl and slightly better weather in Providence. Maybe that's why they named it that. A steel sheen of wind accelerated the erosion of his face. No matter how much he thought of Rachel, Fisher could not warm himself. The thought of food began to jump up at him like a terrible dog. He searched his pockets for money. There wasn't any. What was left of Fisher's cash drifted in furry mud at the bottom of the Charles River.

However he was approaching the seashore which

gave him something to think about. It reminded him of his dream and he pined for a bicycle. Or at least a novelty nose! said Fisher. The tracks turned gently left, then right. They passed over some green knolls and curved in and out of small bays which rested like half open hands lazily thinking of grasping a little part of the Atlantic. No better meal than sea air said Fisher whiffing neurotically. It was good. But not as good as a discarded sandwich in a dirty wrapper would have been. There were islets in some of the bays. Green islets with white houses. Fisher considered approaching a house and begging for food but just plodded on. To ask for food would be to invite suspicion and risk arrest. Besides! he suddenly remembered it was Christmas Day. He would interrupt family events. His shadow at the door casting a silence on the mad unwrapping. Disturbing a viewing of the Big Game. The eyes would strike him down to be sure. Christmas Day! howled Fisher. No wonder the houses were so quiet, so sitting on their folded paws. You're all cats by the fire today said Fisher stopping to shake his fist at a group of small clapboard houses. You're all pipes on the hob, beers in the fridge God damn you! He put his hands as fists in his pockets and walked on. The violin under an arm.

In another hour Fisher saw the coast highway parallel the tracks. And in another hour he distinguished a roadside snack bar facing the sea. Just a short scrabble lunge and bruising dive away he thought. He tumbled down from the roadbed, threw his violin over the fence, wriggled up and over it and approached the snack bar. Head bandage, no knees, unshaven. Violin. Only jacket, no overcoat. Rumpled. Vague thoughts of charity and thievery.

A couple sat eating. What are you doing out here on

Christmas Day? wondered Fisher. They wore overcoats.
No violins. Fisher bore down on them. The woman looked
up and paled. Larry she said. The man looked up and then
at Fisher. Fisher stood in front of them working his mouth
soundlessly. Whaddya want? said the man gathering his
snacks together in a little pile. Uh ah no said Fisher I'm
not a bum. What! the man said. The woman's heavily
made up eyes. Er that is said Fisher I uh look. He opened
his jacket and pointed at the label. So? said the man. Well
said Fisher in irritation Bums don't wear Harris tweed!
What's Harris tweed? the man said gathering his things
still closer together and sliding toward the woman on the
bench. Fisher sank down at a table across from them. I'm
a bum he said. That's more like it said the man. Larry give
im some money said the woman. Fisher looked down at
his feet. His ankles were blue. Ya hungry fella? said the
man not without sympathy. Fisher burst into tears. Go on
said the woman Give mff mfllmpf. Here her words were
lost to Fisher for he put his head in his arms on the table.
Then he felt a crinkling at his ear. Wonderful he thought
My hair has frozen solid and is now being blown away in
chips. No matter. But it was the man trying to tuck a
dollar bill somewhere into Fisher's person. Fisher looked
up and in surprise took it. Thank you he said Thank you
. . . so much. I'm from Los Angeles originally. So what?
said the man. He and the woman walked quickly to a car.
What's your address? said Fisher. Never mind! said the
man. They drove off down the highway very quickly.
Fisher looked down at the dollar. It was green. It was an
islet.

He banged on the plastic service window. A teenage
girl looked at him from inside. Ya think it's OK? she said
to someone hidden behind a machine. She turned back to

Fisher and opened the window a sliver. Whaddya want? she said. Hot dog, black coffee said Fisher as smoothly as he could. The girl grabbed the dollar and slammed the window shut. Fisher stood, unmoving, in the wind. Three minutes later food was thrust out at him and the window slammed shut. What about my change! yelled Fisher banging his turquoise knuckles in agony against the plastic. Comes ta a dolla even laughed the cracking voice of an unseen male adolescent. Dejected Fisher took his meal to a table. From inside he heard hooting.

Fisher's first act was to knock over his coffee and right it only when most of it had vanished in the wind, brown ice. More guffaws from inside. Fisher turned and peered at the greasy window but could see nothing. He picked up the hot dog with difficulty and bit. He was disappointed to see he had eaten half of it. He had wanted three bites. Man bites dog! Tears filled his eyes. The limp white roll stuck to his lips. Other fractions of it blew away. Finished. He lingered over the one cold swallow of coffee, it was almost too sad. He let go of the paper cup and it flew off in the wind.

Fisher picked up his violin and battling a great stiffness he made to cross the highway back to the tracks. Merry Christmas! he said You lovely youngsters. In truth Fisher would have given anything to be in the kitchen with them. Listening to the radio, making coffee and milkshakes, looking at the girl's legs. Talking about cars with the unseen boy. Anything! he shouted in the middle of the highway. He suddenly realized a speeding car was almost upon him. He flung himself across the highway and fell into the gravel against the fence. The car swerved out of the way at the last instant, horn blaring, angry fist emerging and shaking from a power driven luxury window.

Makes a change anyway said Fisher. He lurched over the fence and dragged back up to the tracks. After hyperventilating until near collapse he struck south again.

The cold wind! In his face, biting him at the knees, tearing at his bandage. The bump on his forehead throbbed for the first time since he had received it. Ah now you're awake little fellow said Fisher. More wind! But the scenery drew him on. Although the wiener had been slender nourishment Fisher felt he would be able to gain his destination. Just barely. Walking robotically he shut his eyes and recalled the feel of Rachel's breasts. He warmed! But sightless, he tripped and fell on the tracks, bloodying his knees yet again. Little soldier thought Fisher getting up and marching. South!

It was afternoon. The blistering cold seared the isleted coast into a continuous diorama. The wind and the white flatnesses of clapboard and the odd patch of snow became Fisher's understanding of the world as he walked through it. Then night came to the seashore in the way Christmas night always comes. Depressingly. Finally. As if *it* is relieved and *you* have been making an ass of yourself. Much quicker than night usually falls at the shore. Fisher felt he was getting on but repressed self congratulation. He thought of Rachel and stumped along faster. He was obliged to get off the tracks several times for trains.

Four or five hours into the night Fisher rounded a turn of track and through a bare branched tree saw a brilliant flash which in a leap his stomach told him was the North Point light. Soon he made out a string of lights. The Newport bridge. Fisher felt numb cheer. But now the tracks curved southwest and he was racked with indecision. He stopped and stood in thought and in a rage the wind buffeted him. All right all right said Fisher. He climbed

down from the railway to the sandy verge of the continent
and began to make his way along the shore. He walked
across winter beaches, sand and snow in his shoes. A yel-
lowing unhealthy gibbous moon rose and in spite of the
cold seemed to stink. Fisher paused on a beach to look at
it and to urinate in a clump of seaweed. He had not relieved himself since watering the herbaceous border sur-
rounding General Varnum's house at Quidnessett. But his
fly was frozen and Fisher had to beat at it with a big knob
of kelp until the claws of his zipper relaxed. Then he went
on, picking his way along the small beaches, over rocks,
falling into anemone pools, seafood paradises, blundering
over derelict fences. Seeing lights on the road above after
several hours, Fisher climbed rocks Bump! Crack! with
violin and warily peered across the highway.

Wakefield! Which offered nothing if indeed it ever
does except the glare and threat of an all night doughnut
shop. A shop well known to Fisher. Some months before,
Fisher and a shortly to be introduced character had invaded the place while under the influence of hemp. Even
in this skewed state (or perhaps because of it) Fisher had
taken great umbrage at the discovery that in Wakefield a
baker's dozen meant twelve. He had had to be shouted
down and manhandled. By the soon to be met with fellow.
To make matters worse Fisher and the character ate all
twelve doughnuts in the car before their return journey
was over. They had gone out for doughnuts to relieve the
depression they felt in their surroundings and arrived
back at the surroundings with no doughnuts. With no
proof or memory of having been anywhere. Dope! TV!
Fisher moaned softly and stole away from the glowing
intersection.

But he knew now where to find the road which curved

among piny hills between Wakefield and Narragansett. Fisher began to jog along phumph phumph phumph in the foot of snow that lay on the road. The Newport light flashed regularly through the trees which stood glaring at Fisher with hands on hips. Branches on burls. Phumph phumph phumph. Fisher was dizzy with excitement and fatigue. What a crusty journey. Phumph phumph phumph. Phumph! Phumph! Phumph! At last he reached the crest of the hill. He tottered at the apex. Below him was the elegant curve of Narragansett beach. At the far end the two curious towers connected by the stone arch over Ocean Road. Fisher stood panting. With every freezing dry breath he took his lungs raged for more. He started down, taking less care with his steps, foolhardily trusting his arrival to gravity, falling more frequently. If that could be. In half an hour he reached the cement walk above the beach. Twenty minutes later he was approaching the towered arch.

There are big things in America thought Fisher and he stopped to consider the arch. Its turrets. Big things! like this which to poor thinkers like me put the lie to the Grand Canyon and the General Sherman Tree. They tantalize. If we were but a hair stupider we'd forget from one generation to the next and think they were built by a race of giants. We are but ants on a sticky bun. Great faithful stone dog! said Fisher Big things on the march in America! He put down his violin and with a smile hugged the stone wall. As much as it is possible for a man to hug a large flat surface. While hugging he imagined a strange parade. Doomsday. The monuments of his youth uprooting their stone elephant legs and marching grinding across the land toward ? somewhere, putting awash the Missouri and the Platte and a host of others. Laughing and glassily smiling

Fisher looked up Ocean Road. In fear misery joy and dumb cussedness his breast began to heave up and down. Followed by his stomach. Fisher bent in the arch and in the famous resounding acoustics was dryly deeply painfully sick.

XVI   Windmere

One fifth of a mile from the arch where Fisher stood retching a large yellow house squatted and faced Rhode Island Sound fairly impassively. Its name was Windmere. Named many years before when in newly electric summers Narragansett was choked with mustachioed women in stiff buttoned canvas bathing costumes. At the top of this asymmetrical house were two narrow windows crowned with fanlights. In these windows you would want to see the light of a candle or an oil lamp. Especially if you passed the house in the elemental without. And on this Christmas night there was some small orange bravery, from a candle, there being no oil lamp. The candle was doing its best to stare unblinkingly at the Newport light. Windmere however was so cracked and drafty that there was flicker. And life within.

Under the flicker of the candle in the rented room a meaty hand throttling a terrified ballpoint pen battled its way across a page. It was one of the two hands of Paolo Balluno, a large liquid young man with large liquid eyes. This Balluno was straining to evacuate from himself a long poem in blank verse about his childhood. He had spent most of it tied to a chair in the back room of a grocery operated by his grandparents. So there was not much to say. But Balluno was writing this poem in the vain hope it would be published to worldwide acclaim at the last minute before he would be obliged to enter the ? School of Business Administration. In truth he was neither poet nor businessman. But he was having one strangle off the other. It was his idea of fun.

The section of the poem Balluno wrote this night caused him to heave a great number of copious sighs. He was attempting to liken his grandfather's many years to the rings of a tree and these in turn to the wood of the old coot's cane. However the syntax had got pleurisy and things were beginning to sound as if grandpa was in fact a piece of wood used to beat the squawling Balluno. The poem was in short going nowhere. It stank. To high heaven. It was a tangle of thought Balluno now venomously hated. He was not creating, he did not think. He just sat and watched his big hand write stupid words all over the page, his mind wrestling in a moil of worry over his bleak future. With a disgusted ejaculation Balluno dropped the pen and dully looked up at the flickering candle. It was stuck in a bottle placed on the desk next to an unused fluorescent lamp. A large pool of wax was spreading next to the bottle, threatening to engulf the poem. Balluno could not decide whether to allow the wax this victory. He wondered if he could blame his problems on the candle. He began to fear he had wasted time. That his thoughts would have appeared more rapidly and clearly under the fluorescent lamp. But then said Balluno They would have been harsh blue white thoughts and grandpa and the store were more yellowy browny mouldy. On a slip of paper Balluno wrote Yellowy browny mouldy. He looked at the flame again. And why a candle? he said I can't see a thing.

Balluno was writing by candlelight because of certain mumbled demands made by his friend William Fisher. Who on his last visit to Windmere had drunk seven bottles of Guinness Extra Stout and proceeded to shout about the *feel* of the house. Of all things. Perfect setting! Fisher had roared pitching around. Clapboard house on sea. Balluno. Got to pay. Whuzzword. Homage. Homage to older way of life. Yuh! Don't just snap on lights at five a clock. Light a candle. Get the feel of it. Come on Bloono! So they had stumbled through a week of candlelit homage. Many stimulating discussions, all now forgot. Balluno had done most of the talking while Fisher stared through his stout glass at the flame and tried to remember what he had never learned about refraction. It seemed to him there should always be a rainbow when you look through something at a source of light. Somewhere, a rainbow. He would belabor this point night after night. Then he would crawl around the room on all fours looking for little brown rainbows in the corners. Looking back and forth to his glass! But Balluno liked Fisher in small doses. And now in looking at the candle and remembering Fisher Balluno remarked it had been a number of weeks since he had heard from Fisher. But there were more pressing issues. Balluno's bent wire framed glasses glinted and so did the melon sized drops of sweat on his forehead. The origin of Balluno's sweat was twofold. First, the rigors of literary production. The writing and immediate condemnation. The poem was rot itself. Second, Balluno was struggling to keep a terrible thought from his mind. That Windmere was haunted. This fear had been born in him that morning.

Christmas Day dawned at Narragansett as Christmas Day dawns everywhere. Creepingly slowly. Much more slowly than the blackest winter day dawns at the eastern shore. But that morning Balluno bundled up and slogged through the rimy snow to a Store. A terrible store run by the sourest Yankee alive. A man as human as an unplugged television. Doughnuts, instant coffee, toilet paper. Balluno's Christmas. He was dying to get home and unwrap them. He had made gift tags for himself to affix to his groceries. (Balluno had a family but they had shunned him this Christmas for reasons it would be tedious and cruel to describe.) But perhaps because of the mysterious heart movements of the yule the sour Yankee was moved to speak!

You the fella in Windmere? he said. Uh that's right said Balluno. She lettin you have it cheap? said the man. His face a prune. Straight to the point thought Balluno. He realized if the sour man thought his rent was low he would charge Balluno $2 for toilet paper. Nothing was labeled. Pretty cheap said Balluno. Not surprised said the man poking at Balluno's sack. Yeah? said Balluno Why not? Heard any noises in there? said the man. Noises? said Balluno who although large was like aspic. Balluno was the most nervous big fellow in the world. Usually big men are not nervous. They destroy so many tiny lives with each movement. They've inured themselves, hardened their hearts. But Balluno was big, nervous, confused. Hence poetic. *You* know said the man suddenly grinning awfully *Weird noises!* Balluno reached for his sack. No he said. The man continued to grin. A moment. What kind of noises? said Balluno. Well said the man suddenly catty Ten years ago she rented the place to a bunch of muzicians from N'Yawk. String quar-tet they call it. Three men and one woman if you get my drift. His eyes were slits! Lot of mighty funny goins on. Mighty funny. Really? said Balluno. Ever alert to the possibilities. Ayup said the man. In-fy-delity if you get my drift. I do said Balluno. Well tension mounted said the man Jealousy and who knows what all if you get my drift. Yes? said Balluno tightening his grip on the yuletide sack. Well one night they all up and killed themselves! said the Yankee In a agreement, together. Suicide pack they call it. Yiih said Balluno. And said the man There's those what's rented the place since what says you can hear em . . . *Killing each other?* shouted Balluno. An old woman gasped and dropped her things in the cat food section. Nope said the man but so pleased Nope playin music and like that. Ghostly music if you get my drift. Balluno grabbed his sack and burst out of the shop. He fled up Ocean Road but had stood in front of Windmere for a full hour before summoning the courage to go in. Broad daylight!

Sweat poured off Balluno. Now staring into the flame he was sure he heard music. Not the random hoots and fipplings of the thousand cracks of Windmere which was at times less a house and more a giant ocarina. *Music.* Throbbing. Lilting. 4/4. Haydn's Quartet in E flat Op 50 No3. Balluno screamed and jumped up, knocking the candle over. It went out, dribbling wax on the poem. Wax also flew onto Balluno's hand and cooling felt like a stroking claw. Yiiih! said Balluno. Rooted to the spot! No sound in the darkness. Just the wind. The normal creaks. But music was dying. Had just ended in his ears he was sure of it. Balluno feverishly turned to the window, now the only source of light. God damn gibbous moon he muttered. He was tall enough to look out the fanlight and just as he did the Newport light flashed. Across the road Balluno was surprised to see a wild figure being blown along the walk. The figure halted directly across from Windmere. It faced the house and began to jerk its arms and legs up and down in unison, a wooden monkey toy. It was holding a violin case. It's Fisher! said Balluno in astonishment. The Hell with Haydn. He turned in the dark room and knocking over a table he bounded to the door. He was a bounder. Clomped and boomed down the stairs. Threw open the door with a Bang! in the wind and hurried along the bricks to the road. Fisher! said Balluno. Nugg! said Fisher unable what with hunger and fatigue to make words. Fisher! said Balluno. Fisher put out his foot to cross the road but withdrew it as a swerving screeching car came at him from the south. Even here he thought. He weakly shook his fist at the auto as it disappeared insolently into the mist. He then stumbled across the road to be embraced by Balluno in the stinging cold wet. When Balluno released Fisher from his great hug the little figure collapsed in a heap on his violin. Fisher! said Balluno What are you doing here? No reply. Fisher was not in. Fisher! shouted Balluno. Jesus he said. The wind was awful, the cold worse. Balluno grabbed Fisher by the legs and pulled him along the brick walk. Fisher's head bumped along it. Unconsciously he held his violin fast and it skidded along behind him. Balluno dragged Fisher up the steps Bump! Thump! Bump! through the Crack! door and more quickly up the narrow stairs Bumpbumpbumpbumpbumpbump-bumpbumpBump!bumpbumpbumpbumpbumpbump! into the sitting room.

An hour later Fisher awoke on Balluno's short sofa to find his legs tucked under himself strangely. Hey buddy said Balluno. But Fisher was delirious. Although Balluno could hardly know it was with joy. Mfft! said Fisher meaning My foot but unable to elaborate. Eh? said Balluno. The tracks! The tracks! said Fisher. So that's it thought Balluno He's on heroin now. Balluno had always feared for Fisher on this score. The dark! The dark! said Fisher. His pusher no doubt thought Balluno The swine! So it's really come to this. Fisher writhed ineffectually. Jesus said Balluno. A man of catholic vocabulary. Fisher fell to the floor and began to crawl around the room bumping into things. Ow! he said. Ow! Ow!

Like many large men Balluno was an inveterate hoarder and the jealous guardian of a multitude of physical objects. Periodicals, containers, styli and the bright colored excited his avarice particularly. His rooms in Windmere were cluttered to the point of choking with objects too numerous and too horrible to describe. One could hardly walk without intersecting something. Even the slightest whimsical move when seated sent A crashing off onto B and C and D. Everything was balanced at pinpoint. But big men know the stream of objects in life will splash against them and leave them unhurt. The eddies trap lesser men like Fisher. Ow! he said. Fisher! said Balluno Whatsa matter with ya? He started to follow Fisher, his big hands stretched out around the smaller man's sides but afraid to actually seize him. Ow! said Fisher knocking over a lamp. Finally Balluno summoned courage and tackled Fisher. The big Italian squash. Balluno got up quickly and dragged Fisher to the sofa. He laid him out and then put the Compact Edition of the *Oxford English Dictionary* on him. This quieted Fisher who looked at the big books and then sank back with a groan. I just threw up in the arch Fisher croaked out. My God! said Balluno who had a horror of vomit. In this respect he was similar to Smith and many others although the similarity to Smith ended there. No one lives in Narragansett who could have built such an arch! Fisher pronounced. Then he fell asleep.

When he opened his eyes it was dawn. Balluno was asleep on a large wicker chair. Fisher looked at him. Balluno! he yelled. What! said Balluno jumping up with apprehension. Get this off me! Fisher breathed shallowly. He clawed at the big books on his chest. With some reservation Balluno slowly approached Fisher and kicked the dictionary to the floor. Then he retreated and looked at Fisher. You OK? he said. Yes said Fisher. What's the story? said Balluno Did you walk from Kingston? Why didn't you call me from the station? Hollow laughter said Fisher. Eh? said Balluno. I walked said Fisher From Boston. That is to say Concord. Balluno stared. Get out he said. No fooling said Fisher. Concord! said Balluno Why Concord? Why not Boston? You live in *Boston*. Balluno had an inquiring mind of the irritating variety. Fisher stared at Balluno. Shut up! he said I'm starving! Bring me water! Coffee! Food! Dessert!

Balluno approached with a plate of spaghetti. Fisher ate as though he were vacuuming. And a plate of peanut butter sandwiches. But these Fisher waved away. No! he said No whole grains! When he appeared sated Balluno looked him in the eye. So what are you doing here? he said. Fugitive from justice said Fisher. You couldn't call in advance? said Balluno. No said Fisher It was a spur of the moment thing.

Fisher told Balluno everything. Omitting for the moment his sighting of Thoreau (for whom Balluno nursed a soft spot) and a too detailed description of Alison (who Balluno would call for a date given the chance thought Fisher *I* deserve all the sympathy).

Amazing said Balluno. Appalling. What are you going to do? Nothing said Fisher. The world owes me a living! They dissolved in laughter. FBI! howled Balluno. Can you beat it? wept Fisher. The belly laughs continued as rising sunlight came through the fanlights and made bright seashells on the clean white wall.

Hours later Balluno emerged from the bathroom and looked somberly at Fisher. You're staying he said. Fisher peeked at him queerly over the sofa back. Is that a question or a truth? he said. A realization said Balluno. Silence. The foghorn. Mutual rumination leading to almost nothing. It was Balluno who spoke. You'll be needing an alias he said. In lieu of an alibi an alias will do said Fisher who expected the police hourly. Balluno was standing looking down into the garbage. Cranshaw he said. Featherstonehaugh said Fisher. Doe said Balluno. MacGillivray said Fisher. Public said Balluno. Esquire said Fisher. Smith said Balluno. Your name here said Fisher. We're getting nowhere said Balluno. Erewhon said Fisher. No no said Balluno. MacNono said Fisher. First names first! cried Balluno The character is determined from birth by the first name. It is to that people look, you're strung up on your first name all through life. Balluno wrote all these remarks down on his slips of paper which constantly blew about him like leaves. True said Fisher How true. There is a William personality and I am it. What exactly is it? said Balluno. A bit slack said Fisher. Retiring? said Balluno. A bit more said Fisher. Very shy. Wishy washy. Namby pamby said Balluno Peely wally recoiling escapist! You dog said Fisher. Yes I seem to recall said Balluno. All the Williams. Silence. Well? said Fisher. There is a Paolo personality said Balluno But it is Italian and not a dominant archetype in this culture. Not the same as the Paul personality? said Fisher. No said Balluno. What are you talking about dominant archetype? said Fisher You give me a pain. Yes that's part of it said Balluno. More than one pain upon reflection said Fisher. You're getting warmer said Balluno. Stop! said Fisher. Silence. Although said Fisher Williams charm women. They can't follow through but they charm the pants off them. It's a start said Balluno. Ah! said Fisher But when pants are removed with charm alone there's a doubly desperate battle ahead. Yah! said Balluno. You have no idea said Fisher. Don't I! said Balluno. Silence. The waves. Jim said Balluno. Don said Fisher. Basil said Balluno. Turmeric said Fisher. Obadiah said Balluno. Deuteronomy said Fisher. Leslie said Balluno. That's a girl's name said Fisher. Oh said Balluno. Sylvia said Fisher. Toby said Balluno. Ponkapoag said Fisher. Dale said Balluno. Dale! cried Fisher Dale! Dale!

So Fisher was to be introduced around town as Dale. Balluno magnanimously provided Fisher with a complete set of clothes seven sizes too large. This embittered Fisher but he said nothing. Balluno deemed it too dangerous to send for clothing of the correct size. And too dangerous for Fisher to try to close his tiny bank account by mail. And too dangerous for Fisher to contact his family. Everything too dangerous all around. They'll be looking for someone buying size thirty six said Balluno. But there are lots of thirty sixes said Fisher You don't know! Oh yeah? said Balluno Who? In his bigness he was ignorant of the lives of the small and of the teeming thousands of them.

Balluno went to the store and in doing so was reminded of the ghosts. As they ate a delicious lasagna he explained how he had happened to turn and see Fisher out the fanlight. Rot! said Fisher impolitely. What! said Balluno It happened! Get out said Fisher. Balluno threw down his napkin. Sir! he said. All right all right I believe said Fisher seeing tears well up in Balluno. If it's so vivid then put it in your poem. My poem! said Balluno. He had to put his fork down, racked as he was with sobbing. Sorry said Fisher I didn't know. How long is it expected to live? Balluno looked up vengefully. And you? he said Your violin? No! cried Fisher. Yes! shouted Balluno Ha ha! Play me a Bach partita. Ha ha! said Fisher I can't. No strings. Balluno's triumph lessened. Together they stared at the battered case leaning against the sofa. But Fisher decided to own up. But have no fear he said Even if it were strung with the finest English guts and an E of golden wire I would still be unable. Aha said Balluno but sheepishly. In fact I seem to have lost the relevant cells somewhere said Fisher. In the accident. Which one? said Balluno. You may well ask said Fisher.

As he looked around the room Fisher saw the great problem they would encounter in sharing the place. The objects. So many objects. A pain for each one sizzled up in him. The pathos of clutter! Balluno really was terrible. Chairs, tables, sofas. Metal cabinet. *Television.* Not to mention possibly a thousand magazines and more possibly two to three thousand dried up pens. Already circumscribed! he moaned Death! Fisher began to wonder how he could slowly eliminate objects from the room in which he was doomed to sleep perhaps forever. Forever! What about the statute of limitations? said Fisher suddenly. It does not apply to the truly wicked said Balluno. Fisher brooded. Doubt washed over him erotically. But Rachel he said Figures more prominently in my thoughts than I ever deemed possible. It sounds a bad rub said Balluno And do not make the obvious joke. You can't go back there, they're combing Massachusetts for you. Ah well it needed combing said Fisher. Lie low said Balluno. But to lie lower than I was is nearly impossible said Fisher Assuming one wants to pursue three dimensional life. Three dimensional life he said again. I heard you! shouted Balluno scribbling in a whirlwind of slips. Relax! Fugitive! The end! Fisher sank low in his chair and pondered to beat the band. Balluno was covered in slips. He was stuck in the saddest stage of creativity, trying in desperation to incorporate everything around him into the work at once. Every remark, the slightest diarrheic impression. He grabbed at them like oiled bananas.

They made ready for bed. Bunched up on the sofa Fisher studied the dilemma of it. Amputation is necessary he said. Either my legs or the western arm of the sofa. He evaluated the sturdy western arm and decided his legs would give the least trouble. I need a saw! he called to Balluno. No reply. The lights went out. Fisher decided that for the first night he would try to sleep sitting up. Or at worst slumped forward. Balluno got into his bed under a comforter of slips and shut his eyes. But not his ears.

They roamed and sampled. Fisher's snuffling. The fog-horn. Waves breaking on the beach and against the sea wall. The occasional passing motor. And then, regrettably, Mozart's Quartet in B flat (K 458) ("The Hunt"). Balluno bit his tongue to keep from crying out.

The next day Balluno was gathered unexpectedly into the folds of his family. Although he offended them in the course of the enfolding and was to return before night. But he looked out the fanlight early in the morning to see a car pull up and spew aunts and the like onto the lawn. Quick! said Balluno shaking Fisher's shoulder. How perfect a shoulder for shaking thought Balluno. Quick! he said. Not guilty! cried Fisher jumping up. Hide in the closet said Balluno. Eh? said Fisher. My family said Balluno. So Fisher stood trembling with cold among brooms and canned goods for an hour while All Was Forgiven and Balluno was entreated to spend the day after the day after Christmas with them, cleaning up. No I cannot said Balluno My poem. Fack ya pome said Balluno's aunt. Finally they got him. Fisher heard Balluno being dragged down the stairs. The car drove off. Now is my chance thought Fisher. He dressed quickly in his huge new clothes and stood surveying the room. He took the wicker chair by the arm and marched it out the door down the stairs across the lawn and along the walk by the sea.

The day was blue cold and deep. The beach pebbly and sharp. Fisher now pulled the chair along behind him. He looked at his feet in the enormous Balluno shoes in the sand. Flup! Flup! The tremendous Balluno pant legs. Fisher had thought he was alone on the beach. Dragging his chair. But far up the gentle curve of sand he saw someone doing something. Someone walking back and forth from the seawall to the tide. Fisher continued to pull the chair. It was his intention to scuttle it in the ooze of an inlet he knew at the far end of the beach. Fisher approached the figure on the bright sand. The cold wind! and Fisher still alive with troubles.

On arriving Fisher found the figure to be a rotund man of some seventy years. White hair, a short white beard, eyeglasses. He was doggedly smoking a cigarette in the wind. Flecks of ashes and embers flew at Fisher. The man paid no attention to Fisher who stood very near, still holding the chair. His footprints and the lines made by the chair trailed off in the sand behind. The cushion had fallen off somewhere. The man walked back and forth, inches away from Fisher. It was absurd not to speak. Good morning said Fisher caressing the edge of the chair in shyness. Name's Henry said the man not stopping or looking. He had an armful of pebbles and shells and was walking toward the edge of the water. He dumped his load of rubble and spread it out on the sand. Gingerly, precisely with his feet. Then he began to jump up and down on it. As he did this he smiled at Fisher in a world weary way. Great thought Fisher A maniac. Just what was lacking. What are you doing? Fisher asked finally. Good day for it said Henry. Yes for what? said Fisher. My work said Henry still jumping up and down on the pile of rocks. And what said Fisher regaining some of his old acidity Is your God damn work? Henry stopped jumping up and down and put on a mean expression. Erosion *stupid!* he said. He started jumping up and down again. Explain yourself said Fisher Or I call the police. Standing there in giant clothes after dragging a chair along the beach in 10° weather he said that! You ain't gonna call the police sonny said Henry

Cause I know who you are! Fisher paled. You do? he said.
Yeah you're the guy in Windmere said Henry jumping.
Fisher relaxed. Yes that is I'm one of them he said. Huh!
said Henry *One* of them! Dale's my name said Fisher,
Dale Ponkapoag. Henry stopped jumping and fixed a curious old eye on Fisher. Any strange noises in that place? he
said. Noises? said Fisher. You know said Henry *Weird
noises!* No said Fisher Quieter nor a tomb. I'll bet said
Henry walking toward the seawall. He seized a big log by
one end and dragged it toward the water. What *are* you
doing? said Fisher. I told you said Henry Erosion! Erosion!
Erosion! I get it said Fisher. Erosion. I just kinda help
things along said Henry Ya know the beach gets pretty
messed up. The natural processes. During the summer
with all that suntan oil and Cokes and mustard drippin
down into it and oh Lord at night the wine and sperm and
beer. Er I'll bet said Fisher. So in the winter I come and
get things back into shape said Henry. Ah said Fisher.
Take that rock for example said Henry pointing at a gray
stone. That's been knocked all the Hell out of the ecologi-
cal system by some God damn fourth grade class come to
trample and maraud the place. It's three and a half feet
out of alignment! His voice was choked with emotion. He
carefully picked up the stone and carried it three and a
half feet closer to the waves. Oughta be here! he said
Gettin pounded. Fisher stared at Henry. What ya doin
with that chair? said Henry suddenly. Gonna do some
sunbathin? Er actually said Fisher I came down here to
get rid of it. Yeah? How? Henry looked at Fisher suspiciously. Well I was taking it down to the inlet said Fisher.
The inlet! cried Henry The inlet! He fell to his knees in the
sand. Fisher blushed and looked up and down the beach.
Oh what an infernal mess is the inlet! wailed the old man.

He looked as if he was praying to Mecca on a rug of gravel. Ahem! said Fisher. My work my work groaned Henry. Ah well perhaps you'd like to see to it for me? said Fisher. Eh? said Henry looking up. Well said Fisher if things are uh so bad down at the inlet maybe you could arrange to include this chair in the er scheme of erosion? Sir! said Henry getting to his feet Do you mean it? Well yes uh that is to say certainly said Fisher. I would be most honored! said Henry trembling. Fisher handed the chair to Henry. What a study it will be said the old man It's been so long since an intact manufactured object was given for erosion. Yes? said Fisher. What a pleasure said Henry To see the paint then the weaving and lastly the ferrules go! Yes said Fisher. Erosion! Erosion! cried Henry. Rah! Rah! said Fisher moving off. Oh thank you Mr Ponkapoag! called Henry. Fisher had a thought and turned back toward Henry in the roaring wind. Henry he said I could bring a manufactured object every day. More or less. Oh sir! said Henry That would be . . . He stared out at the sea. I will see you tomorrow Henry said Fisher continuing along the beach. Thank you! called Henry.

Fisher stood at the edge of the inlet. The tidal inlet. Swift navy blue current kept him from a small island. A ruined shack. The dune grass. Pleasing crisp brush strokes of flood. What bothers Henry about the inlet thought Fisher Is the secret erosion. Under the purple silt. Under the cold apple cut birch log sharp New England day, warm soft changes he can't control. Can't even get his hands on. Fisher wondered if the owner of the shack sought a restoring purchaser. On his clumsy way back he found Henry gone but a pile of debris was stacked on the chair.

When Fisher returned to Windmere he found Balluno lying deep in thought. His big legs emplaced like guns on the arms of the sofa. What? said Fisher Back already? It was tragic said Balluno I can't keep my mouth shut for a minute, I'm such a disappointment to them. What exactly happened? said Fisher sitting down and wondering if Balluno had noticed the wicker chair was missing. Upon arriving in the gift wrap strewn house said Balluno I was seized with poesy. I locked myself in the bathroom and began sweatily to compose, getting the runs also with the effort. Handy said Fisher. Eh? said Balluno. Your being in the bathroom I mean said Fisher. Pretty soon said Balluno My uncle was banging on the door. And then his son. And then everybody, banging on the door! Perhaps they needed the toilet said Fisher. They have three said Balluno And anyway all at once? Hm said Fisher. They told me to forget my poem said Balluno Those were their words. To *forget* it! Bad stuff said Fisher. They wanted me to help them clean up and then watch the Big Game said Balluno. I thought the Big Game was yesterday said Fisher Or even the day before. Apparently not said Balluno. Maybe it's so big it just goes on and on said Fisher. My inspiration contracted said Balluno and I reacted violently. So they put me in the trunk of the car and brought me back. Sped off with screeching tires and without a by your leave. Not like my family at Christmas said Fisher But it may be the Paolo/William differences. Wug said Balluno Not even a chance to purloin a bottle of brandy or one of the many cheap fruitcakes dotting the landscape. He wrote all this furiously as he complained to Fisher. My family! blubbered Fisher. Shut up! said Balluno Fugitive! Yes all right snurfled Fisher. You're on your own now said Balluno You ought to welcome it. He glared at

Fisher who slobbered and hoarked for a while in his chair. Balluno rolled his eyes with the effort of trying to recapture his poem from the green and gold bathroom where it had been garotted. Beyond the dunes and some trees, Pasquiset Pond sparkled briefly as the sun set behind it. Inside Windmere deep orange rectangles dawned on the eastern wall.

XVII   The Mosaic of Seaside Life

The New Year came and went without comment from Fisher or Balluno. Balluno's family did not so much as telephone. Fisher wanted to root for a train ride to Providence in order that Guinness might be acquired. But he knew Balluno would say that to buy Guinness would arouse undue suspicion. So Fisher sat on the sofa drinking beer and wondering when he would drag the sofa itself out to the beach for Henry to erode. Fisher had provided Henry with a steady stream of objects large and small. He managed to take something out of Windmere every day. So he was to an extent happy. Even if only a jar or a piece of laughable deskware of the 1940s. Henry dutifully half buried them in the sand. He clucked and cooed over them. Waiting to hail the first traces of erosion. For all Balluno's acquisitiveness he did not notice anything missing.

As the winter days passed and snow whipped dry along the edges of the coast Fisher and Balluno fought their good fights. Balluno dragged out of his bed early each morning and began to beat his breast over his poem. While preparing breakfast his hands and arms would rebel and smash things in frustration over not moving pen on paper every minute. His legs would take him to his dusty desk but with a growl he would return to the sink. This angry clatter would awaken Fisher who would push himself up on the sofa just enough to see his violin case loitering in the morning sunlight. He would then loll and muse on the stringless pity of it all for several hours. While Balluno moaned and searched the works of all previous poets for inspiration. It was quite a jolly little household.

And at night their bugbears. Balluno lying in a sweat wanting only the first bar of any piece of Western chamber music to start screaming. Fisher watching the dim lights passing cars cast on the wall, waiting for the blinking red light he knew must come. William Fisher Arrested In RI Retreat! Fisher Gets One Million Years! Fisher And Hess To Share Cell! Tossing and turning Fisher would finally fall asleep into the jumble of horrendous headlines. Only to be awakened several times each night by the soft moans of Balluno. His rich baritone rose to the notes of the ectoplasmic string quartets trooping naked through the musty rooms of his nightmares.

One afternoon Fisher who had been to the store as Dale returned to find Balluno slumped over the kitchen table. On the table beside Balluno's upper torso head and hands were a bottle of Chianti and eight bottles of Guinness. Guinness! said Fisher running toward the table. I have been reunited with my family mumbled Balluno Even though I have aroused terrible suspicion by asking them to bring this Guinness. Fisher began to hunt madly for a bottle opener. My uncle accused me of going Irish said Balluno But I told him it was a poetic emetic. That shut him up. Fisher overturned the silverware drawer and pawed about in the pile of junk. Already adept at wheedling! cried Balluno The ? School beckons. What's to become of me? I'm damned Fisher! Fisher found the opener and leapt on the nearest bottle. He opened it and commingled. He sighed and looked at Balluno. Buck up! said Fisher Life is bearable when transubstantiation is practiced regularly. Say I'm the Catholic around here said Balluno. He jumped up and ran to his desk. He began to mess furiously with his slips. Fisher finished his bottle and opened another. He then noticed a moving bag of green cloth by the sofa. What in Hell's that? he said. Balluno swiveled angrily from inspiration. Oh that he said Well of course to attempt to secure violin strings would arouse undue suspicion. I don't get you said Fisher staring at the bag which was beginning a slow progress across the floor. So in the true spirit of Yankee resourcefulness said Balluno pausing to write down every phrase he said As I say . . . in that spirit . . . Yes? Yes? said Fisher alarmed and drinking. I have . . . said Balluno, the slips had got him, his poem so near . . . Brought you a cat. A cat? said Fisher. Yes a cat of course said Balluno From which you may fashion the finest of strings so prized by the virtuosi. The beginnings of a cottage industry. He wrote frenziedly on tens of slips! It's not even dead said Fisher. True enough said Balluno But it is very very ill. With a small noise Fisher jumped up grabbed the squirming bag and fled out to the beach.

His immediate thought was to give the bag to Henry who might know what to do with it. Might at least know how to put the cat out of its misery and include it in the erosion if possible. It was only right. Fisher's understanding of natural processes was slim. But Henry was nowhere to be seen. Fisher put the bag down and opened it. A cat ran out and quickly up a pile of rocks to the walk and vanished in the direction of Wakefield. Doesn't look too sick to me said Fisher. He looked at the waves and began to walk toward the inlet.

The day was prismatic. The air, memories of pebbles, music and colors in the sand danced before Fisher's eyes and heart in a pattern which comforted him. He walked and thought within the lines of a big Navajo rug. His days and ideas became a reverberation of successive grey black and white squares, each filled with things he paused to know and then allowed to pass around and through him, changing him, tinting his dreams. Patterns of his own life and those of others shimmered about him, separate for a time. Parts of the moving squares were history, frames of movies, songs, recollections of wood and of lamps he had seen. The seashell of light crept along the white wall in Windmere. The blue of the sky the yellow of the house the damp stones of the arch flowed in his mind, the contrasting forms and colors about him, natural and made by men, reminded him of infinite others: things, places, events from the past and from the future. Gulls squawked and wheeled overhead. There was nothing for Fisher to do, walking on the beach that day, but to kick at the sand and watch recreations of the past in the little clouds of it.